BLACK DESIRE

A KELLY BLACK AFFAIR

CJ THOMAS

cj@cjthomasbooks.com

ABOUT THE AUTHOR

CJ lives in the Green Mountains of Vermont. You can find CJ skiing, hiking, and spending time with family when not typing away on the latest hottest read.

Connect with CJ:

cj@cjthomasbooks.com

FREE NOVEL

Join my newsletter and read my never before published novel, Boss Me, FREE!

QUICK NOTE FROM THE AUTHOR

Hundreds of requests flooded my message inbox over the past year from fans requesting to hear one character's story in particular—Kendra Williams from my On My Knees series.

I could see why she was so popular. Her spunk, carefree, take-no-prisoners attitude resonated with not only me, when telling her best friend Alex's story, but with you as well. That's awesome and why she needs her own series.

Thanks to you, my wonderful and loyal fans, I'm here to tell her story, let Kendra find her love, and fight for the man of her dreams. It's all here in an action-packed romantic suspense that is sure to keep you turning the pages.

If you're not familiar with the infamous, Kendra, I suggest you get caught up and learn her and this series' backstory by first reading both Beyond Tonight and On My Knees series. So, without further ado, here is the much anticipated story of Kendra.

Buckle in, and get ready for one hell of a ride. CJ.

P.S. This book is intended for mature audiences only and contains scenes and flashbacks to childhood sexual abuse, which may cause trigger reactions.

BLACK DESIRE, BOOK DESCRIPTION

I did it for a friend. But he was the reason I stayed.

Criminal defense lawyer, Kelly Black, came into my life as I was on my way out. He was infuriatingly handsome, except the Madam said I couldn't have him. And no matter how many dates I had to keep my mind off of him, Mr. Black was the man who dominated my thoughts.

Then it happened. Ignoring the warnings that he was dangerous, I let him into my life not realizing that his touch would be the reason my broken past resurfaced. Determined not to lose the man who turned my life around, it was up to me to let him know who I truly was. But when he presented me with a demand of his own, I wasn't sure I was ready to agree to his terms.

Submitting was never my strong suit.

1

Kendra

"**S**hut up!"

"I'm not kidding. He really did that," Alex said, giggling like a fool in love.

The driver made a left turn and a block later we entered the neighborhood that housed Madam's office. She said it was urgent and that she needed to see me. I didn't ask any questions. The Madam wasn't a woman you questioned too often. Besides, it wasn't like I had anything else to do today, and it gave me an excuse to see her bodyguard, Jerome. He always managed to make my day brighter.

Alex kept talking my ear off while I exchanged friendly glances with my driver. His eyes were soft and dark with crinkles at the corners that made me think he was a man who liked to smile, laugh, and have a good time.

"And after he slipped the furry socks over each of my feet, he demanded that I go to bed with him."

"Well, nothing has changed there." I rolled my eyes and leaned further back in the solid black leather seat. I was happy for Alex. I really was. What she had with film maker Nash Brooks was what any woman would dream of having. Hell, even in the beginning I'd wanted to sleep with Nash. And that was no secret. Even Alex knew that. But in the end, he had his eye set on her.

"Except it's not what you're thinking." Alex's voice nearly cracked in embarrassment. "He didn't want sex."

My brows squished. "Nash Brooks. The man with the third leg didn't want sex?"

"Nope." Alex's lips popped as if proud of this.

My mind raced to understand. Nash was a man with an appetite. A real man with the kind of muscles to prove it. "Then what did he want?"

"I can't believe I'm telling you this."

I could hear Alex drop her face into her hands. "You can't stop now. You have me heating up. Hell, girl, I'm rounding first base and on my way to second."

Alex laughed.

"Spill it." My voice was firm, meaning business.

"He'll kill me if he finds out I told you."

"My lips are sealed." I held my hand over my heart. "It's me. Your friend who uncaringly tells you everything."

"Okay. All right." Alex paused as if already regretting what she was about to lay down on me. "He said he has trouble falling asleep without me there."

I burst out laughing, taking the phone away from my ear for a second. The driver's eyes locked on me and were perfectly framed by the rearview mirror.

"I knew telling you was a mistake."

I fought hard to control my fit of laughter and, finally, after a minute, I wiped the tears of amusement from my eye and said, "You really have broken this man."

"Hardly." Alex chuckled. "If he finds out I told you this, he'll make sure to punish me."

"Then I'll be sure to tell him." I smirked. For as much shit as I was giving her, it was nice to know that someone like Nash Brooks had a softer, kinder, more compassionate side with the woman he said he loved. That filled me with hope that maybe this world wasn't as fucked up as I sometimes thought it was.

"Where are you, anyway?"

"On my way to the Madam's." I leaned toward the center seat and looked through the front windshield. Town cars lined the street and palms swayed against the gentle breeze. It was just another sunny day in southern California, and we were nearly to my drop.

"You slut."

"Hey now!"

"What?"

"That was my old title."

"And your new one?"

"Still working on it. But I'm a professional now and I think I deserve to be called something a bit classier than whore, or slut." I felt my eyes smile.

"She's working you hard."

The corners of my lips curled into a devilish smile. "Just what the doctor ordered."

Working for the Madam had been incredible. It was the best solution to helping Alex get out of her situation and back in the arms of Nash. And the pay was excellent, too.

But money wasn't my reason for wanting to do this. And I knew that it was early for me to say this, but for me, escorting had been an excuse to go out several nights a week, taste a variety of different flavors, and be taken into worlds I otherwise would have never been invited into. That was it. That was all I'd ever wanted. It wasn't so much to ask, right?

"She has a new date for me," I said, feeling my heart skip a beat.

Alex gasped. It was barely audible, but enough for me to catch it through the phone. "Do you still like it?"

I had a feeling I knew why she was asking me. She didn't want me to regret my decision, and I could appreciate that. But I had no choice in the matter after what I mistakenly got her caught up in. She was lucky to have come out of her ordeal as well as she had. Hell, we were both lucky she was still alive.

"Are you kidding me? This is way more exciting than pushing papers at the corporate law firm."

Alex was far too quiet.

"Alex, baby, you all right?"

"Yeah," she said so softly even I wanted to cry.

"Thank you. I owe this excitement to you." For once in my life I was serious, and it was important that she knew I *wanted* to be here and not because I *had* to be here.

"You're doing it to get laid," Alex said and we both started laughing.

"That too." The driver pulled to the curb, looked me in the mirror, and I nodded. "Now, if only the Madam will let her clients sleep with me, then maybe I'll be able to start sleeping again."

"I'm sure when the right one comes along, she'll give you your snatch back." We both laughed again.

"Hey, I got to go."

"Give Jerome a pat on his butt for me." Alex snickered.

"That boy could use a spanking." Alex dissolved into hysterics. "Call you later," I said as I killed the call.

I stuffed my cell in my handbag, opened the door, and thanked the driver for the lift. "Maybe I'll see you around," he said.

I didn't respond, not wanting to open up any doors that might come back to haunt me later. Maybe our paths would cross again or maybe they wouldn't. In a city the size of Los Angeles, Uber drivers came and went.

As soon as I shut the door he pulled away and took his first right.

With my sunglasses pulled over my eyes so I wouldn't have to squint in the intense sun, I slipped my handbag over my shoulder, looked up and down the block, and marched up the front stairs of the gorgeous red-brick building that acted as the Madam's world headquarters.

I didn't know what to expect. I listened to my heels *clacking* over the concrete. The Madam communicated to her fleet of escorts through a variety of different ways, and being called in for a face-to-face meeting, I could only assume the worst.

My vision tunneled as I focused on the entrance. Time seemed to slow and I couldn't stop the pellets of sweat from falling down the center of my back.

This building brought back memories of the first time I visited. A day I'd never forget. Alex had gone through it before and no matter how many times she explained to me what to expect, there was no way to mentally prepare for it. Being stripped down to your birthday suit and letting a complete—male—stranger inspect my goods for market had to have been one of the most bizarre things I'd ever experienced.

And that was saying a lot.

I was an open-minded kind of girl who'd been around the block. But then again, without going through that initial interview process, I wouldn't be here today waiting to be called in for duty.

I reached for the door handle, pulled it open, and let the cool air-conditioned air hit my face and cool my heated core.

The fact was, I wanted to make a name for myself. It was important I established a reputation, something people would know me for, all while not wanting to disappoint the one woman who gave me the chance to become one of the city's finest highly paid escorts—the Madam.

"Ms. Williams," the front desk receptionist greeted me with a smile.

"Janine, please, my name is Kendra." I tapped her desk as I walked by. "Ms. Williams is my mother."

"The Madam is expecting you." She smiled, turning her attention back to her computer screen.

Nothing gave me the chills like when someone addressed me by my last name. My mother had been absent from much of my adult life, and I preferred to keep it that way. There was no sense in having reminders of why I didn't have a relationship with my own mother. It wasn't Janine's fault. She didn't know, and was doing as she was told.

I walked up the two flights of stairs, cursing under my breath as I neared the top, thinking how the Madam micro-managed every last detail of everyone and everything that entered this building, from how we were greeted at reception, to what we wore on our dates. She ran a tight ship and I supposed that in this line of work, we all had to take it as seriously as she did.

Jerome must have heard me coming because as soon as I hit the floor, heading in the direction of Madam's office, he stepped out, crossed his arms and stood with a wide stance.

I removed my sunglasses and set them on top of my head, smiling. There was a subtle smile tugging his lips when he saw me and I knew he liked me. And not just because he's seen me up close and personal, either. I was sure that helped with his decision but I kept him on his toes and I was sure I was more comfortable around him than some of the other girls.

I sped up and rounded my shoulders back. His eyes moved over me, taking in the dress I was wearing, and I wasn't sure if he approved or was surprised that I disobeyed the Madam and came here wearing my own outfit of a semi-sheer blouse tucked into a gorgeous sun orange skirt. And when paired with my sunglasses, there was no doubt whoever glanced in my direction knew I was making a statement—like, *try to beat this, bitches.*

"Would you like for me to go ahead and strip?" I stopped close enough to easily tug on his tie. There was no doubt the Madam dressed Jerome, but I liked to humor myself thinking that his style was uniquely his.

"Not today, sweetheart," he said with a hint of sarcasm.

My eyes traveled up the center of his broad chest, over his strong jaw, before landing squarely on his light brown eyes. "But then you wouldn't have to look so hard." I bit my lip and angled my head to the side.

That had him laughing as he shook his head.

"Kendra, darling." The Madam stepped out from her office and greeted me with open arms. "What a lovely day, isn't it?"

I looked back at Jerome. "Not bad," I said, winking.

"Thanks for coming down. As soon as I discovered it, I knew that it couldn't wait." The Madam whisked me into her office where she picked up a carefully selected stack of papers, each ear-marked with a brightly colored sticky note. "It seems that a line in our contract was skipped when you first signed on."

I thought back to the seemingly endless papers I signed that first day. "And here I thought you had a special date for me." My gaze browsed her walls. Her office was modern with little décor, but enough to keep things interesting.

"My dear—" She lifted her head and smiled. "I have that for you, too."

I plucked a pen from her desk and said, "Good. Tell me where to sign."

The lines around her eyes crinkled.

"Let's get this show on the road," I said impatiently.

"Please," she lifted a paper up off her desk, handing it to me, "read it carefully before signing. I don't want you thinking that I never told you what was coming."

My gaze narrowed as I read the detailed document line-by-line. The further my eyes traveled down the page, I knew that I would have remembered seeing something like this before. Nothing I read jarred my memory. It was talking about my comfort level and how far I was willing to go sexually. "Is this specific to tonight's date?"

"You're moving up in the world, my dear. Placing you with the right client is essential."

My eyes moved away from the Madam and back to the contract. "Nothing is too surprising here other than the fact that I'm having to sign a contract saying what I'm comfortable doing. Tell me more about my date and maybe it will help me decide which boxes I should tick."

I could tell by the way Madam was looking at me that she was at least entertaining the idea of letting me in on what I was up against. "He's a very powerful man."

I ticked a few boxes and smiled. "Anything else?"

"He holds great influence in the city."

My smile spread to my ears as heat traveled to my core. I ticked a few more boxes. "Is that all?"

"You have a great spirit, darling." Madam pushed off her desk and stood upright. "Remember that this isn't about you. You're to laugh at his jokes no matter if you find them funny." Madam rounded her desk and headed in my direction. "Smile when he looks at you." I watched her hands land on my shoulders. "And make him feel like a God as you hang off his arm."

My brows squished together. "Then why check all these boxes if I'm not going to get laid?"

Madam tossed her head back and cackled. "Kendra, doll," her voice dropped to a more serious tone, "your beautiful cunt needs a rest. You haven't been having sex, have you?"

"My pussy hasn't been this empty since I was a virgin."

"Good." She stepped away. "Tighten it up." She smoothed her hand down the front of her dazzling skirt. Then she looked at mine. "Are you wearing your own clothes?"

My head dropped and I looked at what I was wearing. "You like it? I can tell you where I bought it if you like."

"Throw that shit away," she spat. "And re-read your contract. I can't have you risking my reputation wearing garbage like that."

"Look," I stepped forward, "I have my own wardrobe. Nice things. Expensive clothes. You don't need to keep sending me clothes. I'm a big girl. I know how to dress. Save your ideas for the other girls."

Madam stopped moving and turned to meet my gaze. She was quiet as she stared me down and the longer she went without talking, the more nervous I became.

"No offense." I inhaled a deep breath, wishing that I could go back in time and wear the clothes she'd delivered to my place.

"You'll do as I say. You're mine. I choose what you wear, how you wear it, and how to pair it with what makeup. Remember," she held up my contract, "I own you."

2

KELLY

"I'm across town," I said, answering my cell. "How'd it go?"

"Better than expected."

My heels dug in and I stopped, needing to be sure I heard what Giselle had to say next.

"The case should settle." I could hear Giselle smiling through the line. "Congratulations, Kelly. We won."

I rolled my neck and thought to myself, *finally*. What should have been an open and shut case turned into a year-long struggle to making a deal with the prosecutor. I marched on, heading into the several-story building with a reclaimed bounce to my step.

"I'm leaving the courthouse soon," Giselle said.

Janine smiled at me as I passed reception. "Don't forget we'll be having dinner with the DA tonight."

"On my radar."

I started to head up the stairs with my head down. "Good. I'll pick you up at seven."

"How would you like me to dress?"

"The gown is on your desk waiting," I said, thinking of the sleeveless beaded navy-blue halter gown I'd picked for her to wear tonight. Giselle would look stunning in it and with the keyhole neckline, it would be all too irresistible for the DA to not get flirty with her.

But then again, I'd specifically chosen that for her to wear before we learned the news of our recent victory. Regardless, it would still work to my benefit. All part of the plan at keeping my courtroom enemy in check, constantly establishing my prevailing dominance over him.

"Should I prepare for battle?" Giselle could barely conceal her excitement. And that was why we made such a great team. We both loved a good challenge, weren't afraid to standup and dig in for a good, long, hard fight. And with who we were having dinner with, it was a fair question, too. When dealing with Oscar Buchanan, LA's toughest District Attorney, anything was possible.

But blood wasn't in the waters for tonight. No, tonight was about keeping my enemy close—reconnaissance disguised as dinner.

"Keep your armor at home," I said.

"See you at seven." Giselle hung up just as a young woman come flying around the corner, leaping down the stairs and slamming directly into the center of my chest.

"Watch where you're fucking going." She stumbled backward.

I caught my tongue and got lost in her delicate features. She left me breathless and I couldn't deny how much I appreciated what I was seeing. The woman was a slender tiger growling at me and I prayed to God she was one of Madam's girls. "Pardon me," I said.

She had a dark furrowed brow with fire flaming across her hooded, jade green eyes. "That's all you have to say for yourself?" She cocked out her hip, clearly used to having things her way.

My eyes traveled down her chest, rounding her slender hips, before landing on the floor, staring at my cell she'd made me drop. "You going to get that for me?"

She crossed her arms over her chest and huffed. Her pouty

lips vibrated and made me clench my abs. "You're not even going to apologize?" She gave me an arched look.

"Apologize because *you* ran into me?" My dick grew heavy with the attitude she tossed in my direction. If she wasn't careful, I'd be sure to correct her behavior before she lost sight of who she was dealing with.

"If you didn't have your head down, then you would have seen me coming."

I lifted my brows and pointed at my phone.

"You're an asshole." She tossed her jet-black hair over her shoulder and tried to skirt past me.

I stepped in front of her and she crumbled against me once more. Her nostrils flared as she looked up at me from beneath her brow. I pointed at my phone and got drunk on her intoxicating scent—all fruits and flowers and 100% femininity.

"Fine. Fuck. Whatever." She bent down, picked up my phone and handed it to me. "There. Are you happy now?"

"Couldn't be happier." I tucked the device deep inside my suit jacket pocket and thought that with a little work, this little vixen with an attitude could be trained to obey my every command.

"Now, can I go?"

I stepped to the side and watched her hustle down the stairs until she was out of sight. She had some mouth on her. A mouth that could spout out words unlike any woman I'd met before, and with lips that were pouty enough to fuck. There was little doubt in my mind I had to have her, and I knew just who I needed to ask.

3

KELLY

"Kelly Black." The Madam smiled as she rounded her desk to hug me. "My favorite criminal defense lawyer."

"It's good to see you, Maddy." We greeted each other with air kisses and an embracing hug.

"Please, Kelly. No one calls me by my first name."

I took each of her hands, gently squeezing them, and said, "I just ran into one of your girls." She gave me a questioning look and I hoped that I was right with my assumption.

"Was she nice to you? That one can be a firecracker sometimes." Her knees pulled together as if embarrassed by how she thought I may have been treated.

"She has quite the mouth on her." My lips spread as I felt my smile hit my eyes.

Madam frowned. "That's what I was afraid of."

"She bumped into me as I was heading up." Madam looked worried. "She called me an asshole."

Jerome covered his mouth and snickered.

"I do apologize. You know that's not the culture I promote around here."

My voice dropped as I couldn't let it go. "So, she is one of your girls?"

The Madam slipped her hands away from mine, turned her back, and let the tips of her fingers brush over the top of her expansive mahogany desk as she talked. "A new recruit."

I tipped my head back, rejoicing inside my head.

"Please, Kelly." She spun around with a bright glimmer in her eye. "Other than her mouth, what was your first impression of her?"

My tongue wet my lips and when I started to think about her, what she was wearing, how she wanted to kick my ass, my cock twitched and my nerves tingled with excitement. What I was feeling now had been what my life had been missing for far too long. In a split second, I'd come alive. Something about that girl awakened a sense of arousal I hadn't experienced in what felt like a lifetime. No matter what sexual pursuits I conquered, nothing had me as thrilled as the thought that maybe that woman could soon be mine.

The Madam looked on with a set jaw.

Maybe it was a feeling of having finally met my match. Or perhaps it was having a woman of her size and stature—small and lightweight—challenge a man of my weight and height without an ounce of visible fear. She had my mind reeling with ways I wanted to bend and twist her, bending her strong will into complete submission.

"You can be honest with me," the Madam continued. "It's important I know what men of your class perceive in women like that one."

Images of her legs wrapped around my head as I devoured her sex flashed behind my lids. "Why? Will I be getting a night with her?"

The Madam glanced toward Jerome and he didn't give any indication for me to form a conclusion as to whether my need to have her was even a possibility. Madam collected some loose papers on her desk, formed a pile, and neatly tucked them inside a manila folder before securely slipping them into an empty sleeve in the drawer of her desk. "She's been receiving incredible feedback from the clients she's dated." The Madam's eyes glazed over as she stared at nothing in particular on her desk.

I stepped closer, my brows drawing together. "What is it?"

"It's nothing." She flashed a quick smile and went back to organizing papers on her desk. But I knew the Madam well enough to know that when she lost her train of thought, it was never nothing. There was something she was hiding. "Please, Kelly. Your opinion is valuable to me," she pleaded.

With my hands stuffed in my pockets I shrugged and said, "She's feisty and would be a phenomenal fuck."

The Madam tipped her chin back and hooted. "Always thinking with your dick."

"Here. Don't think that I forgot the reason why I'm stopping by in the first place." I reached inside my suit jacket pocket, pulled out the envelope she was expecting to receive, and slid it across her desk.

Her strong posture bent when her eyes landed on the envelope. "So it's true."

"I'm afraid so."

She let out a heavy sigh. "I'm not sure I have the strength to see them."

I stepped forward and took the envelope back. Opening it, I took the liberty of removing the first photograph from the top of the pile. It was important she saw who it was I called her about earlier. I needed answers and knew that the Madam might just have them. "Just tell me if she was one of your girls."

The Madam squeezed her eyes shut and turned her head.

"I need to know."

She looked over my shoulder to Jerome and motioned for him to leave. He stepped outside and shut the door after him.

I dangled the photo of the beautiful young blonde in front of

Madam's face. Her eyes teared as she studied the girl's delicate features. I must have looked at this photo a hundred different times and not once did I not recognize the life—so bright and true—shining in her promising eyes. And I knew that was what the Madam was seeing now, too. "Was she?"

The Madam swallowed hard.

"If she was, your words are safe with me."

Her eyes rolled up and met my heavy gaze. "Is she the only one, or are there others?"

"She's the only one I'm aware of." A grave expression tightened my face. I wasn't sure if I should be happy that she was the only one and there weren't more, or sad that all it took was one to forever change the world in which we lived.

"Kelly, if working women are being targeted, you would tell me, right?" The Madam's arms flexed and she was back to her strong self.

"You'd be the first to know." My head hung as a part of me deflated just thinking about the possibility of there being others.

The Madam turned to the window and we stood there in silence for a long while before she asked, "Who's your source?"

"Sylvia Neil."

She turned her head to look over her shoulder. "The tabloid reporter?"

"That's the one." I turned on a heel and stepped toward the door. "Call me if you're reminded of anything."

"Kelly," she twisted so that she was facing me, "take the photos with you."

I nodded as I reached for the envelope, slipping the photo back inside and stuffing it away in my jacket. "I'll have them if you need them," I said, opening the door.

"And Kelly?"

I turned to look at the Madam staring at me with round, protruding eyes. "That woman you bumped into—"

My head tipped back and I held my breath, waiting.

"In case you're wondering, she's not for sale."

4

KENDRA

I knew from the box that it was from the Madam. "Thank you," I said, taking the delivery from the courier and shutting the door to my apartment.

The courier was a new face and I was barely dressed, having heard the knock on my door just as I was stepping out of the shower. With a towel wrapped around my head and a soft, cotton bathrobe draped over my body, I pranced to the door trusting the Madam enough to know she would never send just anybody to my apartment without thoroughly vetting them first. This was my house, an address I didn't hand out freely. Few people knew where I lived, and I preferred it that way.

I moved to the couch, the cushions sinking beneath my weight, and cursed the Madam when thinking about the conversation we'd had earlier. She needed to open her eyes to what was standing in front of her. My sense of fashion was impeccable and I could only think that her choosing what I wore was a play of power.

The tips of my fingers pinched the cherry red bow, pulling it free.

I shook my head and clucked my tongue, not understanding

why every outfit before a date had to be delivered in such a ridiculous box. It was thick, sturdy, and a very pleasant cream color. But its elegance was too much.

But then again, that was the Madam described to a tee. And it was how all my outfits arrived so I might as well get used to it.

A tiny squared note fell onto my glass coffee table. Besides the date card, I never received a note like this, so I read it.

Remember, this is my show. ~Madam

"The bitch needs to get off her high horse," I mumbled to myself. "And there is no way I'm tossing my closet in the trash. I love my clothes."

I set the note off to the side, opened the box, and pulled the neatly folded dress out to hold it up in front of me. "Then again, I do like this." I laughed.

The Madam had chosen a gorgeous ivory laced maxi dress and paired it with a white diamond necklace with matching dangling earrings. It was an angelic combination that was sure to knock whoever my date was on his ass.

Speaking of date, I draped the dress over the box and opened the date card. My mouth tugged into a closed-lip smile as I read where I'd be eating tonight. It was LA's best steakhouse in the heart of downtown. A tingle of excitement flooded my senses as I couldn't wait to tell Alex about this one.

My head spun toward my clock near the kitchen and I knew I didn't have much time to get ready before seven o'clock rolled around.

A flutter rolled through my stomach as the clock ticked down. That was another thing about working for the Madam: there was never enough time between when I received my outfit and when I had to leave to pair the night's look with the right touch of makeup.

My cell beeped and I quickly checked to see if it was Alex.

I lowered my head and slinked away when it wasn't. Alex was the only one I had time for. Well, her and the Madam. But I knew the Madam wouldn't be calling, and certainly not messaging. She had other ways to communicate and if it was really urgent, she'd be barging in through my front door to speak with me in person.

I gathered my things and went to my bedroom, taking the box with me. Laid out on my bed was what I would have chosen if I had a say in what I wore. No matter how much I didn't want to admit it, Madam's dress was the better choice. I hung mine back up in the closet and continued getting ready.

As I did my hair I couldn't stop thinking about what Madam said about my date tonight.

He's a powerful man.

He holds great influence over the city.

Most of the men I dated through the Madam were powerful and held influence in a variety of societal spheres. But the way she made it a point of letting me know exactly what to expect, I couldn't help but think that this one had to be different. And as my mind raced to guess what kind of man he was—the mayor, the police chief, perhaps—my eyes grew wider. I leaned closer to the mirror and whispered, "Him."

I gasped and blinked a sort of disbelief as I'd nearly forgotten about him—the man who slammed into me coming from Madam's office.

His dark and somewhat messy hair gave the impression of a beach bum. And so did his sun-kissed skin. But the way his broad shoulders filled his expensive suit had me thinking he was a high-powered executive of some sort. And that wasn't even mentioning the look in his eye. The look that said he was undressing me and on his way to fucking me. Because that was there too. Right up there against his chiseled features and solid muscles. I crashed into him hard and he didn't budge, didn't flinch, just stood there like I was an inconvenience who had gotten in his way.

I dropped my robe and let it fall to the floor, quick to notice my nipples were already tight with arousal. The thoughts of that man had me hot and bothered all over again.

He had some nerve to treat me the way he did. When most men would apologize and pick up their own phones *they* dropped, he demanded I be the one to pick up his. Like it was my fault. It was clear he was a man who got off on telling others what to do. *The balls—*

My sex clenched and I hated myself for thinking—maybe even *hoping*—that he could be my date tonight.

I slipped on a thong and strapless bra before moving through the house. I checked the time, tossed a few essentials into my clutch, and stepped into my dress last. One last glance at the clock, and I was ahead of schedule.

The Madam's words rang between my ears on how to be a good obedient woman. I knew where she was coming from and understood the agreement we had in place. This was her show.

She was right about that, but being a good obedient woman was never my thing. I liked testing authority, pushing people's buttons, and seeing the surprised look on people's faces when I shocked them with my take-no-prisoner attitude that didn't match up with my small frame.

I didn't know what people expected, but that was who I was. Take it or leave it. Kendra Williams didn't put up with shit. I'd learned early on that this world was unfair and if I wasn't careful, people would take advantage of me for one reason or another.

My phone dinged with another message and I hoped it was Alex.

Except it wasn't. "Girl, where are you?" I said, reading my message telling me that my Uber driver was on his way.

I didn't like not hearing from her. I'd put in a call earlier, then messaged her, and still hadn't heard back. Something was up and I hoped that she was okay. This wasn't like her to not at least hit me back with a stupid emoji or something.

I locked up my apartment, took the short elevator ride down

to ground level, and knew from experience that my ride would be already waiting by the time I got to him.

Alex had me worried so I called, not willing to wait any longer. "Hey, babe." She picked up on the first ring.

"What the fuck?"

"Did I do something wrong?"

"Yeah, I've been waiting to hear back from you."

"Sorry. Nash just left."

I could feel her hot cheeks blushing through the phone and I was sure he just sexed her up real good. "I hope it was worth it."

"I'm lonely already."

"Ew, barf." I stuck my finger down my throat for effect.

"What? He's going to be gone for two weeks and I hate it when I can't see him every day."

I rolled my eyes and rounded the next block, picking up the pace. Alex must have heard me breathing hard because she asked if I was jogging. "Briskly walking," I said.

"Where you going? Anywhere fun?"

"This girl has a date tonight."

"Are you still getting picked up two blocks from your building?"

"I am. So what?"

"The world isn't as dark as some people want you to believe."

"And this is coming from the woman who was kidnapped."

"I survived."

The outcome could have been so different, but I wasn't about to remind her of that seeing how I was the one taking all the risks now. "What's it matter, anyway? I like to keep my secrets and there's no way I'd get picked up in front of my place. Too many creeps in this city."

"See? That's what I'm talking about."

"So they meet on my terms, terms the Madam has no problem with me having."

"Oh, I gotta go," Alex said frantically. "Nash is on the line."

"Didn't you just say goodbye?"

"Call you later." She ended the call.

Ring a big freakin' dong.

Alex was losing her mind with that man. He had a big dick and a sizable bank account but I still thought she should have waited longer to tell him that she loved him.

I finally worked my way through the group of people and saw that my ride was waiting. As soon as I slid into the car I recognized the same eyes from earlier today. "Hey, it's you again," I said, closing the door.

"You're a busy lady." His eyes smiled as he glanced in his mirror before beginning to drive.

"A working girl."

"And me, a working man." He laughed.

"Should I be worried about you?"

"I'm in good health, have good eyes, and am always smiling. What is there to worry about?"

"You're not from around here, are you?"

"Uganda."

"What's Africa like? Is it as hot as they say?"

"Hotter," he said making us both laugh.

I was thankful for having him drive me again. He was friendly and made the ride enjoyable. We were downtown and parked outside the restaurant before I knew it. "Maybe we'll meet again," I said, stepping out.

"I hope so."

I watched him drive away, wishing I caught his name so maybe I could request him again the next time I needed a lift.

"You must be Kendra," a friendly voice said behind me.

I turned to find a tall, handsome man heading my way. He was attractive for being significantly older than me—not that age mattered. Perhaps it was the tux he was wearing or the silver hair. Either way, I would be lying if I said I wasn't at least a little disappointed to learn my date wasn't going to be the man from earlier. "And you are...?"

"Your date for the evening." He gripped my shoulders and leaned in to kiss my cheeks.

"Does my date have a name?"

"Oscar." He held out his arm and I hooked mine in the crook of his. "Oscar Buchanan."

The name sounded familiar, but I couldn't place it. We walked to the entrance and he kept stealing approving glances at me. "Your name, it sounds familiar."

He stopped walking, angled his head down, and gave me an intent look. "Have I prosecuted you?"

"So," my eyes narrowed, "you're a lawyer?"

"District Attorney." He flashed a knowing grin at the same time he opened the doors. The smells of meat grilling and onions frying hit my senses and made my stomach grumble. Immediately, I knew that tonight was going to be one for the taking. I'd suck his credit card dry, then if he was lucky, I'd milk him for everything he was worth. But the real question was, what would this elected official want in return?

5

KELLY

Giselle slid into the back of my SUV, joining me in the backseat, and buckled her belt. "I have to admit, Kelly, your sense of fashion is quite good. You really know how to make a woman feel beautiful."

"You look lovely," I said, smiling at the gown I had chosen for her to wear.

A blush crept across her cheeks as she turned her head to look out the window. It was dusk, on its way to night, and we headed downtown with my driver, Maxwell, at the wheel. Not a minute could be wasted in my line of work and more times than not, this was a more perfect time than any to get caught up or prepare for what was ahead.

"I'm sorry for having to drag you away from your boyfriend again." My hand crossed the middle seat and came to rest on hers.

Giselle didn't flinch when I squeezed it; rather, she turned her head to face me and gave me a sympathetic smile under hooded eyes. "He'll learn to forgive me."

"If there is anything I can do to make it up to him..." I rubbed my freshly shaven face, feeling somewhat guilty for always pulling Giselle into work.

"Let's not talk about it," she whispered as I brought my hand back to rest on my own thigh.

We both retreated back into our heads, letting our silence fill the car as my stomach hardened with a sense of remorse toward the demands this job created. I'd seen it happen before in my own life. Giselle's eyes weren't too different from a woman I once loved. The pain, with a dash of regret, was there. Our line of work was strenuous, full of stress, and often times reminded us daily of the dark world that surrounded us all. Like this murder case that had hit our desks recently.

I stared at the back of Giselle's head as she watched the world pass us by outside.

Our work was difficult—as was the case for many demanding professions—to shed at the end of the day and regularly followed us into our own homes and into the arms of the ones we loved. Some of us were able to make it work, but for most of us, it was the reason why we were single.

Giselle caught me staring and I gave her a quick reassuring smile.

I didn't want this life for her. She was young, with a lifetime of promise ahead. From the way she spoke, I could hear the strain, feel the hurt tensing her muscles, and hoped that our job—her choice of profession—wasn't damaging her relationship with John the same way it had to me with a woman I'd given my heart to. John was a good man. He loved her and I knew she loved him more than anything, too. Well, except maybe her job. That was where she and I were both flawed. The job always came first, no matter what.

"Any word from Sylvia since she handed off the original file of photos?" She pulled her cell out from her purse and opened an email.

I shook my head. "Gone completely quiet."

"Don't you think that's weird?" She quickly glanced at me, back to her usual self.

My shoulders shrugged. "My guess is that she's found another story to report on until this one gains some steam."

"Makes sense." She squinted her eyes and read the text that populated her screen. "Julia Mabel is aware of the case but didn't know that Sylvia Neil was our source."

"See if Julia has any information on any other cold cases of missing women."

"Would her publisher have that kind of information?"

"Only if it involves a celebrity." I cast my gaze out the window, realizing we were close to the restaurant. Giselle was typing up an email to Julia when I said, "Then we can match those against the police case files of missing persons, see if there is any correlation."

"Yeah, of course." Her thumbs busily swiped across her screen.

"I need to know what we're working with here. I can't have any surprises come flying at me, threatening to knock me off my feet the deeper we go in this case."

Maxwell parked in front of the restaurant and opened Giselle's door, assisting her out of the vehicle. I met them on the other side and told Maxwell I'd see him in a couple hours. He nodded once and slid back behind the wheel.

"But we don't even know who did this," Giselle said as we stepped up to the restaurant's entrance.

I dug my heels in and stopped, clamping my hands tightly around her arms. "Then find out," I said firmly, in a low voice so others nearby couldn't hear me.

She drew back, making herself appear smaller than she was, and nodded. "I'll do what I can."

We stepped inside to the sounds of meat sizzling on the grill tucked somewhere in the back. Vegetables sizzled just behind the laughter and conversation. My stomach grumbled at the smells and I couldn't wait to finally get some food in my system. I was starved, having not eaten since lunch.

"Mr. Black." The hostess stepped forward, recognizing me. "Right this way. Your guests are waiting."

I followed two steps behind with Giselle on my arm. I liked arriving last, making my guests wait for me, instead of me having to kill time waiting for them. Though this meeting was cordial, I couldn't appear to be weak in front of my colleague.

We weaved through a dozen tables heading toward the back when I found his gaze on me in a sea of faces. The District Attorney was alone and I smiled. He returned my smile, and I knew the reason why he returned it. I had Giselle by my side.

He absolutely loved Giselle. Oscar had his eyes all over her, and I swore that with the way he was looking at her now, she'd be left wearing nothing if he had his way by the time we were seated. And that was why I had her in that dress. It was the right color. *His* color. From the way it caught the light and showed off her amazing natural cleavage to the slit up her thigh. It was a bombshell and she looked stunning. And with it on, she could persuade even a man like him to commit a crime.

Then everything came to a crashing halt when I saw who came up from behind Oscar, choosing the seat next to him. "Oh, shit," I mumbled.

Giselle looked up and gave me a questioning look when she realized I'd stopped dead in my tracks. "Everything all right?"

I swallow hard, straightened my jacket, and rolled my shoulders back. "Fine."

"Are you sure?" Her brows squished together.

"Yeah. Please," I said, holding my hand out in front, motioning for her to take the lead. It was just that I wasn't expecting to see *her* here with the DA. Now I knew tonight was going to be interesting.

"If it wasn't for Giselle joining you tonight," the DA stood, "I'm not sure I'd be so happy to see you, Kelly."

We shook hands. "It's always a pleasure, even when it's not." I angled my head toward his date and winked at the short woman who had me hard.

After the Madam ensured me she wasn't available, I didn't know how I'd find a way to see her again. Then, out of the blue, the heavens opened up and put her at the same table as me tonight. What were the odds?

"I'm glad you could join us," Oscar said.

I couldn't keep my eyes off her. There was a glimmer in her eye that was already cursing me for being the asshole she so easily labeled me as before. There was no doubt she recognized me and, once again, my ball sack was tightening under the flame burning in her sexy gaze. "Any excuse to bust your balls," I said with a smirk, turning my attention back to Oscar.

The DA had already moved on and turned his attention to Giselle, kissing her on each of her cheeks. "Do you two know each other?" he asked when he found me staring at his date again.

"We've met." My core flexed as I burned for her.

"No, I don't think we have." She said it so convincingly, I almost believed her.

"Well, then let me introduce you." Oscar reached out to take her hand, pulling her up on her feet. "Kendra, this is Kelly Black, the city's most ruthless criminal defense lawyer."

So, her name is Kendra, I thought to myself, making sure to give the DA a toast before our meal for that kind of introduction.

"And his lovely assistant, Giselle."

I watched Kendra shake Giselle's hand, letting them get their introductions out of their systems before moving on to my own. When they were done, I made my move, choosing to greet Kendra in the same fashion Oscar did Giselle. "It's so good to see you again," I whispered in her ear. Kendra flinched at my touch, but I wasn't about to let go.

"Wish I could say the same," she murmured.

My lips tugged at the corners. I loved her attitude and wondered if her bark came with a bite. "Don't be naïve." My fingers clamped tightly on her arm. "I know you're one of Madam's girls." She pulled back and looked at me with wide eyes. "And you're just waiting for me to tell you to bend over again."

Her eyes threw daggers as I stepped away, pulling a chair out for Giselle to sit in. I put her next to the DA so I could stay close to my new love affair, Kendra.

Oscar glanced over at Kendra when his and Giselle's conversation died down. I watched Kendra smile at him, beautifully maintaining face in the presence of scandal.

"Kendra, if you ever find yourself on the wrong side of the law, Kelly Black is a great man to know." Oscar laughed.

When Kendra glanced at me, she held her chin high, waiting to see how I'd respond. Inside, I felt giddy for how easy it was for me to get under her skin. "You don't seem like someone who has to worry," I said, looking straight into Kendra's beautiful fiery eyes.

She brought her elbows on the table and leaned forward. "I'm not one to follow the rules."

I bit my bottom lip, feeling my dick twitch against my pants. It was like she was tempting me, teasing me with subtle invitations. "Is that right?"

"Oh, dear." Oscar laughed. "I may have opened up the wrong can tonight."

Kendra's elbows crossed over into my territory. "But I do consider myself a law-abiding citizen so I hope that after tonight we won't *ever* have to see each other again."

Now I was rock hard. This woman had to be punished, and no doubt I'd be the one to lay down the law, teaching her how the world really worked.

I watched Oscar's hand move under the table over to her thigh. Beneath my side of the table, my fist clenched as jealousy burned in my chest. Despite the fact that he was with the woman

I wanted, I couldn't help myself from laughing at the irony of knowing the District Attorney was having to use an escort service like the Madam's.

"I heard your case settled today," Oscar said, smiling at Giselle.

"Are you surprised?" she said coyly.

"Depends." Oscar glanced at me.

"On?"

"On who was lead defender."

"I was," Giselle said.

"Then," Oscar angled his head to Giselle, smiling, "no, I'm not. You're the smart one."

"And that's the reason your office signed off on it?" I asked, curious to hear his thoughts on granting my client the plea deal of a lifetime.

"My office signed off on it because we have bigger fish to fry."

The waiter came to the table, opening a bottle of red wine Oscar had ordered before we arrived. When he got around to me, I covered my hand over my wine glass and said, "Just lemon water for me." The waiter nodded and left.

"Still not drinking, Kelly?"

I turned to look at Giselle and she said, "Kendra, please join me in the powder room, will you?"

Kendra looked at her date and Oscar nodded, giving her his approval.

Together, we watched the women slowly disappear to the front of the restaurant. "She's something, isn't she?" Oscar said.

"Aren't you afraid of having your wife find out?"

Oscar gave me a questioning look, like he didn't know what I was saying. Then I turned back to where I'd last seen the women.

"The divorce was finalized." He set his wine glass down and smoothed his hands down his front. "It's finally over."

"And where did you meet such an attractive young woman?"

His eyes narrowed and I knew Oscar was one to keep the fight at the courthouse—not wanting it to interfere with his public life.

"Forgive me for saying, but I just can't see why someone like Kendra would go out with a man your age."

"Listen to you, never able to leave the courtroom." He chuckled.

I pointed at him and laughed. "Don't worry, Oscar, your secret is safe with me."

He cocked his head, and I nodded.

When I turned back around, I saw the women across the far side of the room, making their way back to the table. "We had an interesting case file hit our desk recently."

The DA leaned forward, listening intently.

"Are you aware of any recent murders involving working women?"

"Who's your client?"

I shook my head. "No one. Yet."

"Then what's your interest? This sounds like the police investigation is still ongoing."

"You may be right. This one just feels...personal." I could hear the women laughing and I knew that Giselle could warm a woman like Kendra up, making her feel welcome in no time at all.

"Not working women, but if you're referring to the young student working in the film industry, then yes, I'm aware," Oscar said, his face firming up to the work tone I was most familiar with.

The women seated themselves, still laughing about whatever it was they were talking about. Oscar leaned closer to me and said, "Let me know what you find out. That case is certainly interesting."

"Kendra, tell Kelly what you were telling me." Giselle smiled.

Kendra started talking, and though I was looking her in her eye, my mind retreated back inside itself. My vision blurred as I was once again consumed by the markings left on the dead woman's body. "Oh, screw him," she laughed, waving me off, recognizing that I wasn't listening. "The three of us will go."

"Is that Wesley Reid's place?" Oscar asked.

I blinked, snapping out of my thoughts. "Mojito?"

"Yeah," Kendra said.

"It is."

"Speaking of Wes." Oscar looked at me and he had that serious expression tightening his face. "Blake Stone's preliminary hearing begins soon. I have to admit, Kelly, I was surprised to learn you didn't accept his case."

"Despite what you may think, I do have a conscience." I laid my napkin across my thighs. "But now that I have one client in the clear, maybe I'll have time to represent him."

He laughed and turned to Kendra. "Criminal defense lawyers are all liars working to free the devil. Don't believe a word he says."

6

KENDRA

"He can wait," I said over my shoulder to Alex.

She peered down the hallway with a longing gaze.

"I like to be bare and smooth before my massage." I untied the fluffy loop around my waist and dropped my robe to the floor, making sure the muscular masseur hiding behind the potted plants was looking. "Go on, honey." I turned back to Alex. "Drop your robe. The man you're flirting with is looking."

She huffed out a disbelieving laugh. "Uh-uh. Oh, no. I prefer to stay covered up, thanks."

"Even with the men you flirt with?" Alex skirted around me, stepped into the waxing room, and plopped her butt down on the empty table. I waved my fingers at the cute masseur, picked my robe up from the floor, and slid on my belly onto the table next to Alex. "Remember the first time you waxed your cunt?"

Alex stared up at the ceiling, a smile tugging at her lips. "Yeah, I remember."

"And now look at you. It's like you know what you're doing." My legs were bent at the knee as my feet kicked through the air.

Aromas of lavender, grapefruit, and eucalyptus filled the air and I felt as comfortable here as I did most places.

Alex's brows creased.

"What?" My feet stopped swinging and I pushed my chest up off the table, rooting my weight on my elbows.

She frowned. "I miss him."

"God. Seriously?"

She nodded.

My forehead crashed down to the table. When I peeked over at her with one eye open, she nodded again. "What's he been gone, like, an hour?"

"Twenty-four." She covered her face and laughed.

I flopped over onto my back, wondering what happened to my friend who was once my wing-woman when hitting up bars. The estheticians arrived and greeted us. I was quick to tell them the work I wanted done, and I told them to do the same on Alex. Alex glanced in my direction and I said, "You are whipped."

She raised her brows. "You would be too if you had what I have."

I gave her an arched look. Her legs were bent and spread but she remained covered in that angelic white robe. Not me, I didn't care about letting it all hang out. Besides, being naked just made things easier. The way I saw it, clothes just got in the way of living. "Please do share. I'm sure we'd *all* like to know what it's like to let Donkey Kong stretch our vagina." The women working us giggled.

Alex winced as her roots began getting pulled. "Well, if you must know—"

"Yes. I must. *We*—" my hands swished through the air in a big circle, "—all must know."

She closed her eyes and a stupid smile spread across her face. "It's amazing."

I couldn't stop staring at her. Was I really hearing her? Was this really the Alex Grace that I knew? The one person I would do anything for? Her face was beaming bright and there was that sparkle in her eye that told me she was head over heels in love. My stomach flipped and I wanted to vomit.

"I wish I could share him."

My head lifted off the table. "Who says you can't?"

Her lips parted and now she was just showing off her perfect teeth.

"Shit, girl. Pass him around. Let us have a taste of this oh so uh-mazing sexual creature that has you acting like a housewife having an affair."

Alex laughed. "I'm hardly a housewife."

"Yet you chose to stay covered because...?" My hand moved the length of her, pointing at her robe.

Alex tossed her head back and yelped. "Christ that hurt. Remind me again why we do this so often?"

"To get fucked," I said, making her laugh. I closed my eyes and got to thinking about my role with the Madam. The job, it was good for me. It kept my life fresh and without routine. I liked that. No day was the same, and when I wasn't working, I had the day to do whatever I wanted. I knew escorting wasn't for everyone, but it was good to me and I could spend days here, at the spa, hearing how in love my friend was. "Baby doll, tell me this," I said, turning back to Alex.

Alex rolled her head to the side and met my curious gaze.

"Does it get boring fucking the same man night after night?"

The woman working me snickered.

"You're unbelievable," Alex said, smiling.

"The heat has to die down. No fire burns forever," I reminded her.

"Gas fires do," she said in a firm voice. "If you let them."

"Yeah, I suppose. But gas fires—unlike wood fires—also have the chance of exploding, too. Is that a risk you're willing to take?"

"That won't be us. With Nash, we're an even hot burn."

I reached over and touched her arm. "I don't know, with him gone you seem cold to me."

She swatted my hand away. "Trust me. I'm hot."

"Aren't you afraid, though?"

Alex turned her head to look me in the eye. "That he'll leave me?"

"No. That's not what I was thinking."

"Afraid of what then?"

"That he'll leave your pussy lips flappy like an old hag."

"You're disgusting."

"I'm serious." My brows knitted tight. "I mean, if he's as big as you say he is—"

Alex gave me a pinched expression. "I'll make sure to keep my young pussy tight just for him."

The woman working me finished up between my legs and I rolled over to stick my ass in the air.

"What about you?" Alex couldn't look at me while on all fours like I was about to take it from behind. "All this talk about sex is making me think you're not getting any yourself."

I reached behind and pulled my ass cheeks apart, not wanting the esthetician to miss a hair. "Finally, you asked. You know, this relationship isn't always about you."

"You're not?" Alex gasped. "But I thought—"

"Yeah, me too." My tongue smoothed over my teeth and picked up some mint flavor left over from earlier. "But nope. Haven't fucked a single date." I rolled onto my back and pointed to my nipples. "Better clean these up too," I said, jiggling them inside my hands. *They still have it*, I thought to myself.

"The money is good, right?"

"It's not why I'm doing this." The hot wax perked my twins.

"I know. But still." Alex opened her robe, revealing her chest to have her nipples done as well.

"There's this man I keep seeing."

Alex snapped her head around and had a glow in her eye that

told me she just couldn't wait to hear more about this man who kept me awake at night. "Go on."

"It's not what you think. He's not a date."

Her brows drew together and her lips pursed.

"First time I ran into him, I *literally* ran into him." My hands joined the conversation. "I mean, here I was, minding my own business, when out of nowhere, this man is blocking the entire staircase. *Smack!* My nose hit his chest. His cell went flying and I stumbled back."

Alex's eyes went big, growing round like golf balls popping out of her head. "What did he do? Did he apologize?"

I barked out a sarcastic laugh, thinking how Kelly Black wasn't a man who apologized. "He made *me,*" I jabbed my chest with my finger, "pick up his damn phone."

"Then what happened?"

"I picked up his phone!"

"No, I mean after that. How did you see him again? You said you keep seeing this man." Alex's voice was loud and fast as she demanded to know more.

"Then, guess who my date is having dinner with last night."

"No!" Alex's mouth circled. "Him?"

I nodded just as we finished up. Alex wrapped herself back up and I draped my robe over my shoulder as our feet hit the ground and we started making our way to the other side of the spa. "What are the chances, right? That's what I was thinking."

"So, who is he?" Alex hooked her arm in the crook of mine as we slowly padded across the warm bamboo floor.

"Well, let's just put it this way." I leaned in close to her ear and dropped my voice down to a whisper so that no one could hear. "My date was the District Attorney."

Alex touched her neck. "And the man you're crushin' on?"

"Criminal defense lawyer."

"Does he have a name?"

"I better not say," I said, looking around at the many faces surrounding us.

She grabbed me by the shoulders and dug her nails into my sensitive flesh. "Does he know your background?"

I shook my head. "And I wasn't about to tell him."

We started walking again when Alex asked, "What did your date think of all this?"

"See, that's just it. This guy stole me away after dinner, insisting that he have the first dance."

"And your date was cool with that?"

My shoulders shrugged. "There was nothing I could do."

"What about the Madam, won't she be pissed?" Alex's gaze was at her feet. "I mean, she's the one who set this up, pairing you with the right man and all."

"You should have seen these two men. They were both more into each other's dates then the ones they went there with. Typical men, jockeying for dominance."

"The DA?" Alex looked at me again with her mouth falling open as if her mind was catching up to everything I was unloading.

I nodded. "Scandalous. I know."

"Do you think you'll see him again?"

"Who, the DA?"

"No. The other one?"

My head bobbed. "I don't know. I sure hope so, because my pussy is in desperate need of relief."

Dozens of missing persons files laid scattered across my desk. I pulled my drawer open and reached for a pair of leather cuffs.

I studied them, holding them up to the light. They were fleece-lined and each had an O-ring restraint to easily attach them to a bedpost or the ceiling.

My fingertip traveled the edge of the leather. It was a tough, ninety-degree cut, but with the soft fleece liner, it should never dig deep enough to cut flesh no matter how tightly clamped around a wrist they were.

My gaze cast back to the photos I had spread across my desk. Each of them highlighted a different area of concern on the young woman's body. There was a picture of her cut and bruised wrist. Another of her ankles. Lash marks between her shoulders, and bruises from being paddled across her upper thighs. They were marks I knew well, marks similar to ones I'd given to my own Subs.

However, there was a clear difference between the ones I gave and the marks I was looking at now. Only an amateur would do this kind of damage.

I licked the pad of my finger and flipped through more photographs.

Her skin had been cut to the point of bleeding. There were signs of struggle, like she'd put up a fight. None of this was how it was supposed to be. For those of us partaking in this underworld of sexual experimentation, we knew the rules, understood the limitations, all of it decided upon by each participant.

But not here. Not with what happened to her.

With her, there had been no rules, no limitations, and it was like whoever did this to her maybe even got off on raping the victim after she was dead.

My stomach flipped and when I shoved my fingers through my hair, I had a desire to shower. I felt grimy and disgusted by what I was seeing. This, what happened to her, gave a bad name to the rest of us. To an untrained eye, it was all the same and could happen to any Sub willing to get bound.

But I knew the truth. It was written across her body. She had been beaten, restrained, raped. None of it was consenting. This wasn't what she wanted and it should have never happened. And that was what bothered me most.

I leaned back in my leather office chair and played with my pair of cuffs, thinking.

Inside, I burned with a desire to help convict the son-of-a-bitch who did this. It was an unusual feeling for me, considering I was generally the one who was making sure criminals walked free, not caring if they were guilty or not. But something about this case sparked a need to do what I knew in my heart to be right, and I'd do whatever I could to help the prosecution once they charged the asshole with the crime.

My arm stretched out and I set the cuffs back down on my desk.

It was in all our best interests to get this one solved—not just pushed under the rug—before word got around to exposing the secret society many influential members, including myself, participated in. The last thing we all needed was for our lifestyle to be easily associated with something as horrendous as murder.

I leaned forward and rested my elbows on my desk, continuing to shuffle through the many other women who had gone missing and whose cases hadn't been solved. There had to be a link between them and this one.

Except I couldn't find one. At least, not with the information I had.

When I glanced up, my breath caught in my throat. I swallowed down the lump and gently smiled back at the only photo I had on my desk, still getting choked up when staring into her soft, loving gaze.

I reached out and let my finger brush over her face. I could still remember the day the picture was taken as if it happened yesterday. We'd just adopted a new puppy and she couldn't have been happier. The leaves were bright green and so full of life after a rainstorm whose scent lingered in the air. It was fresh, just like our relationship. Little did we know that darkness was just around the corner, waiting.

My desk phone lit up and started ringing, snapping me out of my thoughts.

"Kelly, I'm surprised to have you answer so quickly," the Madam said when I picked up.

"You caught me at my desk." I licked my lips and forced myself to look away from the framed picture.

"Fantastic!" She cackled one of her famous laughs. "I won't waste your time."

I turned my head to the window, watching a pigeon perch on a branch. "What can I do for you?"

"I need you to pay Emmanuel a visit—"

"I'm not interested," I said, interrupting her.

"But you haven't heard the best of it."

I rolled my eyes, relieved to know that my lines were secure. I couldn't be caught colluding with clients and helping them get away with whatever crimes they were attempting to commit.

"Perhaps if I open up my new recruit you'd be more open to the idea?" Her voice was full of spirit and I knew it was just one her manipulation tactics. "You'd like that, wouldn't you? For me to introduce you. A proper introduction. The way it should have been in the first place."

My eyes narrowed. "I don't need you to introduce me to Kendra."

"That's because you already did that yourself."

I smiled, appreciating that we could cut the bullshit and get straight to the point.

"You shouldn't have done what you did, Kelly."

"C'mon, Oscar is out of his league with her. You should know that better than I do."

The Madam went quiet and I leaned back, pressing my shoulders to the back of the chair, thinking how I was one of the few people the Madam couldn't control. Sure, she had stuff on me, as I did her, but she couldn't get away with a lot of the shit she could with others. And that was what made our cat-and-mouse relationship exciting.

"Kelly, darling, I'm not happy with you."

That was what made us good for each other. We balanced each other out, kept the other in check. Because if we didn't, then it would be only a matter of time before both our worlds imploded. "Did you hear it from Oscar himself, or did Kendra tell you?"

"Does it matter?"

"I'm a man who likes facts." I tapped the end of a pen against my notepad.

"I explicitly told you that she wasn't for sale."

"That's why you gave me no choice but to steal her myself," I said with a cocky smirk.

The Madam huffed a quick laugh.

"And now that I've had a taste, I want more."

"I'm sorry, Kelly, but I just don't think that that's possible."

"Why not?" My brows drew together.

"She's not a good match for you."

"We can argue this all day," I said, starting to pace the room. "I'll clear my schedule. But you and I both know that you're full of shit and the only thing keeping her from me is you."

"My dear, calm yourself. It's in her contract. The questionnaire you both filled out. She's not willing to do the things you would like her to do."

I stopped pacing and glanced back to the cuffs on top of my desk. My mind was consumed with a dozen different thoughts but only one made sense. "She's new to the lifestyle?"

"I'm afraid so." Madam's words were compassionate, sympathetic even.

Though I preferred my women to have experience, I could make an exception for her. She was no virgin, not with the way she carried a chip on her shoulder. But a BDSM virgin? I liked the sound of that and thought that I could be the one to train her. "I still want her."

"Kelly," I could hear Madam shaking her head, "you're not listening, dear."

"No. You're not listening. I want her. Make it happen."

"She's booked out. Still not for sale. End of discussion." Madam's voice firmed up. "Besides, there's another angel that will be a better fit. Would you like me to introduce you to her? She's definitely more of what you're looking for."

I moved to my desk and trailed my finger around the circle of the cuff. There was only one woman I wanted to strap these to, and it had to be Kendra.

Madam covered her phone with her hand and began talking to what sounded like Jerome's voice.

The second I closed my eyes, images of Kendra getting bound and fucked by me flashed behind my lids, getting me hard. It would be fun, I told myself. She'd make a great student, and when she talked back—which I knew she would—I'd find reason to punish her into being my perfect little submissive.

The voices on the other end of the line got louder. Madam's hand must have slipped from over the mic. Whatever they were discussing seemed urgent. I listened intently before Madam said, "Kelly, you do this small favor for me and—"

"Kendra will be *all* mine."

"I guess you haven't heard."

The muscles in my arms flexed. "Heard what?"

My chest tightened as a flurry of mixed emotions worked its way over my entire body. I couldn't help but feel that she was trying to use me for something, purposely redirecting the conversation in such a way that she maintained the upper hand.

"There is a client who could use your representation."

"Is he already in the system?"

"Oh, Kelly." She chuckled. "First, you agree to do this favor for me, then I'll tell you more."

"Don't forget who you're talking to. I can hear it in your voice. You need me more than I need you. Remember, Maddy—" I smiled, knowing using her first name would only piss her off, "—I've already made myself known to Kendra."

"Business is growing and with it, so will your cut."

I moved to the window, widened my stance, and tipped my chin back. Now I was sure she needed me more than I needed her. She needed me to make sure that everything was done properly—make it look lawful—so that her entire operation didn't collapse. "Tell me more about this client."

Giselle walked into the room and I put the phone on speaker so she could hear.

"Blake Stone," Madam said. "Does that name ring a bell?"

Giselle glanced at me. My brows pinched. This couldn't be coincidence with the DA just asking me about him last night. I wondered how involved Kendra was and what role she was playing for the Madam. "What happened to his current representation?" I asked.

"Apparently, the judge issued a mandatory withdrawal."

Giselle's head dropped into her hand. My mind raced to find reason to why the judge would do that. "How do you know this?"

"Oh, honey," the Madam said smugly. "My girls date clients across the city. Word travel backs to me easily. I know everything."

I wasn't all that surprised. I knew the Madam was the queen of gossip of all things interesting in LA, but now she had me wondering if she purposely placed Kendra with the DA just to see what she might be able to uncover.

"Apparently his hired attorney is also a crucial witness relating to his own case so he had to go."

If Madam was right about anything today, it was that having a case like Blake Stone's fall into my lap was big news. It would be the trial of the year. A high-profile case with more publicity than I could drum up myself.

But there was a catch. I had to win. If I didn't, my reputation would certainly lose.

"I knew it," I said as Giselle met my gaze and nodded once. "They were working together to advance his criminal enterprises."

"I'm not one to speculate," Madam said. "So, do you want it or not?"

"What's your interest in his case, anyway?" I turned back toward the window. "And why me? How do you know he doesn't already have representation?"

"It's not me who will be writing your checks, dear."

I turned to look at Giselle. She was giving me a questioning look. "So, if you're not the one funding his representation, then why do you want me to defend him?"

"Sweetie, I don't want you to defend him." I knew the Madam was smiling by the way she spoke. "I want you to get him convicted."

8

KENDRA

A s soon as I stepped foot inside, Janine gave me a look like she knew what was coming.

My stomach flipped over and I forced myself to hold my head a bit higher after seeing the look on her face. "Hi," I said, gauging her reaction as I passed her desk. She waved me through without so much as a smile and I wondered what had gotten up her ass today.

The entire ride here, my mind reeled with how I was going to explain my way out of this one. I knew I shouldn't have walked away from my date, even if he did basically offer me up to Kelly himself. But with the way Kelly spoke to me, and how he couldn't keep his eyes away, I was more attracted to him and his bad-boy nature than I was to my current date with the district attorney.

I stuck my thumb through the strap on my handbag and started up the stairs. When I came to the exact spot Kelly insisted on getting in my way, I stopped, closed my eyes, and inhaled a couple deep breaths.

It was like he was here. I could still smell his masculine scent and when I closed my eyes, I could see his strong jaw looking at me behind dark eyes, telling me to pick up his damn phone. I laughed to myself, how stupid it all was. No matter how pissed I was for him making me do something I didn't want to do, I still couldn't shake him out of my head. He'd gotten under my skin and had me right where he wanted me.

My feet continued to march up the stairs and by the time I reached the floor, I opened the door to find Jerome perched in the doorframe of Madam's office as usual. "Hey, big boy," I said in my sultry voice, pushing my hips further out to the side as I stepped up to him.

He grinned. "Hey."

"Can you smell it?" I looked to the side and tapped my finger on my bottom lip.

He gave me a questioning look.

I inched closer and leaned into him, letting his thick man thigh come between my legs. "Here, touch," I said, lifting a leg and hooking it around the backside of his knee. He didn't move, just kept his eye on me. Finally, I placed his heavy hand on my thigh and said, "You like?"

He chuckled and shook his head.

"I got all cleaned up—" my lips popped on the letter 'p', "—just for you."

He clucked his tongue and looked away, still smirking.

"Smooth as butter." I dropped my leg and stood on my toes so that my lips were close to his face. "I can show you if you want."

Jerome pushed me off just as I felt his manhood thicken in his pants. *Naughty boy.* "Madam is waiting." He motioned me inside.

"Maybe next time, *dah-ling*," I said, imitating the Madam.

I kicked off my heels, leaving them in front of the black leather couch in the waiting room that seemed to always be empty. I wondered if anyone actually used this room or if it was where Jerome hung out when he wasn't expecting visitors. I couldn't imagine his day was filled with that much activity other than standing around and protecting the Madam. He'd need a couch to twiddle his thumbs. It would be good for him.

"You called?" I said, knocking lightly on Madam's open office door.

"Kendra, doll." She lifted her head and looked in my direction. "Thank you for coming so quickly." She took her eye glasses off her face and tucked a few papers away.

I popped my bubble gum, glancing around her office, before falling into the corner of the loveseat and kicking my feet up. "When I'm called, I come."

Madam stood, rounded her desk, and rested her tailbone on the edge only a few feet from where I sat. Her eyes were cheery as normal until she crossed her arms over her chest. Then they lost their appeal and I knew things were about to get real. "Can I have Jerome get you some water?"

I glanced through the door toward where I knew he'd be standing. I thought maybe I'd accept her offer even though I wasn't at all thirsty. Just to keep Jerome thinking about me. But I decided against it. I'd see him on the way out. "No. I'm fine," I said rolling my head back to Madam. "Look, I know what this is about."

The Madam arched a perfectly shaped brow.

"And it wasn't my fault. You know he ran into me here before the date?"

Madam's other brow lifted. "Oh?"

"Like, literally hit me square in the jaw." The Madam looked more amused than concerned. "You know who I'm talking about, right?"

She gave me a knowing look.

"Then he happens to be on the double date with the client you set me up with." Madam didn't say a word. She just stood there silently listening to me go on and on. And I had to admit, it felt good to just get it all off my chest. I hadn't come up with a good excuse to how I was going to explain myself out of this one so I was left with just being myself. "So, whatever Kelly told you happened, it's probably a lie."

"Are you finished?" the Madam said.

I leaned back and let out a sigh, nodding. "Yeah. I'm done. For now."

Madam uncrossed her ankles, pushed off the edge of the desk and moved to stand in front of her window, looking down to the street below. "Actually, I haven't spoken to Kelly."

My feet dropped to the floor. "You haven't?"

"It was Oscar who called me to let me know how the date went." She twisted her spine to look me in my eyes. "Would you like to know what he said?"

I could have sworn it would have been Kelly to bring me up to the Madam. That man had some nerve and made it clear that he wanted me. Then, I thought about the date and how Oscar and Kelly clearly had it out for each other. But it wasn't like Kelly stealing me away made Oscar all that upset. Besides, he seemed more interested in Giselle than he did me. "Not really."

"I'll tell you anyway." She moved slowly in my direction. "Oscar said he'll no longer be needing my services."

Confusion lined my face. "Wait. What did he mean by that? He's breaking up with both of us, or just me?" I pointed at my chest.

The Madam sat next to me, the cushions folding beneath her weight, and started tucking lose strands of hair behind my ear and over my shoulder. "Sweet darling, Kendra." She smiled. "You need to relax."

"I'm relaxed."

She squeezed my shoulders and shook her head. "Now, you may have thought that I'd forget, but I didn't. Alex played the same kind of games you're trying to play with me now, and I just can't allow it."

Now I was really confused. My body temperature rose and I wasn't sure if I had to defend myself, just Alex, or stand up and fight for the both of us.

"I have a reputation to maintain." Madam's voice was sincere and non-threatening.

"I'm not playing games." I inhaled a deep breath. "It's not my fault. He wanted to dance, so I danced. I was just doing what I was told." A deep breath did nothing to calm me. Instead, it empowered me to have extra courage when getting all I had to say out.

"Which isn't so easy for you, is it?"

My blood pressure kicked up a notch and she was lucky I didn't slap her. We were two hardheaded women who were used to getting what we wanted. And I would have really laid it into her, too, if it hadn't been for the fact that I had her to thank for this gig. A job I was really enjoying. It was easy money. It was fun. And I was free. I'd be stupid to squash the opportunity I had working for the Madam over two men who clearly wanted to come between us only because they wanted to bone me. "You know I wouldn't purposely jeopardize your reputation. I'm just trying to do what I've been told."

"I know, doll." She petted my hair as if I was a lap dog. "And just so you're aware, Kelly isn't an option, so you can forget about him." Her eyes darted across my face. "And, in fact, I need you to stay away from him."

My head pulled back as I searched her face for answers. "Didn't you hear what I just told you? I didn't know he was going to be there. If Oscar didn't want Kelly to dance with me then he should have said so himself."

Madam stood and moved back behind her desk. "I can't argue with you on that." She looked up at me from beneath her brow. "But Kelly isn't the man you think he is. Trust me, dear. I'm telling you this because I care."

The way she said it, like it was a warning, turned my blood cold. There was something definitely dark about Kelly, but I wouldn't go as far as what I thought the Madam was implying— that he was dangerous.

"I have a job for you." She stood straight, her face brightening.
I rubbed my hands together, excited for another date card.

"However, it's not what you think."

"Then what is it?" My shoulders slumped because I was
thinking it had to be related to my next date.

The Madam pulled a key out from somewhere on her desk,
bent over and unlocked a drawer in her desk. I watched her
shuffle some things around before pulling a blank orange envelope out from the back. "I need you to deliver this to a friend but
only when I give you the go-ahead."

"What's inside?" My eyes were glued to the envelope.

The Madam headed straight for me, hugging the package
tight to her chest like she didn't want anyone to see it. "It's none of
your concern."

"Then what's in it for me?"

"More money." She held it out for me to take it.

I studied the sealed package. It seemed normal enough.
Nothing out of the ordinary, and I couldn't imagine there could
be much inside. No big deal. "I have plenty of money. Don't you
have something else you could offer me?"

She pulled the envelope back and looked at me sideways.

I nodded, a glimmer of hope shining in my gaze.

"Hold on to this," she put the envelope out in front of my face,
"don't look inside, and I'll at least think about setting you up
with Kelly."

"So that's a yes?"

"It's a ... wait until I call with further instructions."

"Good enough for me." I shrugged and snatched the envelope
away. Kelly Black wasn't going to be an easy fish to snag, but with
the right hook in place, it was only a matter of time before
everyone agreed he would have to be mine.

9

KELLY

The moment he called, I knew I had to be the one who visited.

The Madam put him up to this. She knew I hesitated in accepting her offer. I didn't want it, wasn't interested, and now she was pulling me further into her scheme I wasn't sure I wanted to be a part of.

I had no choice. I had to go. Because if it wasn't me, it would be someone else and the decisions were too big for me to leave in the hands of anybody but me. I knew the law best, and besides, I needed to see with my own eyes what exactly the Madam meant when she said her business was growing.

With Maxwell behind the wheel, he had me racing across town on our way to Emmanuel's warehouse. It was important I got there before he and Madam decided I was too much of a risk to know what exactly was going on.

My mind was too consumed with longing for the chance to make Kendra mine to notice the world outside.

I needed to convince Madam that Kendra was meant for me. We were meant for each other. Why she was putting up a roadblock between us had my pulse racing to understand. Maybe my meeting with Emmanuel would make her see that I was still loyal to her, and in return she'd give me access to sweet Kendra.

Maxwell pulled off the highway and turned onto the back roads.

We went way back, the Madam and I. Even to this day, I remembered the first time I requested her services. It wasn't long after that first date that she learned my profession and brought me on board to button up her business and act as representing counsel. Not that she needed it. She ran a tight operation that was mostly clean. But, sometimes, it was good to have me there just in case. Soon after, things took off and in return, she'd give me whatever I wanted—except this one request I had for Kendra.

"Park there," I said, reaching over Maxwell's shoulder and pointing through the windshield. He agreed and I had the door open before the wheels stopped rolling. "Wait here. I shouldn't be long," I said, hitting the ground in a hurry.

The warehouse was desolate. It was quiet, no one around. I moved toward the entrance and caught sight of a plastic bag getting picked up by the wind. Each time my foot hit the pavement, it echoed off the high concrete walls and I couldn't wait to get this over with.

I still couldn't crack Madam's interest in the Blake Stone case other than the fact that we all wanted to see him go down for what he'd brought to this city. Maybe that was just it. Hell, even I wanted to see him put away.

It wasn't like I was oblivious to the Stone case. I'd read the articles that poured out after his arrest, kept up on the case files that were made available, and knew what he was up against. He should be easily convicted with what the state had on him, but maybe not for as long as I knew he should be.

That was what made Madam's request interesting. I'd have to sabotage his trial without making it look obvious. I wasn't even sure that I could do that. Never mind the damage I would knowingly inflict on my own career. I was in the business of winning cases and Blake Stone had to lose. Involving me in his trial would be the one factor to guarantee he paid for his crime.

It wouldn't be as easy as it sounded and, frankly, I was more concerned with finding out who murdered Maria Greer than I was in representing Blake Stone, even if it meant putting him away for good. But with him in need of representation, it was our one chance to seal the deal and end him forever, saving LA in the process. I just wasn't sure I wanted to be the one to do it.

I fisted my hand and knocked on the metal door with my knuckles. Without waiting for an answer, I pulled it open and stepped inside. "Emmanuel. It's Kelly Black," I announced.

A truck was parked in the bay and it was clear that a new shipment had arrived overnight. I'd been here before and swore to myself I never would be again. This wasn't part of my job description and the Madam knew it. The place had negative energy and I didn't like the feeling I got when coming here.

Emmanuel emerged from the back. "Mr. Black." He smiled. "What a pleasant surprise."

My head swiveled around as I continued heading in his direction. My gut was telling me that I wasn't being told the complete story to what was actually going on but I wasn't about to start asking questions, either.

"What did the Madam have to do to get you to come back?"

"You know her. She has ways to persuade," I said without any kind of emotion attached to it. I just wanted to get in and get out before anyone knew I was even here.

He tossed his head back and laughed. "Isn't that the truth?" He patted me on the back. "Come. This way."

"Business is good, I see." I peeked through a cracked door.

Emmanuel closed it as we passed as if not wanting me to see more than I already had. Which wasn't much. Just a few people laying some boxes out on top of a table. I didn't catch their faces and it was probably better that way.

"Yes, business is very good." Emmanuel smiled proudly.

"Women and their beauty products." He laughed. "It's almost too easy."

If it wasn't for my burning need to see it for myself, I would have told Madam to find someone else. But there were too many questions I had to not be suspicious of what she had up her sleeve. A small part of me doubted that all this was just the Madam funding Emmanuel's growing business. The pieces of the puzzle were scattered on the table, I just hadn't put them all together yet to see the bigger picture.

"Tell me, Mr. Black," Emmanuel glanced behind his shoulder, locking eyes with me as he crossed the threshold into his back office, "what did she tempt you with? Women? She has herself a talented harem. Many beautiful women working for her now."

"Something like that," I said as I took in what he had hanging on his walls.

They were mostly empty except for a few framed photos of the first salon he opened. He had the first month's paycheck framed like so many first-time business owners did, and alongside that hung a business certificate awarded by the mayor. It smelled of the hair products he sold, and industry magazines filled a corner of his desk.

"Please, sit. Let's talk." He spun the big light brown leather chair around and slid in behind his desk.

I pulled out the hard plastic chair opposite him, noticing how he appeared to get swallowed by his own chair. He looked smaller than when standing next to me just a moment ago and I couldn't figure out why. "The Madam is curious to know if your new salon is open for business."

"You saw for yourself on the way in. All that product outside will have to be sold somewhere." He flashed a toothy grin, stealing a glance at the briefcase I set by my feet.

"I assume she's contacted you about the reason I'm here."

"She's an active investor. I knew money was coming to me today."

"And Madam was the one to tell you to give me a call?"

He nodded and smiled. I cursed the Madam for playing these games. Anybody could make this delivery. Why did it have to be me? Was it just to get me to work for what I wanted? Or was there something more than that?

I turned my attention back to Emmanuel. He steepled his hands beneath his chin, reeling through his own thoughts. "Mr. Black, tell me—" his eyes rolled to my face, "what is your record for getting your clients off?"

"Why?"

He shrugged. "I'm a curious man."

"I'm the best there is." My eyes narrowed. "And that's all you need to know."

He wagged his finger at me and chuckled. "The Madam speaks very highly of your work."

"Well, let's hope that you won't have to hire my services. I'm not a cheap man."

"I can imagine." He leaned back and eyed me. "Now, tell me how much she sent you with today."

"She didn't tell you?"

"I'm afraid these matters are best discussed in person."

"I couldn't agree more." I nodded and said, "One-hundred G's."

He turned his head toward the little window sucking sunlight into what would have otherwise been a very dark office and let out a heavy sigh. "It doesn't seem enough, does it?"

"Six figures," my tongue slid over my lip, wetting it, "a month is not enough?"

His head snapped over to me, his brows raised high enough to pinch his forehead. "Business is growing fast and it's important I keep up with demand."

"The Madam is willing to work with you on this. However, she's going to need 10% of net profits. Can you handle that amount?" I could see him thinking, crunching the numbers. "So, are you in, or are you out?"

"I can handle that amount." His grin spread to his ears. "I just don't like the rate."

My fingers played with the handle on the briefcase. "I see."

Emmanuel rolled his gaze back toward the window. He was deep in thought and I didn't let the silence filling the room get to me. My stomach clenched, knowing that that kind of money was a hell of a lot for what seemed like an otherwise typical small business. The details behind the curtain didn't matter. Not today. All I cared about was getting this message delivered and getting back to convincing Madam to allow me to see Kendra. That was my goal and the only reason I was here in the first place. Ever since I bumped into her, it had been all about her—making Kendra mine.

"What is it?" I asked.

"It's getting ugly out there," he mumbled. "With Blake Stone waiting for a court date, rival factions are scurrying to claim his old turf."

I leaned back, tugging my suit jacket, as Stone's name was once again mentioned. It wasn't worth telling him that Stone's preliminary hearing had been set.

I pulled back slightly, cracking my knuckles, waiting to see where Emmanuel was going to take this conversation.

Emmanuel turned to meet my gaze. "Stone's loyalists are working to keep things the way they were."

"What does this have to do with us?" My brows drew together. Was he saying what I thought he was saying? Was this what this meeting was about? Had the Madam fooled me into thinking it was something else?

"It will soon be a bloody mess on the streets, Mr. Black." His voice was calm, somber even.

I didn't like what I was hearing, but I also didn't see how this related to the reason why I was here in the first place. "Why are you telling me this?"

He dropped his chin to his chest and started laughing. He rolled through a fit before finally settling down and saying, "New opportunities. A new game to play. I don't know, maybe someday I'll request your services and need you to do what you do best."

"That's not why I'm here, Emmanuel, and this isn't how that works," I said in a calm, unwavering voice.

His jaw set as we stared each other down.

"The Madam needs an answer today." My fingers drummed on my thigh.

"And I'll tell her when I know what it is." He turned his head, nodding.

"Is that right?" I gave him a questioning look even though I knew we were both thinking the same thing. I didn't want to jump to any conclusions or share any of my assumptions with someone I barely knew, but I saw it in his eye, the way his lines deepened across his face. The Madam could trust him with this, but his loyalty was with her, not me.

"You just tell the Madam she doesn't have to worry about me. I'll accept her offer and can start receiving the monies as early as next week." He stood, moved to the door, and opened it before escorting me to the exit.

"Thank you for your time," I said, leaving the warehouse, the briefcase heavy in my hand.

Emmanuel watched me slide into the back of my waiting car. I nodded to Maxwell and he started the engine and drove away with me reeling to make sense of what the hell just happened.

The Madam wanted me to convict Blake Stone through false representation. Emmanuel said the streets would be getting bloody as factions tried to fill Stone's absence in the drug market. And, on top of that, I couldn't help but think that the Madam might be the one to instigate this power struggle unfolding around us, playing me like a fool. With Stone out of the equation, there was a bounty of opportunity waiting for someone to take it.

I just wondered *who* that someone would be.

My head hit the back of the seat and I felt nauseas for thinking that I was being used—that Madam was only telling me half the story. Because the last thing I wanted was for me to get sucked into a quagmire I couldn't get myself out of.

I reached inside my jacket and pulled my cell free. My thumb swiped over the screen, searching for Madam's number. Once I found it I hit dial, and when she picked up she said, "Did the meeting go well?"

"Depends."

"Did you make him the same offer we discussed?"

"I did."

"But?"

"I need more."

"Kelly—I will get you your client. Your firm will be compensated extremely well and I'll help you in every way I can."

"It's not what I want. I could give a rat's ass about Stone." I sat up. "I want the girl."

Silenced filled the line but I held out, knowing she was still there mulling over her options. "Fine," she barked. "You can have Kendra."

"Then we're open for business." I grinned. "Now don't send me here again."

10

KENDRA

"I'm not sure," Alex said as she lightly shook the envelope next to her ear. "Is there even anything inside? It barely weighs a thing."

"I just want to open it." I stepped toward Alex, taking it back.

"Maybe it's a note. Like one of her date cards." Alex moved to one of the half-eaten cartons of Chinese food we'd ordered. Just like all the times before, we ordered far more than we could eat.

"It was in the way Madam said it." I shook my head. "This is different."

Alex scooped another bite and chomped at it as we tried to decipher what lay inside. With Nash away, she insisted I pick up food and bring it over to her apartment. Really, it was Nash's place because he technically owned the building—including this penthouse—but whatever.

"So she didn't say what it was, but she trusted you with holding and delivering it?"

"Pretty much." I shrugged. "She had it locked away inside her desk drawer. I saw her pull it out. She used a key."

"Do you think it's dangerous?"

My brow wrinkled as I rubbed the back of my neck, thinking.

"Like, what's that white powder terrorists send to politicians?" Alex's tone was excited, like she was really getting this whole sleuthing business down.

"Anthrax?" I glanced at her out of the corner of my eye, jutting my chin.

She snapped her fingers and pointed at me. "That's the one!"

"I don't think so," I said, biting my fingernails.

When I couldn't sit still any longer, I stood and began pacing the apartment. I really liked what she'd done with the place. Nash had given her the ultra-comfy couch as a housewarming gift, but all the plants and paintings she'd chosen herself. Alex had an eye for detail. I shouldn't be surprised by that seeing as she was already well on her way to making a name for herself in the entertainment industry.

The next time I turned around, Alex was still diving into the carton of chicken cashew and I just had to know. "Is Nash making you pay rent yet?"

"He won't let me." She swallowed down a large bite, wiping her mouth. "He insists on taking care of me."

I didn't understand the whole paternal, fatherly thing these men had when it came to the women they loved. Like us women weren't strong enough to take care of ourselves or something. Alex's easy-going attitude must have overpowered her independent streak to let Nash get away with that. And, besides, she was always receiving gifts from him, so what did it matter? Maybe I was just clueless. Or jealous. Certainly one of the two, but I couldn't decide which.

"In fact, he sent me a gift today." Alex plopped the container down on the coffee table and said, "You have to see it."

My tongue moved over the top of my teeth, picking out all the food left behind, as I nodded. Just as I was thinking. Another gift, and I was sure that Nash would have another one coming tomorrow.

Alex pranced back to the living room and came out with the most gorgeous lingerie set. "Look at this. Isn't it amazing?"

"He's brave," I said, moving in her direction to get a better look. There was hardly any fabric there and what little there was, was see-through.

Alex looked down, staring at her new gift for a long second before glancing up and giving me a questioning look. "What do you mean by that?"

"What man would give his woman something like that when he knows he's going to be out of town? Shit, woman. Even I'm getting wet imagining you wear that sexy-ass outfit."

Alex looked down at her chest one more time, her face flushed. "He wants me to wear it when we video chat."

My brows shot high on my head. "Will you?"

"I'll do anything he asks." She looked up at me with hooded lids, biting her bottom lip.

"Whatever you both need to get off." I fell onto the couch, kicked my feet up, and stared at the ceiling, thinking more about this envelope. "Am I unknowingly getting myself involved in a criminal activity?"

"Madam wouldn't do that, would she?"

"Do you think it's possible, though?"

"Not too long ago I would have said, no. But now, after what happened to me—"

"You're right. She has Jerome to do her dirty work. There's nothing I should be worried about," I said, not wanting Alex to have to relive what she'd gone through. And especially not while Nash was away. But of course it was possible the Madam was secretly involving me in something I shouldn't be getting myself into.

"You're just doing your job." She set her new video chat outfit on the table and sat in the chair next to the couch.

"I'm now Madam's little bitch."

Alex snickered.

"No different than what I walked away from." The backside of my hand came to rest on my forehead as I let out a heavy sigh. "And here I thought that this gig would be better than pushing papers defending unethical corporations who polluted the environment." When Alex didn't respond, I rolled to my side and found her staring at her little slut costume. "Argh. Really?"

"You know, I missed him so much last night," her eyes were full of sparkle, "I just couldn't help myself."

I turned my head further to get a better look, knitting my brows.

She turned and met my gaze. Her cheeks were flushed a deep shade of red. "I played with my dildo last night," she admitted. "I hadn't done that since before I met Nash."

"Good for you." I rolled my eyes and plopped over onto my back again. "At least you're getting off. Madam seems to be wanting me to revert back to being a virgin. There's no way I can even think about fucking a dildo. Let alone a real penis."

"It was fine," Alex mumbled. "But nothing can replace Nash."

I could only imagine. "I'm so horny I can barely sleep through the night."

"What about that guy?" Alex dropped her feet to the floor and leaned so close to my head she was practically hovering over me. "The one you were telling me about."

I brought my knees to my chest and flung them over the side of the couch until the pads of me feet rooted into the floor. "I'm working on him. Hey, did I tell you the Madam mentioned you by name today?"

Alex angled her head to the side, lines of confusion crossing her face as she rapidly blinked.

"I couldn't believe it either."

Alex gasped, her hand flying over her mouth. "Oh, my God. Does she know?"

The crown of my head pulled toward the ceiling as I furrowed my brows. "Know what?"

"How we pushed our way into the business?"

My lips pursed as I gnawed on the inside of my cheek.

"Because if she ever found out, we'd both be screwed."

"I can't wait," I said, rolling my eyes. It had been so long since I'd been fucked, I barely remembered what it felt like.

"No. Really, Kendra. I'm serious."

"I'm serious," I said, my voice cracking. I'd be digging my own grave. But her? She had Nash to protect her.

"Then think about it." Alex leaped to the couch and sat right up against me. "I mean, what are the odds she'd take us. Two strangers off the street to work for her?"

"Two, amazingly beautiful women," I corrected her.

"You don't think it's possible?" She got right up in my face as if I couldn't see what it was she was thinking.

"Sure it's possible," I said, leaning my shoulder into hers. "But what does it have to do with anything?"

"What would you do if the Madam ever found out how you first came across her name?"

I hadn't thought about it. It seemed irrelevant now. "There's something I didn't tell you," I said cautiously.

Alex's eyes widened as I felt the fear that quaked down her spine vibrate the cushions.

The side of my face scrunched and winced. "I stole the file the firm had on the Madam."

"Kendra!" Alex pushed me away. "Why did you do that?"

"With you going to work for her, I thought I better know everything about who she was."

Alex paced to the window, took a quick glance outside, then turned around and said, "Do you still have it?"

"Of course. Like I'd get rid of that." I snorted a laugh.

"Is there anything revealing?"

My head shook automatically. "She's pretty much a mystery."

"Maybe that's what this is about," Alex said, staring at the envelope. "The Madam knows what you did, what *we* did, and whatever is inside that," she pointed to the envelope, "is her way of hitting us back."

My muscles twitched as I ran my sweaty palms down the tops of my thighs.

Alex looked at me. I looked at her, and our minds raced as we both thought the worst. Then, when my phone beeped with a text, we both jumped.

"Oh. My. God." Alex breathed, her face going pale.

I picked it up off the coffee table and said, "Relax. It's only Jerome."

Alex fell back into the couch, closed her eyes, and let out a huge sigh of relief.

"But—" I showed her my screen, "—it's the address of where I need to take it."

11

KENDRA

If I wasn't so serious about seeing Kelly again, I would have totally opened the envelope just to cure my burning curiosity. But I needed the Madam to see him again so I couldn't disobey her rules.

I hit the sidewalk, leaving Alex's apartment in a hurry.

This stupid thing had taken over my life, I thought as I walked quickly down the street. Even though I wasn't coming from my place, I still instructed my lift to pick me up two blocks away, not leaving anything to chance.

The Madam and Jerome made it very clear that I kept this confidential and not tell a soul what I was doing. They were clear instructions I could follow—with the exception of telling Alex—but it did little to settle my stomach. I hated the secrecy behind it all.

When I rounded the corner, I recognized his car right away. I put on the brakes and slowed my walk, looking around before deciding that it was only coincidence. "Now I'm going to have to call the cops," I said, opening the door and sliding into the back seat.

He turned his head and gave me a worried look.

"I'm just playing. I wouldn't do that."

The same Uber driver from my last lift had managed to be the one to pick me up again. He locked gazes with me and I held it for a minute before smiling. Then he tipped his head back and laughed.

"But seriously, dude, you creepin' on me isn't very cool."

"Do you not like me?" The lines across his brow deepened.

"I'm starting to," I said with a straight face.

"This is only coincidence. I have many customers besides you. They all love me."

"That's good." I pulled the belt across my shoulder and buckled myself in. "But you shouldn't let it get to your head."

He turned back around, faced front, and looked over his left shoulder for any oncoming cars. When it was clear, he pulled away from the curb and we were on our way.

"I promise to be quick."

"Take your time. Being quick is not a quality any man should aspire to," I said to an oblivious recipient.

Settling into my ride, knowing that I had at least a good fifteen minutes in this car, I pulled out my cell and stared at the screen lighting up. I had to double check the address, even though it was seared into the front of my mind. It matched what was on his GPS so we were all good there.

My hand dove back inside my tote, feeling for the envelope I knew was secured inside but I just needed to reassure myself that I still had it and hadn't dropped it somewhere between Alex's place and where I was picked up. After all the speculation Alex and I had done surrounding this stupid delivery, I was beyond nervous.

My fingers shook like I'd drank a gallon of coffee and I couldn't sit still.

"You look nice." His friendly eyes caught mine in the rearview mirror and I wondered if he did this with all his passengers.

"Are you hitting on me?" I quirked a brow.

He let out one of his famous boisterous laughs. "Just being friendly, is all."

"If that's all it is, then thank you." I turned my attention to the world outside and stared out the window, thinking what, if anything, the Madam did have on me. Because I knew she had to have something. Something she could use as a bargaining chip to control me. Otherwise she wouldn't have trusted me so quickly with adding me to her list of clients to date, or with delivering whatever highly classified material hid behind the seal of this packet.

My fingers drummed and I kept checking my phone for no reason.

"On your way to work?"

"Something like that," I murmured.

It wasn't like there was anything from my past she could use to manipulate me. But I wasn't stupid. If I was the Madam I'd make sure to keep dirt on all my employees. Just in case. Sure, I had my closet full of secrets, but everything I could come up with wasn't enough to bend me to her will.

Except for that, I nodded as the thought hit me. My attraction to Kelly.

The Madam knew I wanted him. No matter what words came flying out of my mouth, it was no secret that I needed to explore more of who he was. He'd gotten under my skin, inside my head, and soon, if I had my way, he'd be between my legs, too.

It didn't matter what the Madam said about him. I could ignore her warnings and run off of instinct. My gut had gotten me this far in life, so why would I deny my own intuition now?

Kelly Black.

The name itself sparked a kind of darkness that only a woman like me would find completely irresistible. There was a mystery behind the man, and I couldn't wait to brush off the dust that hid what rested beneath his many layers.

The pad of my thumb stroked over the ticking pulse in my

wrist and I snapped my knees shut the moment I caught the driver staring. "You're creepin', dude."

His eyes crinkled at the edges as he turned off the highway and headed into a part of town that always made me nervous.

"Are you sure you know where you're going?"

He tapped his GPS screen and said, "As long as this device does not lie, then I know where to go."

"This doesn't seem right," I said in a barely audible tone I was sure only I could hear.

"Trust me."

I hated those two words. Whenever someone said to trust them, I wanted to do the exact opposite. I mean, think about it. Why would anyone have to convince you to trust them? If they just did what they were supposed to do, then trust wouldn't ever be an issue.

Today sucked. I fucking hated it. I didn't want to be here, and I should have told Madam to shove it.

Time slowed to a crawl and my head spun as I just wanted this delivery to be done with.

I was so not myself and hated the feeling of being weak. That wasn't who I was, but something was off and I couldn't shake the feeling.

This was proving to be the longest ride of my life and I wondered if this was the most direct route to wherever I was going. It didn't seem likely. Maybe he was lost and didn't want to admit it. I didn't know.

The further he drove, the more I convinced myself he was definitely lost. No one in their right mind came to this part of town unless they had any business in doing so. This was the area that always made nightly news. It was grimy and crime-ridden and had a reputation of being plain bad.

I held my breath and worked to smooth down the gooseflesh that managed to cover my entire arm.

We exchanged a few more glances, and as soon as we crossed over into greener pastures, I let out a heavy sigh of relief.

"You okay back there?" he asked.

"Fine," I said, unable to look him in the eye.

It wasn't like he would get paid any more by taking the longer route. Maybe he just liked my company as he couldn't stop talking. Whatever.

"Ah, here we are," he said, straightening the wheel as he turned onto a busier street.

I liked busy. I appreciated the chaos of being surrounded by engine rumbles, car horns, and all the comforting noises associated with a city. And, besides, this driver was really growing on me.

But that detour was weird. Or maybe that was just the story of my day.

He talked mostly to himself the rest of the ride and when we arrived he said, "Thanks for flying with Uber. We have now reached your destination."

That made me smile as I gathered my belongings and opened the door. With one foot already on the ground outside, I paused and said, "Would you mind waiting for me? I shouldn't be long."

He must have seen the uncertainty on my face because he asked, "Shall I escort you to the door?"

I held his gaze for a moment before smiling. "Forget it."

"It's no problem."

"I'll be fine."

"Are you sure?" He frowned.

"Yeah." My other foot hit the ground.

There was concern in his eyes when I shut the door and I regretted saying anything at all. I'd be fine. This was just jitters talking. I didn't know what had gotten into me, or why I was so out of character, but whatever it was, I knew that it was all because of this stupid envelope.

I watched him drive away and once he was out of sight, I

turned and faced the building. It was simple without many windows. I turned and watched the stream of pedestrians flow across the street to my left. Having them there gave me a sense of comfort and strength I so desperately needed. Because where I stood now, it was deathly quiet.

My cell rang and I dove to retrieve it from deep within my tote. "Hello."

The line was silent.

"Hello," I said again.

Then whoever called hung up.

"Fucking asshole," I mumbled.

Instead of putting my cell back inside the bag, I kept it in my hand, ready to call for help if I needed it. With the package sticking out the top of my tote, I took a deep breath and started heading for the door.

The sounds of my clicking heels hitting the pavement swirled around me and my senses were on high alert.

The only thing I could think about was the day Alex was kidnapped and how that was what was going to happen to me right now. I'd walk inside this building and disappear. No one but the Uber driver, Alex, and the Madam knew where I was. And what did a driver care about anything more than a paycheck? I was just one client in a long list of many. My employer on the other hand...

My legs continued to carry me closer to the door as blood thrashed between my ears.

So many thoughts swirled around my head, my vision blurred. I had no idea what was waiting on the other side of the door I was heading straight for. It could be anything. The Madam could be setting me up. Just like Alex speculated. Maybe the Madam had had enough of my antics and she'd decided kidnapping me was her way of severing ties.

I felt the sweat on my palms for the first time when I reached for the door and opened it.

The air inside was stale and the lights were off. I held my breath and listened before saying, "Hello?"

"In the back," a familiar-sounding male voice responded almost immediately, but my legs refused to move.

It all seemed so sketch. None of it felt right, and yet, here I was.

I thought about asking if I should come to him—whoever he was—but I already knew what the answer would be. "All right. Fuck it," I said, taking the first step, thinking that this wasn't what I signed up for. I much preferred the dates over this.

The place went quiet again and I couldn't stop thinking that I was walking directly into an ambush. One foot in front of the other, I walked down the hallway that seemed to get narrower the further I moved to where I last heard his voice.

I glanced at the dark purple walls which were decorated with framed erotic pictures. It was strangely familiar but I knew I'd never been here. And when I came to the only open door, I peeked my head inside and nearly jumped out of my skin.

"Surprised to see me?"

12

KELLY

I didn't know what she'd been told, but she looked scared. Then anger replaced her fear as I saw it flash across her eyes.

"You have something for me?" I asked.

"What's going on here?" She looked around. "Is this some kind of sick joke?"

"The envelope." I held my hand out, palm to the ceiling. "Give it to me."

Her gaze narrowed as she looked me up and down. "I can't be seeing you."

The corners of my lips curled up. "The Madam tell you that?"

She nodded and her chin dipped to her chest.

"The envelope." I pointed again and she dug around in her bag, pulling the package out and handing it to me. I twirled it between my fingers, seeing that it was still sealed, and handed it back. "Now, open it."

Kendra hesitated a moment before taking it back, suspiciously eyeing me as if she was questioning whether or not she could trust me. "Did you set this up?"

My manhood thickened as I raked her over. She was practically spilling out of her tight tank that rode just a little off her tight jeans, exposing a sliver of her mid-section that I wanted to lick.

"Open it, and we'll see." I stepped forward, closing the gap that separated us.

She looked so delicious, I just couldn't wait to have a taste. The Madam had to have orchestrated this and, if that was the case, I was happy to know she'd finally seen the light. None of her other clients could handle a woman like Kendra. They preferred the cultured women who kept her mouth shut, agreeing to all the stupid things they said.

Not me.

No, Kendra's spunk was what initially caught my eye. It was what kept me hard when she was around and, besides, I didn't want my woman to keep her mouth shut. Mouths were made to be opened, fucked, kissed, and maybe that was all the reason Madam needed to put Kendra here with me today. She knew I could break her and earn her submission.

Kendra peeled the tab back with her nail, exchanging glances between me and the envelope. I watched carefully, thinking that my meeting with Emmanuel was totally worth it—the risk, the frustration, everything I needed to go through to have Kendra standing here in front of me as we both gritted our teeth in anticipation of what was hiding inside.

She flicked her gaze up at me and I licked my lips, watching.

My own curiosity kept me on edge and my heart pounded harder against my chest as she ripped the seal, finally opening the package and pulling out a single folded piece of paper. Her eyes darted across the paper, reading it. Then she looked up at me and said, "What the fuck, Kelly?"

My hand flew from my side as I pinched her cheeks between my fingers. "Careful how you talk to me."

She flipped the paper over and shoved the note in my face.

I let her go and stole the paper from her hand. I recognized the letterhead and font within seconds of reading it, knowing exactly what it was. "Son of a bitch," I mumbled. It was a date card. The Madam had actually done it. She'd handed Kendra over to me. "It appears the Madam listened to both our requests," I said, spinning around to face Kendra.

"What do you mean *both* our requests?" She folded her arms and jutted out her hip, giving me an arched look.

I stepped close enough for me to hear her stop breathing. She gazed up at me as I hovered over her, saying, "You didn't ask to be mine?"

Her shoulders drew up, causing her elbows to tuck into her sides. She watched my hand come to rest on her shoulders as I smoothed down the guilt tensing her muscles. She didn't pull away and I swore I felt her melt into my palm as my desire seared into her skin. We were made for each other. I could feel it.

"I don't request clients," she said all snootily. "They request me."

She said it with such certainty, but I knew it was a lie. Madam would have never placed her with me if she didn't feel like she couldn't stop the impending collision Kendra and I were both on. No, this was no accident. Kendra was a loose cannon who needed to be wrangled in, and I was the man to do just that.

"Take a look around," I said, placing my hand on the small of her back, twirling her around. She needed to really see why she was brought here. This wasn't just any old place. No, like everything I did, there was a method to my madness—even if I didn't fully expect it to be her to bring me the package I knew the Madam was sending.

Kendra's head swiveled back and forth, taking the time to really check the place out more than I already assumed she had.

The building was one of my favorites. An exclusive nightclub that catered to a certain clientele. Men like me, and women like her. It was why this place was born. Kendra might not know it now, but she would soon.

"Why this place?" Her hair draped over her shoulder as she spun around to look me in the eye. "I mean, you're not denying that you requested me. So why did you want to meet me here?"

"It's where I told the Madam I'd be." My voice was deep and husky as a flood of old, suppressed emotions came to surface. Once, long ago, I was a regular to the club but hadn't been back for quite some time, not having the urge to explore my darkest fantasies since the accident. I didn't think I'd ever be back, and if I was being honest with myself, I wasn't entirely sure why I thought Kendra would be the one to make me want to live that lifestyle once again.

Kendra shook her head in disbelief. "So why the secrecy? If there's nothing to hide, then just come out and say it."

"You should know by now." I stepped forward, meeting Kendra where she stood. "Madam's business is kept confidential for a reason. There is always something to hide when going to work for her." I smiled, stuffing my hands deep in my pants pockets.

Kendra rolled her eyes and let out an adorable little huff through her pouty lips I wanted to seal with my own. I could understand her curiosity to want to know the details behind everything the Madam did. She was a woman of mystery and, naturally, that was what made her such an interesting figure.

"Besides," I took one step closer, "how many dates through the Madam weren't a surprise?"

"All of my dates are a surprise."

"My point exactly." I could see the pulse tick in her neck and I knew I had her right where I wanted her. "No different than this one."

She tucked her hair behind her ear and was still throwing daggers at me with her eyes. I reached out and clasped my fingers around her forearm, smoothing her flesh until reaching her wrist. "This is different," she said. "None of them was like this."

"How so?" I cocked my head to the side.

"Delivering that envelope, for starters," she said, holding up the now empty package. "You should have heard what Madam said about that thing. My head was spinning trying to decide if this delivery was a suicide mission."

I tossed my head back and laughed, still playing with her fingers inside my hand. "Sweetheart, it wasn't what was inside that was dangerous. No," I dropped my chin and lowered my voice, "it's me who is dangerous."

Kendra shifted her feet and glanced around me to gaze at the soft glow coming from beneath the entrance door at the front of the building.

"Relax." I squeezed her hands. "There isn't anything you have to worry about."

"I'm relaxed." She openly stared. "I'm not worried."

A chuckle worked its way up my chest. "Besides, you need a little adventure in your life, don't you?"

Her eyes widened with surprise and darted across my face.

She couldn't answer me because we both knew it was true. We'd known it the first time we locked eyes with each other and, ever since, our sexual attraction simmered hot enough to leave scars. She swallowed the lump in her throat and asked, "Did you have the Madam set this up?"

I bent over and placed my lips close to her ear. "I always get what I want." She swallowed hard, her lids hooding her eyes. "You can deny you didn't want this, but I can see it in the way you look at me."

"I'm not denying anything," she whispered.

"Good. Because the moment you do, I'll have to punish you for it." My voice was dark and husky, causing a shiver to work its way down her arms.

She turned away, slipping her hands out of mine, and pretended to study the walls. My dick was pressing against my zipper and I was close to taking her here, now, relieving the pain drawing my balls tight.

I knew she was wet, completely aroused by me. And as I watched her explore, it didn't take her long to realize what type of club this was. It was dark and completely out of the way—the kind of place stories were made.

"Tell me this, Mr. Black." She turned and glanced in my direction, holding her head high. "If this was Madam's idea, why would she want me to be with you?"

"Because I'm the only one who can handle you."

"You? Doubtful." She huffed out a laugh, rooting her fist into her hip. "I've seen Madam's client portfolio. There are plenty of men who would pay top dollar for this." She lifted both her index fingers and pointed at her chest.

"You're right." I inched my way to her. "Madam has an extensive list of clients, however, none of her employees—and that's what you are—would still be breathing if they made a client like Oscar Buchanan walk away from her services entirely."

Kendra's ears turned red with embarrassment.

"Everyone knows that you ditched Oscar for me." I smiled.

"That's not how it happened, and you know it!" She grinded her teeth, jabbing her finger into my chest.

"Imagine how it must seem to someone who wasn't there." The crinkles around my eyes deepened.

"You're unbelievable." She stomped her foot and growled.

"You see, it's not what happened that matters."

She gave me a questioning look.

"It's how the story is told." I placed my hands on her perfectly formed hips, smiling. "Remember that."

"Maybe Oscar was right." Her tongue wet her lips. "Criminal defense lawyers can't be trusted."

I stared into her gaze, determined not to be the first to look away. She needed to know who the dominant one was. "Come. Let me show you something," I said, taking her by the hand and leading her down the dark hallway and stepping into another room, needing her to see what a future with me entailed.

"So if you're so good at telling stories, tell me this." She threaded her hand around my waist, pulling herself up on me. "What were you doing at her office the other day?"

My hand cupped her face, brushing her cheek lightly with the pad of my thumb. She was so beautiful, she had no idea how dangerous it was. "I was there for the same reason you were."

"Does Jerome inspect you for market, too?" Her eyes flashed with amusement.

I dropped my head and chuckled. "Not exactly."

She pressed more of her weight against me, raking her eyes over my face as she played with my tie, tugging and pulling where she saw fit. "Are you her lawyer?"

"I'm lots of people's counsel."

She dropped her gaze to our feet and nodded. "So, what's next then, Counselor?" She angled her head up to meet my gaze.

"Reach inside my jacket and find out."

Her eyes danced with mine as she debated whether or not to trust me with my first request.

"It's all right. I'm not asking for you to reach inside my pants."

"Maybe you should," she teased as she pulled out a perfectly folded piece of paper. "What's this?" Her heels hit the floor as she stepped back to open it up.

"A contract."

Her shoulders slumped. "Why?"

"Because, then," I reached out to gently tug her hair, "you won't be able to ditch me like you did Oscar." I tugged again as my free hand came to rest on the small of her back. "Or sell anything you learn about me to the media."

"I can't even read it." She looked down at the paper. "It's too dark in here."

I reached behind me and flicked a switch, stepping away from her. Slowly, Kendra's eyes peeled off the paper and widened into large discs as she took in her surroundings.

"Because dating me will be like dating no one else you've ever dated before." I reached up and tugged on a chain hanging from the ceiling. "Once you agree to this," I jabbed the contract she was holding in her hand, "there is no going back."

"Kelly," she mewed, "does the Madam know about this?"

"I'm not interested in only having arm candy for fancy dinner dates. I can get those without them signing their freedom away."

"But you want me to lick your lollipop," she said without thought.

Her response was pure, genuine, and how could I not laugh? Kendra had a way with words, and I knew she and I would make a great team. "I want you to be mine—*fully.*"

Her eyes dropped back to the document as I made my way to the toy chest. "But I've already signed a non-disclosure with the Madam."

I reached down and picked up a wooden paddle, slapping it across the palm of my hand a couple of times, feeling the sting awaken my skin. Then I turned around and moved back to Kendra. Her eyes were glued to the paddle when I said, "That's to protect her."

"Then who's to protect me?"

I slapped the paddle down hard across my hand again. "You're looking at him."

13

KENDRA

"You told him you'd think about it?" Alex tucked her feet up underneath her and gripped her wine glass with both hands.

"Yeah. What's wrong with that?" I gulped down a thick swallow of my own wine.

"No reason." Alex averted her gaze. "It's just, I thought you liked this man."

"I do." I peeked over my rim. "Like, a lot."

"Then I don't see what the big deal is."

I lowered my glass. "You don't see what the big deal is?" My neck craned out as I felt my eyes widen. "No. You're right. It's not a big deal." I waved my hand through the air and dropped my voice down to more of a conversational and less accusatory tone. "Except for the fact that the moment I sign it, I'll be his possession and I'll lose all my cards."

Alex stuck her tongue out at me. How could I not love her? She was my voice of reason and the one person I could trust when in need of life advice. And with Kelly wanting me to sign my life away, I was in desperate need of advice.

I set my wine glass down on the glass coffee table and picked up the contract again. Between the two of us, Alex and I must have read it a million times. But I read it again for the hell of it, pacing back and forth in front of the windows, thinking of a way to hit him back. I had nothing and was feeling defeated. I finally collapsed into the fluffy corner of the couch, letting out an exaggerated sigh.

"You know, Nash likes to be in control, too," Alex reasoned, but I wasn't listening.

It was impossible to not be attracted to Kelly. And that was half the reason why he was so frustrating. He was the type of man who commanded a room the moment he walked inside. Men like him controlled the conversation with style and grace, sprinkled with a dash of dominance that left me yearning for what it would be like to completely submit.

Alex kept talking about Nash and I nodded when it was appropriate but mostly I was stuck inside my own head.

Nash wasn't all that different from Kelly. I'd give Alex that. They were both alpha males who would fight tooth and nail to get what they thought was rightfully theirs. Nash did that with Alex, and now it felt like this man, Kelly Black, was determined to do the same with me.

Except there *was* a difference.

I'd seen it in Kelly's eyes. The dark shadows that glimmered against a moonlit night. That look he kept giving me made me both curious and terrified to know what the cause of it was. Kelly was damaged and I wasn't sure that I was the right one to fix him.

Nash didn't have that extra baggage. Or, at least, not that I knew about. And what was with the Madam contradicting herself? Was Kelly really as dangerous as she made him out to be? And if he was, then why would he admit it himself? Maybe he was a dangerous man, but not in the ways that I should be worried about. He was a lawyer. Weren't all lawyers dangerous?

"Are you even listening to me?" Alex said.

I glanced at her and she was pretending to not be staring a

hole into the side of my head. "You remember when we thought Nash was cheating on you?"

"I'd like it if we didn't talk about that. I'm still embarrassed by it."

I dropped my feet to the floor, leaned forward, and rested my elbows on my knees. "Just hear me out."

"Fine," she said, hiding behind the rim of her glass. "But only because I love you."

"So, we thought he was cheating only to find out that it was his daughter kissing his cheek."

"I still can't believe I overreacted like that." She cleared her throat. "Thanks for reminding me how pathetic I am. I don't deserve him." Alex glanced at the calendar with a longing look on her face and I knew she was counting down the days until Nash was back home, tucking her away safely inside his arms. "What's your point?"

"Maybe we need to do some research on Kelly."

Alex tossed back the rest of her wine, set her glass down, and pranced across the room to take her laptop between her hands. "On it!"

She was way too excited for this, I thought as a small pang of regret twisted my gut.

"Do you think we'll find something juicy?" Alex wiggled her brows.

All the warning signs were there for us to find something on him. Hopefully it wouldn't be something that I didn't already know. Kelly Black was dark, precarious, and completely mysterious. "Doubtful," I said, snuggling up next to Alex's shoulder as she typed his name into the search query.

Kelly's face populated the screen like a billboard advertising his services. Next came his law firm website. Information about him or his firm came up as some of the top results. We skimmed a click here, a click there, and he was clean as a whistle.

"Has Nash taken you to Mint yet?"

Alex snapped her head in my direction and gave me a look. When my eyes widened, her cheeks flushed and she said, "No. He hasn't."

"Oh." I frowned. "Was that not an okay question to ask?"

She turned back to the screen. "I prefer the softer side of romance."

I laughed. "And what the hell does that mean?"

"You know ... vanilla."

I clutched my stomach and fell back laughing. "You're so full of shit."

"Okay. Maybe a part of me is interested in exploring more of that lifestyle."

I pointed at her. "I knew it!"

"What about you? Why are you asking, anyway?"

"I know we followed Nash there that one night, but I guess I'm just curious to know if that's the only location or if there are others. I thought maybe you would know by now."

Alex's head slowly rolled back to me and knitted her brows. "More than one location of Mint?"

I nodded. "Do you know? Is there?"

"What's going on? Are *you* getting into the lifestyle?"

I didn't want to answer that right now so, I thought it best to deflect her question and get on with our internet search. "Here, type *Kelly Black tabloid news*."

Alex's fingers tapped away and, once again, our internet search produced nothing worthwhile. "I don't know." She cocked her head. "I think you might have found a winner. He seems pretty boring."

Alex didn't look too closely at the face I saw. Besides, the Kelly I knew in person versus the Kelly on the internet looked quite different. And maybe she was joking, but I knew that Kelly was a catch.

She nodded as she read the site she opened up. "He's an incredible defense attorney. Looks great in a suit. Oh, and look here—" Alex angled the screen so I could see, "—he even drives a fancy car."

"This is worthless," I said, falling back into the couch. "He's squeaky clean. At least on the internet, and even that should make me suspicious enough to question his intentions."

Alex pushed the laptop forward and said, "I say sign it."

"I can't."

"Why? He's perfect. Look at him."

She wasn't even looking. This was just her ploy to get me involved in experiences worth gossiping about. I was all she had left now that Nash had her on lock down. And with Nash out of town, it was up to me to bring home the stories. "None of this adds up. I know there must be some kind of dirt on him."

"Not everyone is like you." Her lips flattened.

I shot her an arched look.

"Besides, what's the worst that can happen?" The lines on her forehead deepened when she raised her brows.

My body lurched forward, swiping the stupid contract off the table in front of us, and I said, "The Madam's agency already has this kind of paperwork in place."

Alex's chin scrunched into her neck as she leaned away from the flailing papers I had stuffed in her face.

"Okay. I get it." She swatted the papers away from her face. "Why the need for his own unless he's into some really kinky stuff? Is that what you're asking?"

I bit the inside of my cheek and shrugged. "Yeah. I guess so."

"Oh. My God." She gasped. "That's why you were asking about Mint."

"I was set up." I stood, needing to work the adrenaline flowing through my veins out of me. "The Madam set this all up, and he told her where I should meet him."

"So they were both in on it?"

I crossed my arms, thinking. "It certainly seems that way. But I don't think she knows about this contract he wants me to agree to." I turned to face the window, unfolding one of my arms and bringing my hand to my mouth. "I don't think I was at Mint—" I pinched my bottom lip, "—but it certainly was a place just like it."

"Are you interested in that stuff?"

I glanced over my shoulder. "Like you're not?"

Alex nodded, thinking about it. "Would you do it if that's what he wanted?"

I turned back to the window. "I've done some things, but I've exaggerated. You know this. We both know this. When I think about the way he makes me feel when I'm around him—like I'm living in the tropics, all hot and bothered—I know I have no choice but to sign it."

"And is that your head or your heart speaking?"

"You know it's not my heart," I said firmly, pushing my fears to the side, knowing that the excitement I was after when going to work for the Madam was within reach. "It's just that ... I'm scared."

Alex pushed the papers to the closest edge to where I was standing. "Sign it. Be with him. Clearly, there is something there between you two."

I knew she was right. But that wasn't the reason I was afraid. I was terrified of what he wanted to do to me and how far he'd take it, or even if I could handle it. "First I need to message him." Alex watched me type up my text to Kelly.

Signed and sealed but need to know where to deliver it.

Not a minute passed before he responded.

"What did he say?" Alex sat on the edge of the couch with a straight spine.

I lifted my gaze up away from my screen and said, "He'll take it when he picks me up for our date tonight."

"Holy shit. This guy doesn't mess around."

14

KELLY

Okay, I'll be waiting.

I smiled at the message I'd just received from Kendra, confirming where I'd pick her up for our date tonight, when Giselle entered my office.

"Sorry to interrupt, but I think you oughta see this." Giselle pulled a new case folder out from under her arm and handed it over to me.

I pointed at the empty chair across from my desk, wanting her to stay so we could discuss any questions I might have. She settled in and watched me scan over the documents, beginning with the files on top. "His name is Mario Jimenez, and he's charged with the murder of Maria Greer," she began filling me in.

I glanced up at Giselle.

She nodded. "Looks like we found our guy."

My heel tapped wildly beneath the desk as I went back to reading his case file.

"And guess who he's requested to have represent him?"

"Did he request us specifically or was he referred by someone?" I asked, continuing to read more on this potential new client of mine.

Giselle crossed her leg over her knee and shook her head. "Unknown."

"What about the deceased? Have we learned any more about her?" I licked the pad of my finger and flipped through a few more papers. "Was she a working girl or just an unlucky one?" I looked across my desk at Giselle from under my brow.

"Still working on it. I'm also not sure if there was more to her story or if she was just in the wrong place at the wrong time. Too many unknowns to form any kind of conclusion. But we'll get there soon. I have our people working on it now."

"Good. Let's get there soon." I pulled out the images of Maria. "There's no time to waste." The photos twisted my gut just like they had the dozens of times I'd stared at them before. It wasn't a pretty sight, nor one easily forgotten. Not all cases hit me like this one did. I hadn't been able to push her murder from my mind, no matter how hard I tried.

A vein pulsed in my temple and my hand balled into a tight fist as it rested on top of my desk.

With Maria, it always came back to the bruises and cuts on her wrists and around her neck. Giselle was probably quietly wondering what it was about Maria that had me by the balls. And a small part of me wanted to confess my reasons to her. But I couldn't. Not without looking guilty myself.

Giselle sat quietly as she watched me do a side-by-side comparison of both the victim and accused.

Mario had a smug look on his face and parted his lips just enough for me to recognize a gold tooth. "Ever hear of this guy before today?" I asked.

Giselle's swinging leg stopped. "New face and name for me, too."

"Does he have a record?"

"Nothing. No record of employment either. The little I know about him is in that thin file I handed you. The man's a mystery and I'm not entirely sure he's guilty, either."

My gaze bore a hole through his photo, making sure I stared at him long enough to sear his image into my brain. I hadn't recognized him, and based off of first impressions, he didn't seem to be one who could have had access to the nightclubs—the ones where members paid upwards of $100K in monthly membership fees—that offered up the BDSM lifestyle that could possibly inflict the types of injuries found on Maria.

"What do you want to do?" Giselle asked.

I ran my hand over my face, thinking. He was dirt. He was trash. That much was apparent off of my first impression of the man. And if it wasn't for the crime he was accused of committing, I would happily swoop him up and put him on my list of clients to represent. But, *if* he did kill her, he deserved to get locked away forever.

"I don't know," I said, just as my cell started ringing. I glanced at the screen to see who was calling. "Excuse me. I need to take this."

Giselle left my office, closing my door on her way out as I answered the call.

"Not even a thank you note?" the Madam cackled through the line. "After the trouble I went through to give you exactly what you wanted, this is how you treat an old friend?"

"How do you know I don't have flowers on the way?" The corners of my lips curled into a thin grin.

"Because, dear," her southern accent was a nice touch to normal SoCal flare, "you only give flowers to the women you fuck."

I leaned back, turning my gaze to the window, and laughed. "You might be right about that."

"Might? Oh, hun. I know you better than you know yourself," she said proudly.

"Then consider yourself one of the lucky ones, because not many do know me that well."

"So?"

I arched a brow.

"I'm waiting." Her voice rose as she wouldn't give up on demanding I thank her for finally giving in and handing Kendra over to me.

"I'm courteous." I wet my lips. "But I'm not polite."

"Kelly..." She sounded so disappointed by my behavior.

"Besides, what you did, don't you think what you put her through was a bit excessive?"

"Hardly. I just like to keep my girls on their toes. Keeps them sharp." I heard her heels clacking as she drifted across the hardwood floors of her office. "It's a good state of mind for the business we're in."

"You scared her half to death," I said, remembering the look on Kendra's face when she arrived at the club.

"The girl could use a good scare."

"Well, let's just hope that it won't ruin my date with her tonight."

"For you, I hope not either," she said sincerely. "But this isn't why I was calling."

"Then what can I do for you?" The tension in my neck released as I looked forward to seeing Kendra again.

Glancing at the clock, I knew that I had to get going if I wasn't going to be late. Standing, I pulled my jacket off the back of my chair, taking my wallet inside my hand as I walked myself out of the building.

I knew Kendra would come around to agreeing to my terms. All I needed was to shield myself in case of any kind of fallout. Then once I had that guarantee in place, it was fair game to gently lead her into my world.

"I'd like to start making investments to Emmanuel. Today." The Madam was back to business.

"Can't happen." All the excitement I was feeling only a second ago vanished and I felt my face harden. "It's too early. I thought we discussed this already? He needs a week to get prepared."

"A week is too long," she urged.

Her impatience was new. Madam was a woman who planted seeds, nurtured them, and watched them grow, only to harvest the fruit when it was good and ready. It was skilled manipulation and no one did it better. Madam nearly always got what she wanted. Just like me. But her urgency kept me feeling unsettled.

"By then we'll be backed up and we'll be playing catch up," she told me as I found Maxwell waiting on the curb. "You know I don't like a rough start. Go talk to him again. Make it happen, Kelly. You know better than most. Money doesn't wait."

I gave Maxwell a quick nod as I slid over the smooth leather seats in the back of my SUV. "This isn't my problem. I told you I'm done negotiating for you."

"After all I did for you?" Her voice was soft and sweet like I'd hurt her feelings. "This is how you repay me?"

"If you need advice pertaining to our original agreement, I'm here." Maxwell sat behind the wheel and started driving. "Anything else is off the table."

"I'm not liking what I'm hearing, Mr. Black."

"You can find someone else to handle those types of transactions," I said, knowing that I was getting under her skin. Madam rarely used my last name. When she did, she made it clear that she needed me more than I needed her.

"I gave you Kendra, but I can still hold off on giving you Blake Stone."

And there it was. Stone's name was dropped without me hinting toward it. Now I knew something was up, as it seemed the worst of my fears were coming true.

I closed my eyes and the moment my vision darkened behind thick lids, I saw Maria's lifeless body and I wondered if her death had any connection to Blake Stone and his associates that everyone around me couldn't seem to stop talking about.

When my eyes opened, I stared at the world outside, not wanting to know any more about what the Madam was up to.

Because she definitely was up to something. Something that my gut told me I shouldn't be a part of. Whether or not she was the one to be fueling this impending drug war on the streets I was hearing about, this was one corner of her business I needed to bow out of. Solving Maria Greer's murder and keeping my focus on Kendra was my top priority. Nothing else mattered.

"Can I ask you something?"

"Darling, please." Her voice was cheery. "You know you can ask Madam anything." I could almost see the sparkle in her eyes the way she spoke.

"Do you feel your business is secure?"

"My girls are safe with me, if that's what you're asking."

"No new competition that may be after you?"

"Not in this town." I could hear her shaking her head. "I squashed that long ago." She laughed. "Why are you asking, anyway? Do you know something that I don't?"

"No. I'm just trying to find answers to that young girl's death. The one I showed you photos of."

"Tragic." Madam's voice went quiet. "But I didn't recognize her face."

"It's an ugly world in which we live," I murmured.

"Blame Blake Stone. He's the one who fucked this city long ago," she said coolly. "That's why we need to be sure he never walks free again."

"Is that why you want me to represent him? Revenge for what he did to our city? Or is there another reason you're not telling me?"

"You know me, honey. I just want what's best for everyone."

She was right. I did know her. And I knew that what she really wanted was what was best for her growing empire. Maintaining power was a daily struggle and no path to riches didn't involve a little blood. Now, whether or not the Madam would go on the offensive and start a war to annex a little more of the city she was trying to own herself, that was still undecided. "And may the best man win," I said, just as Maxwell turned into the neighborhood I was picking up Kendra in. "I gotta go."

"Do keep me posted, Kelly. I'm as interested as you are to get to the bottom of what happened to that girl."

"You know I will."

"And I'll forgive your impoliteness today. But only this one time."

"You're so kind," I said as she laughed, ending our call.

Kendra was already waiting on the corner block, and fuck me, she looked stunning. I couldn't wait to have my hands on her and as soon as the car stopped, I stepped out and took her by her wrists. "My God. Look at you." My eyes traveled the length of her.

She sucked her pouty bottom lip into her mouth, taking it between her teeth, and let me continue fucking her with my eyes —one long lingering gaze at a time.

She was wearing an angelic long-sleeve club dress that fit her tight as a glove. Her gorgeous tits spilled out from the deep V-neck that easily provoked the nastiest of thoughts a man could conjure up. My core heated and all the blood traveled to my groin.

"Do I have you hard yet?" She tilted her head to the side.

She was so damn sexy I couldn't stand it. Slowly, I leaned closer, inhaling all of her feminine scent that went straight to my head, making me dizzy. "Painfully stiff," I said as I kissed both her cheeks.

"You don't look too bad yourself." She leaned back, still holding onto my hands, taking me in.

We were made for each other. There was little doubt that once I fucked her, the passion between us would be explosive. "The Madam sure knows how to dress her women."

"How do you know I didn't choose this dress myself?"

"I don't doubt you could. I'm sure you have a fine sense of fashion."

"But you don't think I did?"

I shook my head.

"Confidence can be sexy, but I can't decide if you're confident or just cocky."

"Would you like to feel for yourself?" I brought her hand to my flexed abs, tempting her to reach between my legs and feel how cocky I was. "Besides, you think the Madam wouldn't mark what she considered her own?"

Kendra's gaze narrowed as she angled her head to the side.

"Only women working for Madam have the privilege to wear the rare stone Tanzanite in their ears." I gently pinched and tugged the lobe of her ear. The blue-purple gem was as immaculate as my date. But, together, the combination was absolutely gorgeous.

Kendra blushed and I knew that I'd managed to render her speechless.

"Lucky me," I said, reaching into the backseat. "I chose wisely."

Kendra watched me pin a blue orchid flower to her dress.

"It's beautiful, Kelly. Thank you." She looked down, smelling the flower petals. I squeezed her hand and led her into my waiting vehicle. "Careful with me, Mr. Black. You might just get what you're after."

15

KENDRA

I glanced over my shoulder to find Kelly on the sidelines schmoozing with another couple who'd come up to greet him.

He caught me staring and flashed me that confident grin that clenched my sex.

Never had I expected to have so much fun at a charity ball. It really wasn't my scene. And though my bank account was comparable to many of the people who were here in this room, our personalities didn't match up which generally made me feel like the black sheep who wasn't invited.

But not tonight. Tonight, I felt free as I moved through the room, stealing bites to eat as they passed, swaying to the live music playing against the murmur of conversations the swirled around me. People danced, laughed, and the mood was light.

A server passed with a platter of bacon wrapped scallops. The scent of bacon and sea water filled my senses and I just had to steal myself a taste. It was succulent and tender when I bit through the meat and I let out a pleasurable moan. When the tray of drinks passed, I plucked a flute of strawberry champagne between my fingers and headed toward my man.

Kelly noticed me coming for him just as he was finishing up his own conversation. I bit my bottom lip, loving watching him interact with so many different faces. He was a real charmer, that one, and indeed, I needed to be careful.

"Need some rescuing?" I asked, shortening my step as I closed the gap between us.

His devilishly handsome eyes darkened as he closed his fingers around my elbow. Leaning close to my ear he whispered, "Don't tell anyone. But I can't wait for this to be over."

I gave him a look, somewhat surprised to hear it. If asked, I would have sworn he was enjoying himself by the smile on his face.

His other hand clamped around my arm, sending trails of desire shooting across my body. "That dress is killing me."

My breath hitched as his hot breath swirled over my ear, drawing my nipples tight. "And here I was under the impression you weren't interested in arm candy for fancy dinners."

The crinkles around his eyes deepened. "I'm not."

I leaned more of my weight into his heavy body, appreciating a man who could take a little smack talk. My finger trailed down the center of his chest, feeling his muscles dance against my touch. He looked deliciously handsome all dressed up in a black tuxedo he'd put on just before we arrived.

"Just a means to an end." He slid his hand possessively around my waist, stopping only when it hit the area just above my ass crack.

I knew what he meant, and what was on his mind. The dress I was wearing would undo any man with the dark desires I knew Kelly Black harbored. Anticipation of where he'd take our night flooded my senses, and though I was having fun mingling, eating all sorts of gourmet foods and drinking all I could get my hands on, just like Kelly I couldn't wait to get back to it being just the two of us.

"Is that a promise?" I asked.

He shook his head. "A guarantee."

I smiled. "Keep this up and I'll make sure that our night never ends."

He pressed his thick lips against the center of my forehead and chuckled. "My God, woman. I swear you will be the end of me."

I closed my eyes as lust filled my body with warmth. I hated how attracted I was to him. My intention was only to sleep with him. Show him a good time. That was it. I knew I shouldn't be falling for him as quickly as I was. Even if the Madam said to keep my legs closed, with Kelly doing what he was doing, it would be impossible to deny him.

My fingers tugged on his shirt, tucked tightly into the waist of his pants.

Determined to keep my heart out of the equation, I had to remind myself that our relationship was nothing more than a transaction set up by the Madam.

Kelly's lips finally pulled off of my skin, sending my heart into a flutter.

It wasn't like I was falling in love with him. But there was definitely something different about him that made him so much more magnetic than all the other men I had been with before. His wealth was the most obvious differentiator. But beyond that, it was his confidence and the way he worked the room, like he owned the building and the conversation that came along with it. Secretly, I wondered what it would feel like to be his only.

He spun me around and dug his strong fingers into my shoulders as his arousal pressed against my ass.

I stole a tiny sip from my drink as we stood there simply watching the ebb and flow of the room. We didn't have to talk. As long as he held me and kept me close, that was enough to get me through the party. Kelly was possessive of me, acting as if he didn't want to share me with anyone else. And that feeling of being owned by someone like him actually surprised me with how much I was liking it.

Maybe Alex was on to something with Nash, I thought as I reached up, needing to touch Kelly's hand resting on my shoulder. He kissed the crown of my head and a delicious shiver worked its way down my spine.

For generally wanting to be the one in charge and control the situation, for some odd reason I couldn't fully explain, I was more than fine trusting Kelly to lead the way.

"Kelly Black," a tall man with a strong smile said as he approached us from the side.

Kelly reached out and shook his hand. "James."

"I'm so glad that you could make it tonight."

"Anything to help." Kelly's hands squeezed my shoulders as he talked.

"And your generous donation tonight certainly helps a lot." James's smile spread across his face as he locked eyes with me. "I'm sorry, I'm not sure that we've met."

"James, this is my date, Kendra Williams," Kelly said.

I held up my hand and James bent his spine, bringing my hand to his lips, kissing my knuckles. "You are truly lovely."

"Thank you," I said, stealing a glance at Kelly, making sure that he was okay with what was happening between James and me.

He nodded once and flashed a closed-lip smile.

"Kelly doesn't deserve you." James released my hand, gently laughing.

"You may be right," I said. "But maybe one day he'll earn his keep."

Kelly's rough hands smoothed down my arms, pulling me closer to him. His sudden possessiveness over me was a welcome feeling, and certainly something that I could get used to.

"No, really." James slid his hands inside his pockets, glancing at Kelly before letting his gaze fall back to me. "Kelly is a wonderful man and I can assure you that you'll never be let down so long as you treat him right."

"That's what I'm learning." My cheeks blushed for how wet Kelly had me.

"It was good to see you, Kelly." James shook Kelly's hand again. "Kendra." He nodded.

"Nice to meet you." I smiled, watching James stop to greet another friend standing in a circle not too far from where we were.

I liked hearing the praise Kelly was receiving tonight. It made him more human and less of a dick like the first time I met him. He was real and I could feel the power he held radiating off him as we stood watching the party unfold in front of us.

As the evening drew on, I grew more and more attracted to him. When he left my side, I moved closer, needing to fill the void of what was missing when he wasn't there.

Kelly seemed to know everyone. And everyone knew who he was. He was well received and I liked that the party didn't feel stuffy as I imagined so many events like this did. He was obviously well respected, a prominent member in his community, and I started to see him in a completely new light.

I finished my drink and felt slightly embarrassed when I noticed that I was the only one of us slamming these drinks down like they were water. The band picked up the tempo and began playing a tune easy to move to. I started to dance and said, "Kelly, you should be drinking with me."

He watched me twirl around him. "Not interested."

"C'mon. Let loose." I bumped my hip into him, trying to entice the man into dancing with me.

He shook his head and my feet stopped moving.

"C'mon. I don't know anyone here." I hooked my hands on his shoulders, hung off of him and begged, "It's not fun to drink alone."

"Stop," he snapped, clamping his strong hands around my thin wrists.

My throat tightened and made it painful to swallow.

A darkness washed over him and made me shiver as he stared into my big, round eyes. I didn't know what I'd said, but clearly I pushed him too far.

"Quit asking." He leaned back, his tight grip releasing from around my arms. "I don't like having to repeat myself."

I lowered my gaze and turned away. I'd touched a nerve and wasn't sure what that was about. Fear paralyzed me and, just like that, I no longer wanted to be here.

Out of the corner of my eye I saw Kelly's chest expand just before he let out a long, controlled breath. "Kendra..." his fingers closed around my arm once again and I fought the urge to pull away from him. "You want to dance?"

My tongue slid over my lips as I swallowed down the tension that buzzed between us. When I looked up at his face, his eyes were soft again and I nodded. "That would be wonderful."

Kelly took my flute of champagne and set it on a passing silver platter. I didn't want things to get awkward between us. I had high expectations for the night, and I was certain he did too. I breathed a sigh of relief when he threaded his fingers through mine, leading me to the dance floor.

My mind spun with regret.

I should have never asked him to drink.

It wasn't my place to dictate how the night went. If he didn't want to drink, fine. What I'd done was totally uncalled for. I was his date, not the other way around. I'd forgotten my place and I was glad that he corrected it so easily.

Kelly towed me through the crowd as I watched the sea of people part once they saw him coming. Faces smiled and nodded, and a path easily cleared for us. Not everyone was blessed with such respect as people clearly gave Kelly. I wanted to know how he earned that kind of respect.

Or if I was mistaking respect for fear.

He glanced back at me and I loved the feeling he invoked inside me. The feeling of importance I got when knowing that I was his date and not some other bimbo here tonight.

Once we hit the dance floor, Kelly twirled me into his body, holding me tight against his solid muscles. He was firm, and so tight, it didn't feel like he had an ounce of fat on him. "Hang on," he said in a sexy, husky voice.

My palms spread flat against his chest and traveled up his body until my fingers hooked around his neck. Slowly, he began to move. "Do you like to dance?" I asked.

"I'm liking dancing with you."

He was graceful with his movements, calculated with his response. His protective hands were exploring and possessive as they roamed my body. His steps, deliberate and calm, yet I could feel his hunger, so full of desire by the way he held onto me.

"Are you enjoying yourself tonight?"

I tipped my chin back and nodded. "I am."

"That's important to me."

"Is it?"

"Certainly."

"What if I said I wasn't?"

"Then I'd find a way to correct it."

And that was who he was. I got that feeling from him from the get-go—that he was a man who liked to have things go his way. He'd make sure everything was perfect. Pleasing everyone he came into contact with, doing whatever it took. "Do you attend these types of events often?"

"I do." I felt his hand splay across my back. "But tonight is special for me."

I cocked my head to the side, curious to know why. I knew that it was a charity to raise funds for an underprivileged school, but beyond that, I didn't know the details.

"I like to help the community when I can."

It wasn't the answer I was going for. I was hoping to learn more. But with what happened after asking him to drink with me, I was already walking on thin ice and didn't want to press him into having to explain himself.

We both drifted inside our own heads, dancing in slow circles, holding onto each other like we didn't want to let go.

My entire perception of who he was kept being shattered with each new revelation that presented itself tonight. It was funny how that worked when you got to know someone. He wasn't at all the person I thought he was when we first met. No. I liked him so much more and actually saw myself wanting to pursue him beyond just *arm candy* that made him look better than he already did.

My thighs tightened around his leg, needing to relieve the agony in my swollen clit. He pulled me close, circling his hips as I writhed on him.

The Kelly I was witness to tonight—minus that one moment of weakness—was a man I could see myself with. I was curious to know how he would kiss. What it would feel like to have his tongue sliding over mine, and if he had it in him to be gentle when I needed him to, and to fuck me good and hard when the urge was there. I needed a well-balanced man to deal with my own highs and lows. Someone who could pick me up and keep me from falling down.

My head dropped to his chest and I liked how I fit to him. He was slowly earning my trust and I liked his approach. It felt natural, and that was important, considering the situation.

When the song faded out, he hooked my jaw and tipped my chin back. Our eyes danced as I labored through heavy breaths until he finally crashed his lips over mine. I parted my lips, eagerly sucking him into my mouth.

I had been waiting for this moment all night, and now that it was here, sparks flew from behind my eyelids and small explosions set my body on fire.

He swirled his tongue over mine, deepening our kiss.

I was broken, desperate, and I knew that I wanted to fuck him right then and there. Lifting my leg, I knew that if he fucked half as good as he kissed, I was in trouble with this one.

He thrust his tongue over mine, causing me to whimper softly into his mouth.

"Well, I guess I shouldn't be surprised to find you two here," a familiar voice said.

Kelly pulled away and I felt his body go stiff. Slowly, I turned my head, dropping my heels back to the floor. I was startled to find Oscar Buchanan approaching.

"I suppose I should have seen that one coming." Oscar's eyes narrowed. "Not the first thing Kelly has stolen from me."

"I'd hate me, too," Kelly said, hugging me close as I felt his gaze drift over to Oscar's date. "And who is this lovely woman you have on your arm?"

Oscar's date had been eyeing me from the moment she arrived. We both exchanged glares, sizing each other up, and I wondered if she was an escort, too. Everything about her told me there was a chance—from her dress, to how she had her hand constantly on him, to how she smiled, nodded, and pretended to be genuinely interested in what Oscar was saying. Madam had plenty of us under her harem, so my assumption wasn't all that far-fetched. Though rumor was that Oscar was through with her services after his date with me.

"Angel." She held her hand out and Kelly shook it.

Angel. The name was more prostitute then it was escort. I wondered if it was her real name or just a name she used when out on dates. Older men probably ate that shit up, but I could see right through her. She caught me glaring and scowled.

"Kelly, have a moment?" Oscar held his arm out, not even giving me any kind of recognition. And I guess in a sense I deserved that.

"Excuse me." Kelly kissed the side of my head. "I won't be long."

As soon as the men were out of earshot, Angel toed closer and murmured, "You don't know what you're getting yourself into with that one."

I glanced at her. She stood about a half-foot taller than me and she was beautiful. I could see what the DA saw in her. A full bust, long legs, and a flawless face.

Angel folded one arm over her midsection and lifted her champagne flute to her lips. "Then again, maybe you already know."

"I'm sorry, do you two know each other?" By the way Kelly introduced himself, I was under the impression this was the first time they'd met.

"Kelly Black has a reputation," she said behind the rim of her glass. "And I hate to be the one to break the news to you, but I just assumed that you already knew."

Well, I didn't. At least not whatever gossip she was hinting toward. I watched the men talk as struggled to figure out what it was she was referring to. I didn't have it in me to ask and my hope was that all she was referring to was something other than what I thought it was. "I'm not following."

She rolled her eyes over to me and huffed. "Sweetie, look. Kelly is charming and easy on the eyes. But if you're expecting the honeymoon to last, don't."

"This is our first date," I mumbled, wondering why I was even bothering to tell her anything at all.

Her brows raised. "Then it's good you're hearing it now."

My face pinched. "I don't know what you're talking about or why you're telling me any of this."

She turned to face me. "Then I'll dish it to you straight. From one girl looking out for the next."

My hand slowly crept toward my neck.

"Once that man fucks you, he'll toss you to the side just as he has done to countless women before."

I turned to look at Kelly. He caught me staring as my fingers played with the jewels around my neck, wondering if what she was saying was true. And if Kelly could be trusted.

"Don't take it personally." She shifted her weight over to her other foot. "Just don't let your heart get involved if you do fuck him."

I looked up at her.

She shrugged. "Whatever he tells you, it's him who has the commitment problem."

16

KELLY

"Are you sure? We don't have to do this if you don't want," I assured her as soon as the elevator doors closed.

Kendra melted into my side, letting her head rest over my breast. "I want this."

Something with her was off. She was quiet the entire ride from the charity event to the hotel. I didn't know if she was just tired or if something was said that made her go silent. I hoped that it was just exhaustion. That would be a much easier fix than the alternative.

I kissed the top of her head.

The last thing I wanted was for her to not be herself just before I surprised her with what I'd been dying to get to this entire evening.

She hugged my waist. "Is Oscar ever going to be able to forgive you?"

My hand moved up and down her arm as I wondered if that was what was bothering her. "We butt heads constantly. It's been like this for a while. He and I are always trying to beat each other. But it has nothing to do with you. It's just the way it is."

She lifted her head off my chest and looked up at me with extraordinary jade green eyes. "I don't want to be the cause of a war between you two."

I tipped my head back and laughed. "When you're in law, it's always a war to beat your opponent. That's all this is. You have nothing to worry about."

"I know." She wedged her hands beneath my jacket, letting her fingers curl over my hips, hugging me tight.

"Is that right?"

She nodded.

"And how is that?"

"I studied law." She smiled confidently.

My smile vanished in a flash and I felt my eyes go big. "No shit?"

She laughed. "You didn't know that about me?"

I cupped the back of her skull and petted her incredible long black hair that held more body than anybody else I knew. "There's a lot I don't know about you." My neck craned as my lips pecked at hers. "But you studying law is certainly surprising. I'll give you that."

The elevator slowed to a stop and the doors dinged open when we reached the top floor that housed an executive penthouse suite.

Kendra turned her head as the doors opened and she slowly drifted away from me like a balloon being released into the air. "Kelly Black, did you do this?" she squealed.

I stepped out of the elevator car and into the hallway, bending down to pick up one of the several dozen pink and blue orchids that lay scattered across the floor. "That would be one hell of a coincidence," I said, holding an identical flower next to the one I had pinned to her dress earlier tonight.

Her fingers pinched the fabric of my jacket, gave it a hard tug, and stood on the tips of her toes to give me a kiss. "You're something else." Her eyes half closed, filled with lust.

I held her at the waist, loving the way she felt as I dug the tips of my fingers into her flesh, steering her toward my waiting suite. "Follow the path."

"Yes, sir."

Kendra was giddy again and it was good to have her back. That was the woman I craved. The one who made life fun. And that was exactly what I needed because for what I had planned, I needed her to be spunky and alive.

She tugged me along and I followed, one step behind. A sense of euphoria washed over me as she kept stealing glances over her shoulder as if to make sure I was still right there with her. As soon as the path of flowers ended at the door, she stopped and I had her pinned up against the wall.

Her green eyes darted across my face as I reached up to touch the racing pulse traveling through her neck. "Tonight has been amazing," she said.

"It's not over yet." My lips crashed over hers.

Her tongue curled over mine as she sucked me deeper into her mouth. She tasted of alcohol and I liked the way she softly whimpered into my mouth as I pushed my tongue against hers.

I lifted her leg and she hooked her ankle around me.

Her tongue thrashed and my hips thrust hard against her pelvis. When I pulled back she snapped her teeth like a crocodile, hungry for more. I fell into her, pressing more of my weight against her as my mouth fell to her neck, nipping and sucking her sweaty flesh.

She shoved her hands in my hair, clawing and digging, tipping her head back to open up more of her neck for my tongue to explore. Slowly, I peppered open-mouthed kisses over her jaw until locking on her mouth once again. "Shit. This is what I was waiting for all night," I growled.

Kendra's fingers clamped on my skull and pulled me back to her mouth where she kissed me furiously. Our tongues dueled, starving for more.

When my hand grabbed her tit, roughly squeezing it, I was so painfully hard I couldn't take any more. This needed to happen. It couldn't wait. If we didn't get inside now, I was surely going to fuck her here, in the hallway, up against this wall. "I could fuck you here," I said as my fingers closed over her neck.

"Why don't you?" she tempted me.

I pulled my keycard from my back pocket and swiped it in the door, opening it up to smells of freshly cut flowers. "Because I plan to torture you slow tonight. And a hallway is no place to sex up a queen."

Kendra pushed me off of her with a force that didn't match her small size. "Holy shit. This is your place?" Her head swiveled on her shoulders, taking in the spacious entry way.

"My home away from home." The door closed behind me and I watched Kendra stop in front of a large mirror, fluffing her hair and checking her makeup. "Make yourself at home."

She pulled herself away from the mirror and continued perusing the place. "Kelly, this is incredible." Her eyes shined like a woman buying shoes.

I knew it was. The place was over-the-top and filled with the luxury only men like me could afford. Expensive, and furnished with state-of-the-art technologies, stuff that made a statement. It was all here.

There was a large living area, a chef's kitchen, and floor-to-ceiling windows that boasted a perfect view of LA's skyline. It was sexy, modern, and the perfect pad to fuck.

Kendra kicked off her heels, pranced around barefoot on the exotic stone floor, and twirled around to the song playing inside her head.

I stood back, observing how she moved fluidly without a hint of hesitation.

My lips curled upward as I watched her rake her fingers over the sectional couch before coming to a dead stop in front of the bottle of champagne I had waiting in a bucket of ice.

She studied it, and from the look on her face, I knew what it was she was thinking. Instead of two glasses, there was only one. "Go on. Pour yourself a drink," I said, walking to her.

She reached out and touched the one and only glass. "Kelly," her voice was soft, "about earlier." She turned to meet my gaze. "I'm sorry for pressing you to drink."

My shoes clacked over the marble flooring as I closed the gap between us.

Her eyes fell to the floor with embarrassment. "I shouldn't have done that."

Once I was an arm's length away, I dropped my chin to my chest, hid my hands inside my pockets, and sighed.

Her eyes found my face and she softly said, "I know people who have struggled with the disease."

With my gaze cast at my feet, I nodded. But what I couldn't say was that I wasn't an alcoholic. My reasoning for not drinking was so much worse than anything she would ever want to hear. When I finally lifted my head, she was staring at me with the most compassionate eyes. "Let me pour you a glass."

"Kelly, really—" Kendra's hands hovered over her midsection, "—I don't need to drink."

"Nonsense," I said, stepping forward and popping the bottle open. She watched me pour a glass and hand it over to her. She accepted it without a fight and I plucked a fresh strawberry off the platter of fruit, bringing it to her mouth. "Fruit tastes so much better with a little bubbly."

She opened her mouth, holding my gaze, and sliced her teeth through the soft fruit. Her eyes closed and her lips curved. "It certainly does." She swallowed the bite down, laughing as she covered her mouth. "Shit, that was good."

I tucked her hair behind her ear and leaned in to press my lips against hers. She tasted sweet and sugary, just like the strawberry I'd fed her. "I told you."

"So you don't lie all the time then," she teased.

"Only when it benefits my pursuit." I leaned in and kissed her again.

"Tell me this, then," she said, plucking another strawberry from the plate. "Do all attorneys get their dates through the Madam?"

My lips pressed together. "Let's not talk about her," I said as my hands ironed down her sides before coming to rest on her ass.

Her ass was beautifully round with hips that would be perfect to grip as I slammed into her. I couldn't stop touching her. She was so receptive and I could only imagine how she'd be once I had her naked.

She took a sip and set her glass down.

"What kind of law did you study?" I asked.

"Corporate." Her face was stoic and full of strength.

It was clear to me that she would have made a fantastic lawyer. "And why aren't you pursuing a career in corporate law?"

"Because it's boring." Her eyes flickered like a candle in the night.

I laughed. "And working for the Madam is more exciting?"

"Only after I met you." She smiled and pinched a third strawberry between her fingers.

My hand traveled up her body, grazing the side of her boob before reaching behind her back and tugging on her hair. There was a glimmer in her eye that spoke volumes to what it was she was thinking. "You want me to fuck you, don't you?"

Her tongue traveled across the front of her teeth. "You have no idea."

I took her face in the palm of my free hand. "But?"

Her eyes fell to my flexed abs. "The Madam—"

"—won't let you." My thumb brushed over the pink in her cheek.

She shook her head and I could only imagine what it was she was feeling. Like she was forbidden from doing the one thing her body was screaming for her to do. "But she didn't say I couldn't do this." She unzipped me, reaching her hand inside to pull my steeled rod out.

Every single muscle in my body tensed at the sensations of what it felt like to have her hand pumping me. "You can do whatever you want to me," I said, pushing her down to her knees. "I won't tell."

Kendra adjusted herself until she was comfortable and I watched her mouth go round just before she hid my pulsing shaft under her thick, soft lips.

My eyes rolled to the back of my head as bolts of lightning flashed behind the lids. "Fuck," I growled. "That feels amazing."

She knew what she was doing and I liked that she had experience. That would make her progression into my world move quicker than if she didn't. It was perfect. She was perfect.

My fingers worked to undo my belt, letting my pants fall down my thighs so I could widen my stance and expose all of the areas I wanted her to touch.

Kendra kept one hand at the base of my shaft, stroking me tight and hard between cupping my balls. Her other hand reached around my body and she dug her nails into the muscles of my ass, positioning herself for me to charge to the back of her throat with each lap of her tongue.

"That's it," I murmured as heat spun at the base of my spine. I was close but I grinded my teeth, fighting back the urge to come, wanting instead to watch her work.

She popped me out of her mouth. "You're so big."

And her mouth was small, tight, and totally hot. "You have a sexy little mouth."

I didn't give a fuck what the Madam said Kendra could or couldn't do. I'd dictate that. Shatter Kendra's expectations and destroy Madam's silly rules. Nothing was going to stop me from taking what I wanted so badly tonight.

My hips bucked forward as her teeth grazed over a sensitive area.

But before any more fucking occurred, there was something I needed to check on. "Did you bring the contract with you?"

Kendra closed her eyes as she pulled me out, tortuously slow, from the back of her throat, stopping at the tip to slurp up her saliva. And when I thought maybe she was ready to answer, she looked up at me and circled her tongue over my purple tip as if to show me she had the power to unravel even a man like me. "I have it."

"Good." I plunged my cock back into her mouth, twitching as it slid over her hot tongue.

She hollowed her cheeks and bobbed her head, taking my full length like we'd done this thousands of times before. When she spit me out, she looked up at me behind doe eyes. "But here's the thing ..."

"Excuse me?" My brows furrowed.

The lines of her forehead twisted. "I didn't sign it." She bit her cheek and looked at me, ashamed.

My fingers tangled in her hair as anger and disappointment filled my head. I thrust my cock back into her mouth, plunging hard and fast, furious to hear that the contract hadn't been signed.

She gagged and chocked as I continued my assault.

Kendra had told me it was signed. That all she needed to do was deliver it. I'd come into tonight with that expectation and she'd failed me.

I thrust hard until I felt my body begin to spasm. When the first hot ropes of semen streamed from the tip I released my grip and shot it across her face, pushing her off of me.

Kendra tumbled back onto the floor and said, "I can explain."

I took my cock in my hand and squeezed it tight. My head shook as my spine bent forward. *What the hell did I just do? And why didn't I check that all the paperwork had been signed?*

"I had questions I needed answers to." She breathed as her

tongue circled the rim of her mouth. A white pool of my desire dripped down her cheek, but she didn't seem to care.

"Like what?" My chest heaved.

"That club we were at." She wiped her mouth with the back of her hand. "What was that?"

"It doesn't matter," I snapped, hardly able to look at her.

"It does matter." She pushed herself up onto her feet and smoothed down her dress. "Because I'd like to know what you want to do to me."

My eyes narrowed as I gave her a questioning look.

"Kelly, people say that you're dangerous."

I stroked my cock. It was still painfully hard and I knew that there was only one way it was going down tonight—after I fucked that tight pussy of hers and let her know she was my possession and she'd do what she was told.

"Even the Madam has warned me to stay away." She slowly inched her way back to me.

I laughed. "Of course she would say that."

Kendra stepped back, clearly wondering why the Madam would warn her to steer clear of me.

"Don't you see what's happening here?" Kendra's eyes fell to my raging cock. "It's a ploy. We're Madam's game."

Recognition flashed across her eyes and I knew that she was starting to see the bigger picture of what was actually going on.

"You were a bargaining chip to get me to do something for Madam."

"What are you talking about?"

"I wanted you. She wouldn't let me have you."

"And what did you have to do to have me?"

"It doesn't matter." I stepped toward her, the sudden need to touch her pulling me closer in her direction. "All that matters now is that I have you."

"I want to sign your contract." She took one step closer to me.

"And I'm aware that it will strip my voice away once it's complete. But I have no intention of hurting you."

"Once you sign it, your lips will only open for me." I tugged her bottom lip before nipping at it. I pressed my tongue against the seam of her mouth and she welcomed my kiss without a fight. "I don't want you even thinking about being with another man."

"I still need to know what you want to do to me." The palm of her hand smoothed down the side of my face. "What has you so worried that I might discover?"

"Sign it—" my hand reached between her legs, finding her hot, damp mound, "—and I'll show you."

17

KENDRA

I held my breath, too afraid to breathe.

My heart thudded hard against my chest as I shut the door to Kelly's penthouse suite as quietly as humanly possible. I couldn't afford to have him hear me leave. Because if he did—

The door slid into place, latching as I winced.

Then I turned on bare feet and padded silently on the tips of my toes, hurrying down the hall to the elevator to make my escape.

With each step I took, my face pinched and my shoulders cringed, thinking that I was being too loud—that somebody would hear me and stop my pursuit.

I turned to glance over my shoulder.

It was still just me—all alone in a narrow hallway that closed in on me.

Another stride and I reached out to hit the button that requested a cart to come and retrieve me.

My hair swished across my face when I snapped my head around, looking to see if he was coming.

The hallway was still empty.

His apartment door, still closed.

"C'mon. C'mon." My thumb was relentless in the pressing of the elevator button. "Fucking, c'mon," I pleaded under my breath.

Then I heard a noise.

I froze.

My ears perked.

But it was nothing more than my fears making up sounds, keeping my nerves rattled.

I paced back and forth in front of the closed metal doors, debating whether I should seek the stairs or not. They might be faster to reach but surely they would be slower in taking me to the lobby on the ground floor. So I stayed and impatiently waited for my chance to flee.

I didn't have much time. The clock was ticking. It would only be a matter of minutes—maybe even seconds—before Kelly noticed that I was gone.

My jaw clenched as a primal scream ripped inside my head.

I splayed my fingers and slammed the palm of my hand hard against the closed metal doors. A deep thud filled the shaft as I spit through a series of curses under my breath.

My throat tightened and I wanted to cry. And I would have, too, right then and there, if it wasn't for the renewed hope I felt expand in my chest when I heard the elevator cart approaching my floor.

I took one step back, glancing once again toward Kelly's front door, and scrambled inside the elevator as soon as it arrived.

When the doors closed I crumbled to the floor. Hugging my knees to my chest, my face twisted in humiliated pain as I refused to cry.

The cool tile floor spread over my bare feet and traveled up to my head, causing me to shiver. I felt so cold. So afraid. Realizing that my ride could stop on any floor, I forced myself back to my feet, slipping my heels over my toes, collecting my thoughts.

Kelly was going to be pissed.

He'd come after me.

That much was for sure.

After all the promises he whispered in my ear, the feelings of ecstasy that jolted my heart alive, everything gone in a flash.

I breathed and rubbed my hand over my face. Circling my tongue around the rim of my mouth, I could still taste him on me. Coating me with his masculinity and everything that made him the dark and complicated man that he was.

I didn't expect to run, but a trigger set something off inside me. A dark secret that should have been snuffed out long ago—something that hadn't surfaced in a very long time. It was up to me to leave before Kelly saw the truth that hid inside me. I couldn't let him see me like this. Because if he did, it would change everything.

The floor numbers seemed to go down impossibly slowly. This was turning into the longest elevator ride of my life.

I crossed my arms, then let them fall to my sides as I couldn't find comfort in any stance.

I twisted the rings on my fingers, constantly shifting my weight from one foot to the other. My palms were sweaty as fears that Kelly would catch me before I had a chance to leave the building rolled through me.

I closed my eyes to memories of tonight flashing across the forefront of my mind.

When Kelly said he needed to freshen up, I saw my chance. Leaving me in his apartment, alone, I felt the vulnerability and pain bubble up inside me and I knew that I had to leave. It wasn't worth saying goodbye. And even if I wanted to, I couldn't.

That stupid contract had pushed us too far. Our relationship hadn't even rounded first base and we were already broken. Maybe he'd realized it, too. If not then, maybe now, and certainly once he recognized that I might not have it in me to come back. But after what happened, he would have come to the same conclusion—that me leaving was what he would have wanted, too.

I smoothed down the front of my dress, ironing it out over my thighs, and shivered with the reminder of how his hands felt on me.

This was for the best.

My lungs expanded in my chest as I inhaled a deep, calming breath.

It wasn't his fault. He didn't know. Hell, even I didn't see this one coming.

I caught my blurred reflection in the chrome wall, stepped close, and fluffed my hair. "Get your shit together, Kendra," I mumbled to myself, understanding that I would soon be facing a lobby full of strangers.

The doors opened as soon as the cart stopped on the ground level. I stepped out with as much confidence as I could muster and walked with long strides, my head held high.

But inside I was breaking down as my nerves were aching and raw.

My head turned to the right. A young man lifted his head from behind the front desk he was working.

I gazed to my left. A couple strolled casually from the hotel restaurant, holding hands and laughing.

It seemed as if people stopped to stare, like they knew what had just happened and why I left Kelly Black's place in such a hurry. Their accusatory looks were enough to make me want to run.

I walked past the bar and a man in a three-piece suit lifted his drink, winked, and smiled.

My skin felt clammy, like it needed a good soak after a night like the one I'd had. The room spun around me, making me dizzy, and with each step closer to the exit, it only seemed to spin faster and faster until I lost all focus on what was happening around me.

I felt ashamed as I marched through the lobby, like I had done something wrong. I attempted to do everything in my power to avoid any kind of eye contact with the many strange faces swirling around me. I didn't feel like myself at all.

When I took my last step before reaching the exit, I lifted my heavy arms, reaching out to push past the gold-trimmed glass revolving doors, and inhaled a deep breath as soon as the outside air hit my face.

The night air washed over me and, immediately, I shed the weight of all that was inside that building—the people staring, Kelly Black, my fucked up reason for leaving—as the tension in my shoulders began to relax.

I tipped my head back, closed my eyes, and took a deep breath as if I'd nearly just drowned in my own emotional wreck.

Then I snapped back to reality when my shoulder was accidently bumped.

"Excuse me." The man stopped to apologize and when I waved it off as no big deal, he placed his cell back over his ear and continued on his way.

The peace I momentarily felt was gone just like that. Sirens and horns honking filled my ears as I reached inside my clutch to pull out my own phone.

Quickly, I scrolled to find Alex's number, putting in a *911* text to her.

Fear lined my face and I didn't feel like I could trust anybody but her. She was my lifeline, and though we hadn't talked about what would happen if I ever needed to be saved, I knew she'd understand my text and not hesitate to get in her car and come swoop me up.

Alex.

I sighed.

I was thankful to have her. And not just because she was the only person I could trust to tell everything to, but also because she was the only one I could deal with right now.

Where are you? Alex responded in a flash.

My hands trembled as I looked up at the towering building shooting up to the sky.

I knew exactly where I was, the cross streets and everything. But this was the last place I wanted to be waiting for Alex to come save me. It was too close to Kelly—too close to what just rocked my soul nearly to death.

There was a café a couple blocks away and I told Alex to meet me there. LA never slept, so even at this hour a café was a safe haven. She said it wasn't a problem and that she'd be there as soon as she could. I hoofed it to the café, never once looking back.

This night needed to be over. I needed a break. A rest from everything. Ever since going to work for the Madam, my life was moving too fast to process and finally it had caught up with me.

All I wanted was to curl up into a tight ball and make myself a cocoon I could stay in and hide forever.

The bells above the door jingled as I stepped inside the mostly empty café.

Smells of freshly roasted coffee filled the room and once again I felt like everyone was looking at me. I spotted an empty seat near the window, giving me the perfect view to watch for Alex, and took it before it was gone.

Alex would be here soon. It wasn't that far from her apartment, and even though I knew it was late, it had to be her who picked me up. I didn't want an Uber or have to find myself some other kind of lift. It needed to be Alex. She was the only one who would understand—the only one who could see me so vulnerable. She was my best friend and if anyone was going to see me this fucking weak, I knew that she would be the only one to understand.

Because, I wasn't weak.

No. I was strong.

The free-spirit who didn't let things get to me.

But the way I was feeling tonight was so out of character, I didn't even recognize the girl staring back at me in the window's reflection.

A man's voice snuck up from behind and made me jump.

I yelped and covered my mouth, fighting to maintain control over my wild emotions.

"Sorry. I didn't mean to startle you," he said. "But did you want to order something?"

I should have expected that something like this would happen. These types of places hated having people fill their seats who weren't paying customers. Unlucky for him, I wasn't in the mood. Nor did I want to be anywhere else while I waited for Alex to come save me, and certainly wasn't going to risk being seen by standing outside, in the open.

"I'm waiting for a friend." I managed to say in a calm, small voice.

He nodded. "I'll be back then."

"Thanks," I whispered, retreating back inside myself.

My arms hugged over my chest as I closed my eyes, fighting back the tears that threatened to spill. The faint pounding of my heart echoed around me like a bass drum off in the distance, mourning for a life taken.

This wasn't how I'd expected my first date with Kelly to go. It wasn't supposed to be like this. It was supposed to be magical. I was supposed to fall in love. But now, when I thought of him doing what he did, it was impossible not to shiver and have my entire body be covered in rotten goose-flesh.

By the time I opened my eyes, Alex was pulling up to the curb. I gathered my things and ran out. She had borrowed one of Nash's cars and instead of caring about any of that, I slid into the passenger seat, barely able to look her in the eye.

"Are you okay?" Alex stared at me with concerned eyes.

I shook my head and hid my face inside my hands. Then I started to cry.

18

KELLY

I clutched my hardened stomach at the pang of guilt I felt for how last night went down with Kendra.

My fingers twisted the top of the plastic bottle and I shook the container until two antacid tablets fell into the palm of my hand. I popped them in my mouth, munched, and washed them down with water.

I should have known not to leave her alone. Especially after learning that she didn't sign the contract. It was a simple, straight-to-the-point document. Words to shield me in the event of a fall-out. Nothing more. Nothing less. I didn't understand why she was so concerned when it came to scribbling her signature.

One-by-one, my fingers crawled across my office desk as I couldn't escape the memories of last night. Picking up an orchid flower, I stroked each petal and was reminded of what was supposed to be.

Maybe Madam was right. Maybe Kendra wasn't ready to delve into the dark lifestyle I wanted to introduce her to. Or maybe she was interested but wasn't a good match, like the Madam said. Our personalities didn't align. After all, what did I know? It was Madam who had the paperwork on all her women—the intuition to properly place them with the perfect clients. After what happened last night, it was clear I knew nothing.

My hand closed over the flower and I squeezed it into a tight fist, feeling the plant crush against the pressure. Then I tossed it in the trash and glanced at the clock on the wall. It was nearly time.

I stood. Pulling my jacket off the back of my chair, I stepped out of my office to find Giselle on the phone. She held up her finger and from what I was hearing, I knew I had to stick around and listen to more.

"Thanks for calling. We'll be in touch soon." Giselle set her receiver back in its spot and gave me a look.

"I have to step out," I said, pushing my arms through the sleeves. "It shouldn't be more than an hour."

"That was Mario Jimenez." Her brows raised.

"Oh yeah?"

She folded her hands on top of her desk and nodded. "Requested you by name."

"Why didn't you put him through?" I scowled.

"He doesn't want to talk on the phone."

"Then what did he want?"

"He requested you meet him in person."

"What did you tell him?"

"That you'd get back to him." She tilted her head to the side. "Kelly, he's curious to know whether or not he should shop around for another lawyer or not."

I tilted my head back and rubbed my hand over my face.

"We need to give him an answer." Giselle's eyes widened. "What do you want to do, Kelly?"

I stepped toward the exit and pulled the door open. "Anything from Julia Mabel?"

Giselle dropped her gaze and shook her head. "Came up empty."

I turned back to the door and let out a heavy breath. Then I stepped out and started walking.

"Kelly! What do you want to do about Mario?" Giselle yelled through the closing door.

I lifted my hand and waved her off as I leaped down the stairs.

Mario deserved a meeting. I'd give him that. But, unfortunately for him, the woman I had a crush on left me last night and I was hoping the Madam could at least tell me that Kendra was okay.

The sun hit my face as soon as I stepped outside. Flicking my wrist, I checked the time. Madam was running late and I hoped she would be arriving soon. I hated having my time wasted. Madam knew that better than anyone and I was sure she did it on purpose just to piss me off.

I moved down the sidewalk, thinking that if Mario *was* guilty, then I wanted him to rot for what he did to Maria. However, if he *wasn't*, then I wanted to know why he thought he was the one to be charged with her death.

My hand slid inside my pocket, pulling out my cell. I dialed Giselle's desk and as soon as she picked up I said, "Set up a meeting."

"You got it."

"And Giselle—" I turned to look up the street, "—don't make any promises. He's going to have to sell me on why I should represent him."

"Of course." Giselle ended our call just as I caught sight of Madam's limo.

It shined like it had been recently waxed and the windows were as dark as black paint. She traveled around the city like a stealth bomber, blending in and going undetected, collecting recon. As soon as it stopped at the curb, Jerome stepped out. "Mr. Black." He nodded, holding the door open for me to slide inside, which I did.

The inside smelled of a mixture of polished leather and

heady scents distinctly Madam. The leather couches faced each other with Madam facing the front, hiding behind a wide-brimmed hat and donning white gloves. "Kelly, darling. How do you do on this fine afternoon?"

Jerome shut the door and we pulled onto the road, leaving him behind. "Aren't we forgetting someone?" I pointed in the direction of Jerome.

"It gets crowded in here with him. He's such a large man." Madam laughed. "Besides, he could use a break from me." Her hand reached over and patted my knee.

Naturally, I wondered, why the secrecy? Because, let's be honest, that was really why Jerome wasn't invited to come along. "What's this about?" I asked.

She sighed and flashed me a thin-lipped smile. "I hate to bring it up. I know you like to think things over before making a decision. Especially when they're as big as this one, but I'm afraid I'm losing my patience."

My eyes narrowed as I couldn't help but be curious about what she was referring to.

"Kelly," her eyes flickered, "if you don't act now, I'm scared of who will end up representing Blake Stone."

"We still have time. These things don't happen as fast as you may think."

She dropped her chin to her chest, causing her forehead to fill with deep lines. "So you're going to do it?"

There was a glimmer of hope in her eye, so it hurt me to say, "I'm a bit preoccupied at the moment."

She lifted her brow, turned her head, and said, "I see."

"What's that supposed to mean?"

"It means that I see."

"See what?"

"See that you're not interested."

"What you're asking me to do is risk my entire reputation to purposely commit a man to a lifetime behind bars." Heat flushed through my body.

"Kelly, dear. That won't happen." She smiled.

"My job is to get people off. It's the prosecution who are supposed to convict."

"I know that, hun." She batted her lashes at me.

"Then trust the judicial system to do its job." I glanced down at my hand on top of my thigh, balled in a tight fist. "I've seen the case files. He'll need a fucking good lawyer to get him off with what the state has on him."

"And leave it up to a handful of jurors?" Madam's brows raised as she smirked. "I don't like those odds."

She hemmed and hawed her way through our conversation and I knew that she wouldn't let this go until I agreed to her request. Madam was a woman who was used to having her way. And I knew her well enough to know that she wouldn't stop until she was convinced she was going to win.

"Kelly, you're acting like you don't want to see Blake Stone go away."

I cast my gaze out the window. Traffic was insane this time of day, and though I'd been sitting in this car for a good fifteen minutes, we had barely gone more than a couple of blocks.

"Should I remind you of the lives he ruined?" Madam leaned forward, resting her elbows on her knees.

"You don't have to tell me what that asshole did. I get it. And trust me when I say I would like it if I never saw his face or heard his name again."

Madam pulled in a deep breath as she sat back in her seat. "Me too, sweetie. What that man did to the reputation of, not only this city, but the entertainment industry—"

"I know."

"Then do it. Be his friend."

My brow arched.

"Then bring him down." She held a high chin as she intently stared.

I closed my eyes and pinched the bridge of my nose, thinking.

I'd make enemies no matter what decision I made. Whether I won or lost, people would come for me. Too many powerful people wanted to see Stone go down. And many wanted to see him walk. If Stone was convicted, his people would hunt me down. And if he walked, I'd feel like I let my city—the city I loved—down.

There was no winning this one.

"Kelly." Madam reached out to touch me again. "What's wrong? Is it Kendra?"

I slowly lifted my head with knitted brows. There was a knowing look on her face and I wondered what she knew that I didn't.

"I know you took her to your penthouse." She crossed her legs and folded her white gloved hands on top of her thigh.

"Did she tell you that?" I held my breath.

"I thought about it some more. You were right. I think she will be good for you. A step in the right direction. I can only imagine the pain you must be feeling. The anguish knowing that a heart can only give so much love before there is nothing left."

A stone formed in my throat. I stared back at Madam with my eyes beginning to water. I hated her for saying that. Despised her for bringing it up. She didn't know what it was like; what I'd been through—was still going through. "Remember those photos I showed you of that young woman, murdered?" I asked, needing to change the subject before I let it go any deeper.

Madam cleared her throat, nodding.

"The man charged with murdering her called my office today."

Her eyes sparkled. "I know."

"You know?"

"Mario Jimenez." She didn't miss a beat.

"It was him. He did that to her." I watched as she dug in her purse. She pulled out a compact mirror and opened it.

"I told him to call you." She reapplied her lipstick.

"And why would you do that?"

"Because he has something that we both want."

"What would that be?" I frowned.

"Meet with him. Talk with him yourself. You might be surprised with what you learn."

The limo stopped in front of my office building. Jerome was standing in the shade and slowly approached the vehicle when he saw us arrive.

"There is reason for me to believe that Mario may be connected to the cartel Stone was working for," I said.

"Yes. You see? We should be thanking him for getting caught. Such a pity." She frowned. "Meet with Mario, then get to work on Stone."

Jerome opened the door.

"And if I don't?"

Her face lit up. "I'll find someone else to do it."

19

KENDRA

Nightmares robbed me of sleep.

There was nothing more I wanted than the night to be through.

I blinked. My eyes were finally dry. No more tears, the heaviness gone. And though I still felt numb, a renewed hope filled me as I watched the bedroom floors grow brighter with the sun.

The bedroom door squeaked open but I didn't move. I knew who it was. Who was coming for me.

Alex lifted the covers and cuddled up behind me, spooning me with her tiny arms, hugging me tight. No words were exchanged. She didn't have to speak. Her actions were what mattered. From the way her cheek pressed firmly against the middle of my back, I knew that she was here for me no matter what.

I just laid there, staring at the polished wood floor, thinking how the navy blue comforter was a perfect match against the solid white walls. Those bright colors were exactly what I needed to get me back to feeling 100%.

"I have coffee for you when you're ready."

I liked that Alex didn't ask questions. She knew that if she waited long enough, I would find the courage to say what it was I knew I had to say. I told her everything, but still, this time it was different.

"I'll be out in a couple minutes." I hugged her hands tight over my heart before she freed them, leaving me alone in bed. "This bed is too comfy to leave." I tried to sound as playful and carefree as possible but it came out half-assed.

"You should try sleeping in my bed." Alex laughed behind me. "Now that is a bed difficult to roll out of."

I flipped onto my back and turned my head to find Alex nodding. "Nash." She smiled, tilting her head to the ceiling with her hands over her heart. "He's so good to me."

I laughed as I watched her leave. I wasn't ready to roll out of bed quite yet, but after a minute I tossed the covers, knowing that staying in bed would do me more harm than good.

Alex's guest bedroom was becoming my home away from home. With how broken I'd felt last night, I was thrilled that Nash was away. It made it easier for me to come back to Alex's without having to hide behind my swollen eyes just to make an appearance in front of her boy-toy.

My feet hit the floor and I padded to the nearest wall covered in framed pictures, my hands tucked firmly under my armpits.

When we got in last night, Alex asked if I wanted to talk about what happened, and when I said I didn't, she just turned on the water and filled the tub. That was why she was the best. I soaked in that thing for a good couple of hours, refilling it with hot water every 20 minutes, collecting my thoughts and scrubbing off all that made me feel dirty and used.

A photo caught my attention and I reached up and pulled the frame from the wall, needing a closer look.

It was filled with members of Alex's family, everyone smiling against the bright blue back drop. The trees were neon green and full of life. They were happily enjoying catching up, laughing, sharing stories at what appeared to be a family reunion.

Her entire family seemed to be there. Everyone minus her parents.

I frowned.

Alex was so strong, a true inspiration, for having gone through what she did with the death of her parents. I couldn't imagine it was easy for her to visit extended relatives knowing that it was her parents who she really wanted to visit with again.

I hung the photo back on the wall and continued perusing more family photos. She was really making herself at home here, and I liked her confidence in settling into Nash's place, adding little mementos of her own. It meant she believed in their relationship and saw a future, one she wasn't going to leave. Even I couldn't have predicted them lasting as long as they already had, but I was happy for her, for them.

That was what made Alex such a relatable friend. We were both without parents. And though mine weren't technically dead, they might as well have been to me. All I had was Alex, and I counted on her to help me work through my problems, just as she would me.

A shiver worked its way up my spine and I hugged myself, feeling slightly better about what transpired last night. There was a chip on my shoulder and that could only mean one thing; I was starting to feel like my glorious self.

I moved down the wall one small, slow step at a time.

The longer I stared into the many faces of her extended family, the same people who shared her DNA, I wondered what it would be like if I still had a relationship with my parents. Would they even care who I was? What I was doing? How I was spending my time? Probably not. Besides, I knew that I would never be able to forgive them for what they did—or in my case, didn't do.

Pushing these thoughts out of my head, I slipped on a pair of grey sweats and found Alex in the kitchen pouring two cups of coffee.

"I haven't been shopping since Nash left." She turned to hand me a full mug. "But I thought maybe we could grab breakfast at that new joint up the block?"

My lips pursed near the rim as I blew the steam off the top. "I'd rather not."

"Sure. Okay." She turned to the sink and mixed some cream into her cup.

It wasn't that I wasn't hungry, I just wasn't ready to face the world yet.

"Maybe after this caffeine gets in my blood I'll change my mind." Both my hands cupped the hot mug as I took a sip. "Thanks again for last night."

"Don't worry about it." Alex tucked a loose strand of hair behind her ear. "That's what I'm here for." She stared into her mug, unable to look me in the eye.

"It wasn't as bad as it looked," I whispered.

I knew I shouldn't be, but I was embarrassed for breaking down piece by piece last night once Alex rescued me. As tears streamed down my cheeks, my best friend had looked on with worry, and rightfully so. But it wasn't what it seemed. Kelly didn't mean to hurt me. He didn't know. It was me who was fucked up. This was my fault. Not his.

"Do you want to talk about?" Alex's voice was soft and non-threatening.

"Not really." I pushed my tailbone off the edge of the stool I was resting on and walked to the living room couch.

Alex followed me and took the corner opposite me. We drank in silence for a long time but I knew better than to think that her mind wasn't on anything but me.

"I've never seen you like that." Alex's pained gaze peered over the rim of her mug.

"I know." I cast my eyes into the black abyss of my coffee.

"If someone hurt you," she paused, shaking her head like she couldn't believe she was even thinking it, "I want to know about it."

I brought my feet up and hugged my knees to my chest. I thought whether or not I was ready to have this conversation. Because once I started it, I knew there was no turning back. Finally, I said in a dull voice, "Someone did hurt me."

"Shit, Kendra." Alex's lips parted and she looked at me like she couldn't believe what she was hearing. "Was it a date? Never mind. Don't answer that. I know it was a date. I knew I shouldn't have let you do this for me. This was a bad idea."

"It wasn't a date," I said, hoping to calm her down.

Alex snapped her head away and shoved a hand through her long, beautiful hair.

My chest expanded and I held my breath for a couple seconds before letting it out. "I was raped." I sighed.

"Fuck." She straightened her arm and settled her hand on my knee. "I should have taken you to the hospital, not here."

"It didn't happen last night." My eyes were round as I looked at her. I knew I was the cause of the dark circles under her eyes.

"Oh, my God, Kendra. You don't have to be doing this."

I sipped my coffee, knowing that this would be how she'd react. Alex didn't know. I hadn't told her about my rape. Hell, I hadn't thought about what had happened to me for a very long time. "It happened to me when I was just a teenager. I don't like to talk about it."

Alex let out a sigh, falling back into the couch.

I couldn't look at her, but I felt her staring. The way Kelly touched me set off a trigger. It had nothing to do with him and everything to do with me. This was all my fault. When I should have been sleeping off the hotness of last night, I was here telling my friend that I had a secret I hadn't shared with her yet.

"Kendra?"

I lifted my gaze.

"Will you tell me? I'd like to help."

My heart pounded against my ribs. I felt helpless and afraid. There were no words to describe the shame I still dealt with for what happened to me. And I hated that Kelly was the one who'd dug up those feelings. He was the last person who it should have been, and just when we were getting our relationship started. It couldn't have come at a worse time.

"Kendra," Alex said again. "Will you?"

My cell dinged with a message.

We exchanged looks and she must have known that I was going to avoid having to relive that dark, dark day. I set my mug down on the coffee table and ran to the other room, knowing that she knew I was purposely avoiding having to discuss the secrets of my past. By the time I came back, Alex was still waiting for an answer.

"It was the Madam," I said. "She needs to see me."

20

KENDRA

Jerome had his eye on me the moment I stepped onto the floor.

He looked like he could use some cheering up so I bounced my hips, twirling my tiny purse through the air as I approached. "Why so sad?"

He licked his lips without responding.

"Madam working you too hard?" I stepped up to him and he only stared. "Talk to me, big boy." I reached behind him and slapped his hard butt.

He caught my arm, closing his fingers tight enough to pinch my flesh in his nails, and he led me inside the office with brute bodyguard force. Pushing me over the edge of the couch, his strong hand began spanking me.

"What the fuck?!" I swatted his hand away but he kept spanking me. "Jerome!" I cried as the stinging pain rippled down my legs.

Only when the Madam stepped out did he stop. Jerome pulled me to my feet and stepped back.

"Thank you, Jerome." Madam leaned against the doorframe with folded arms. "I'll take it from here."

I smoothed the wrinkles out of my dress and fixed my hair. "What got into him?"

"Kendra, doll." Madam looked me in the eye. "You've been a bad girl."

My brows furrowed. "So that's how you punish me?" I glanced over my shoulder to find Jerome smirking.

"No, honey." Madam smiled. "That's how Jerome punishes you."

"And what did I do, exactly?"

"Come into my office." She waved me inside. "Take a seat, and I'll tell you."

I followed the Madam into her office and fell into the empty chair.

"Kendra, baby."

"Yes?" My eyes were wide as I looked around, feeling like I was receiving a lecture from the high school principal.

"How was your date with Kelly?"

I let out a shaky breath, afraid to learn what may have already gotten back to her. "It was fun." I bit my bottom lip and nodded.

"And he took you back to his hotel suite?"

My brows pinched. "How do you even know this?"

She looked to the side and laughed. Then she turned her attention back to me. "Did you sleep with him?"

I cast my gaze to my swinging foot. "And if I did?"

"See there." Madam angled her head. "Your lip is the reason why Jerome had to punish you." She pushed off the desk and stepped behind me. When her hands came down on my shoulders, I cringed. "Let me remind you, you're arm candy. That's it, unless I say otherwise." Her fingers worked to soften my deep tissue.

"Did Kelly say something?"

"Is there something that he should have come to me with?"

I shook my head.

"Don't be naïve, sweetheart." She bent down and placed her

mouth close to my ear. "All news travels back to the Madam eventually."

My breath caught in my throat and I hated not knowing for sure what she knew about me, my past, and what happened last night. I was certain Kelly would tell her that I bounced, but maybe he hadn't. And if he hadn't, I wondered why.

Madam lifted her head and stepped around to her desk. "The reason I called you here is because you have a new assignment."

I bit my lip, wondering what kind of package she wanted me to deliver this time. I watched as she opened a side drawer to pull out a date card. My eyes closed as I let out a sigh of relief. She handed it over and a part of me expected it to be another night with Kelly. "Am I allowed to sleep with this one?" I asked.

She pointed at me. "You don't learn, do you?"

My shoulders shrugged as I opened it up. I wouldn't have given her lip if I didn't expect to see Kelly Black's name written on the inside. Except where his name should have been, Timothy Parker's was there in bold letters instead.

"I'll have your wardrobe delivered this afternoon with any important details of what to expect."

I stared at Timothy's name, unable to look Madam in the eye. There was so much that I needed to resolve with Kelly I could hardly imagine entertaining anybody else until he understood why I'd left last night.

"Is everything okay?" Madam asked.

My tongue circled my lips as I hung my head, nodding. But everything wasn't okay. I knew I shouldn't have let my heart get attached, but Kelly brought a strange familiarity to my life that made me feel whole. It was dark. I know. But it was the truth.

"And Kendra, darling?"

I lifted my head and locked eyes with Madam.

"This one I want you to fuck."

21

KELLY

I licked the pad of my finger and turned the page.

When I should have been preparing for my meeting with Mario, I had my mind on Kendra. Everywhere I looked, I was reminded of her. She had me second-guessing everything I did. And that was why I was back to the non-disclosure I asked her to sign. *Was that the reason she left?*

No matter how many times I considered it, I wouldn't change things. I needed it done. Needed the protection put in place. There was no negotiating this one. If she wanted to leave, then that was her choice. Besides, there were plenty of women in this city I could seduce—*just none could come close to comparing to Kendra.*

The door opened and Emmanuel burst into my office, breathing heavily.

I lifted my eyes off the paper I was studying and glanced up at him from beneath my brow. "Did we have a meeting I missed?"

He wiped his mouth, pacing around my office, rubbing his arms.

I stood, hiding my hands deep in my pockets, glaring at him. "What can I do for you?"

He stopped and turned. "Madam didn't tell you?"

I shook my head, noticing that his pupils were tiny pin pricks. "Tell me what?"

"You were supposed to deliver the payment she promised."

My brow furrowed. "I'm sorry. I'm not aware of any payment."

He stepped forward, locking his eyes intently on mine. "So it's not here?"

"I think you were mistaken," I said as I heard Giselle get back from a late lunch.

"Fuck!" He bit his knuckles as he cursed.

I'd never seen him like this and it had me on edge. With the way he was acting, his behavior was completely unpredictable. Emmanuel was irrational as he paced nervously back and forth. Pellets of sweat formed on his brow and, by the looks of it, I would guess that he hadn't had a decent night's sleep in days.

"She said it would be here," he growled.

"Well. It's not."

"Why would she lie to me?" I watched as he slammed his fist down on my desk.

"I think it's time for you to leave," I said, stepping around my desk, ready to muscle him out the door.

"Fuck you!" He stepped away from me. "I'm not leaving until I get the money."

Giselle ran into my office just as I was about to manhandle Emmanuel. "Kelly!"

I turned to find Giselle holding up a briefcase. My face twisted, wondering how she got that and what it was doing in my office.

"Madam dropped it off earlier," she said.

Emmanuel tried to side-step around me, but I blocked him with a sharp elbow to the gut. The only thing that made any kind of sense was that the Madam did this on purpose. I'd seen her play these kinds of games before, just never on me.

But I wasn't stupid. I knew what her angle was. It was her way of pressuring me to do what she wanted—agree to represent Blake Stone.

I took the briefcase from Giselle, needing to feel the weight myself. There was no doubt it had the money inside. Just as Emmanuel said. "Get some rest. Clean yourself up."

He reached for the briefcase and I pulled it back.

"Maybe even get yourself laid."

"I don't need the Madam's girls," he sneered.

There was more going on than I cared to know. "Take care of yourself," I said, finally releasing the briefcase over to him. "Don't do something you might later regret."

He looked at me and smirked.

"And, Emmanuel," I said as he was on his way out, "don't ever barge in like that ever again. If you need representation, you're free to call or schedule an appointment."

He hurried out the door, leaving me giving Giselle a questioning look.

"I'm sorry. I should have told you." She averted her gaze. "I thought the Madam would have given you a heads up."

"Don't worry about it," I said, excusing Giselle to her desk.

With everything happening around me, and somehow it all being connected to the Madam, I knew that I needed to step away and find reason behind the madness. Because if I didn't correct course soon, this shit would explode and maybe take me with it.

"I'm working the rest of the day from home," I said, passing Giselle on my way out. "Hit me on my cell if you need me."

I leaped down the stairs and hurried to my car parked out back. There was only one person who could help me sort through this mess I'd found myself somehow entangled in.

Once settled in behind the wheel, I turned the key and revved the engine.

I knew she'd be happy to see me. It had been a very long time since our last visit. We had a lot of catching up to do. And maybe I'd even bring flowers.

22

KELLY

The grass crinkled beneath my feet as I approached. My legs were heavy and I could barely pick my feet up off the ground to take the next step. My shoulders pulled low as my pulse raced. The emotions that pounded through my heart contradicted themselves. I was filled with regret and unconditional love—the same emotions I felt the first time I laid eyes on her—and that was all on top of a heavy sadness I was sure I'd never be able to overcome.

I peeled my heel, that felt more like a brick, off the ground and stomped it down, one step closer to her.

The beat of my own heart thrashed between my ears. I was lightheaded and dizzy. I hated myself for deciding to stay away. She deserved better. A selfish decision I'd made long ago in an attempt to heal my own wounds. I'd promised her the world and, in the end, I tried to forget about her because it was easier that way.

But here I was ...

My hands tightened their grip on the stems of the flowers I held. They began to shake the closer I got to her headstone.

When I glanced down at the fresh, colorful bouquet I had brought for her, I smiled.

Each flower produced heady scents that nearly choked me with tears.

It was all a blur. The last few steps, I couldn't remember. My mind went blank and I felt numb. But as soon as I reached her plot, the ground where she was buried, my strength fell away and I collapsed.

The bouquet of flowers fell with me and I began to sob.

"I'm sorry, my love." My chin trembled with the deep pain I was experiencing. "I'm here now. Everything will be all right."

Even as I heard myself saying all those things, I knew them to be a lie. All except for the one about me being sorry. Because I was sorry. More than anything. If I could take back that day, I would. I deeply regretted that I couldn't save her—do something —before it was too late.

"This is all my fault," I cried. "I should have been there for you. But I wasn't."

Tears streamed down my cheeks. Inside, I was hollow. Completely lonely and incredibly depressed. My body filled with aches and pains as I thought about how much I hated this cruel world. It wasn't fair. Wasn't kind. And it seemed like no matter what I did to try to make it a better place, it only got worse.

"I let you down and I hope that you can forgive me." I tipped my head back, wailing into the cloudless sky.

I didn't care if anyone heard. This was my grief, my way of dealing with the loss of my wife. I could give a fuck about anything else right now. The only thing that mattered was her.

Reaching inside my jacket, I pulled out the handgun I had tucked away in its holster beneath my arm. I looked at that thing, thinking through my situation and how I could choose to end the intense suffering right here, right now, with a pull of the trigger.

My chest heaved through my cries that seemed impossible to

stop as my thumb stroked the black metal of the gun. I thought I could do it. Join my wife in the afterlife. But I couldn't. It wouldn't be what she would want. And besides, *would she even be happy to see me?*

Tucking my weapon away, I wiped my eyes dry, blinking away the swollen grief that clouded my vision. "You're right," I said, nodding to my wife's name engraved on the rock. "You're right."

I crawled on my hands and knees, cleaning off the gravestone before reaching back around and laying down the fresh flowers I had bought for her.

"For you." I smiled, laughing a little.

We shared a moment in silence before I looked around, thinking that the view wasn't what it once was, like when she first came to rest here. It had changed considerably but it was still beautiful because she was here.

"I'm sure she was beautiful," a familiar voice said behind me.

When I looked to see who it was, I found Adrianna Eastman approaching. She was wearing a leather jacket with white slacks and had her hands hidden inside her jacket pockets.

I stood and wiped my face, knowing that not too many people knew about my wife because I was ashamed of how she died. "If Wes knew you were here, he'd kill you."

"He doesn't know," she said, stopping in front of the gravestone. We both stood there staring at the flowers with our heads down as if silently praying for peace to comfort us through the pain. "I came alone."

"How did you know where to find me?"

She turned to look at me. "You're not the only one who suspects the Madam is up to something."

The crease between my brows deepened as I stared back at her.

"I've been keeping an eye on Emmanuel. When I saw that he stopped by your office ..." She dropped her gaze back to my dead wife.

"Why didn't you come inside?"

"I saw you leaving—"

"—you followed me here," I said, interrupting her.

She nodded. "I'm sorry for your loss. Even after all this time, I can't imagine it gets any easier."

My chest tightened, thinking that she had no idea what it was like to be me. "The Madam is definitely up to something."

"What do you think it is?"

"You don't know?"

The wind picked up and blew hair across her face. "I'd like to know what it is you're thinking."

My eye caught a seagull floating nearby. I watched it ride the drifts of air, plunging before soaring, and I said, "I hate to be saying this, especially to you, but I believe the Madam wants to be the one to fill the gap Blake Stone left in the market."

She hung her head and frowned. "That's what I was afraid of."

No one wanted to see Stone rot more than Adrianna. He set her up, got her hooked on blow, and it was amazing that she made it out as strong as she had—completely clean.

"Look, I'm sorry that I had to follow you here." She turned to look at me, smiling. "If you need anything—even just to talk—I want you to know that I'm here for you."

I nodded as she smoothed her hand down my arm, then she left.

"What are you going to do?" I asked.

She spun around, her hair blowing wild in the wind. "Tell Wes. He needs to know about this."

23

KENDRA

Timothy Parker brought his A-game.

There was nothing I didn't like about the man. And I *tried* to not like him.

Believe me. I did.

Hell, I even went into tonight with plans on how I could sabotage the date just so I wouldn't have to make an excuse of why I couldn't sleep with him like the Madam had asked me to do.

He had a slender neck with a sharp Adam's apple that cut through the center of his throat. I'd never seen such shiny silver hair like he had. It glimmered like the mined metal and though he was old enough to be my father, it was impossible to not imagine what it would be like to fully step into his world of luxury.

"This steak never disappoints." He smiled as he cut through his nearly finished slab of meat.

I nodded, fully enjoying my own meal of braised lamb shanks.

Alex was pissed that we didn't have our talk, but how could I possibly talk about something so dark when I had this amazing man sitting across from me to look forward to?

"You know," he lifted his head, still holding a fork in one hand and a knife in the other, "you remind me of someone I know."

I swallowed down my last bite, clearing my plate. "Oh, yeah? I hope she's nice."

"The funny thing is, I can't recall who that person is." His eyes smiled as he chewed with his mouth closed.

"Maybe it's me," I said, dabbing the corners of my mouth clean with my napkin.

He finished chewing and smiled, showing me his teeth. I couldn't help but notice how good he looked. Or maybe it was the restaurant, the soft glow of seduction swirling around him that made him seem so handsome. Whatever the reason, I liked my view tonight.

"I suppose it could be." He sipped his wine.

"Except we haven't met until tonight," I reminded him.

"Isn't that a shame?"

"Ask me tomorrow." My eyes narrowed as I grinned.

He chuckled as he worked to finish his own plate. "What's your last name?"

"Oh, no. I don't give out those kinds of details until the third date."

His eyes sparkled when he lifted his head. His gaze was as steady as his posture and with his pupils big and round, it was clear that he adored my company as much as I did his. "I can wait then."

"A confident man." I pinched the stem of my wine glass, picking it up from the table. "I like that." My lips curled over the rim as I stole a sip while keeping my eye on him.

"And I like that you're cautious." He grinned. "Have I told you how amazing you look tonight?"

The candle flickered in his eyes as they drifted over me. "Not nearly enough," I teased. A man could compliment me night and day. It would never get old, I thought, as long as they did it in a classy manner.

"Well, you are absolutely stunning." He couldn't take his eyes off of me.

All night he peppered compliments about something he liked about me. Whether it be the amazing dress Madam had given me to wear, or the diamond earrings that complemented the shade of red lipstick I wore. Timothy found reason to share his desires whenever he got the chance. At first I didn't think much of it, then when he did it again, I knew his words to be sincere.

"Do you always wear three-piece suits?" I asked. I liked how well he fit into his tailored clothes.

"Every day I'm at the office." He pulled in a deep breath.

When I finished my glass, Timothy reached for the bottle and held it up, asking me if I wanted more with his eyes. I nodded, watching him pour my glass half full, realizing we were close to polishing off a second bottle already.

"Tell me, Mr. CEO," I brought my glass close to my mouth as I smiled, "what is work like for you?"

Timothy leaned forward and started talking about his business empire. It was made clear to me that he enjoyed talking about himself, so I did him the honor of being curious about what it would be like to be an entrepreneur who worked around the clock, seven days a week.

I could appreciate the ambition but the schedule seemed grueling.

His hands waved through the air as his story of empire building continued. It was unbelievable, really. Incredible what a little bit of ambition could achieve. He had his hands in real estate, fashion, start-up technologies, everything under the sun. Some of which were sure to take off and be the next greatest thing. But as he talked about his own accomplishments and the celebrities he knew, all I could think about was Kelly.

My finger circled the rim of my wine glass as I pretended to listen.

I knew I needed to talk to Kelly. It would be stupid of me to think that this would just pass. Or that he'd let it go. He needed to know that it wasn't him, but me. I was the reason I ran.

My fingers pushed the hair out of my face as the thought alone left a sour taste in my mouth.

There was so much I still needed to know about him. And I hadn't forgotten Angel's catty comment about how I should be careful to not get hurt if Kelly left me after first finding his way into fucking me. *It's him who has the commitment problem,* I could still hear her say.

"Hey, are you okay?" Timothy reached over and touched my frown.

"Yeah." I smiled. "I'm fine." Except now I was thinking about that fucking contract Kelly swore I needed to sign before allowing our relationship to go any deeper.

"Anyway, enough about me." Timothy's fingers walked their way over to my side of the table. "I was thinking of ordering dessert."

I glanced down at my empty plate, completely stuffed. The meal was exquisite but I couldn't refuse dessert. But when I flicked my gaze up to him, I wondered if he was even thinking about food.

"Dessert, you say?" I twisted a lock of hair around my finger, debating whether or not to reach out and touch his hand that was clearly trespassing on my side of the table.

"We can eat it here," he flipped his hand palm up, "or we can take it to-go." He smiled.

He had the whitest teeth I'd ever seen. They glowed like bleached coral and if I didn't know what he did for a living already, I would have guessed he was a dentist.

He was waiting for an answer and I was thankful the waiter came to clear the table. I was saved from having to decide, at least for another minute. A tab was left and despite all my thoughts being consumed by Kelly, I needed to remain present for the man who'd paid for my company tonight.

"What would you like?" I asked, letting my hand fall into his.

I watched as his long fingers closed around my bones, stroking my moisturized flesh with clear intention. He was hungry for more of me, but even with the Madam specifically instructing me to fuck this man, a man who most definitely pulled out all the right stops and deserved a good romping, I couldn't.

"I want what you want."

I dropped my gaze and thought about how best to respond.

It wasn't his fault that I was dragging my feet. Only days ago I would have totally done it. And despite his relentless attempt at seducing me, Kelly was the man who deserved to be wrapped up between my legs. Not Timothy.

He squeezed my hand and craned his neck forward.

I shifted uncomfortably in my seat, my heart beating wildly in my chest.

"Kendra, beautiful Kendra."

I flicked my eyes to his but couldn't hold his strong, curious gaze.

"Where did you go? Have you left for the evening already?"

"I haven't gone anywhere." It was a lie, and despite my best efforts to hide the truth of what it was I was thinking, I couldn't fake it. He'd read between the lines. It was written all over my face. "I'm not ready for dessert, but I would like another ride in your car."

Timothy's sports car was the hottest thing I'd ridden in. It was a classic 1955 Ford Thunderbird that had all the American ingenuity and muscle packed into one engine.

He rested his other hand on the table and I let him pull me to my feet. "Where would you like to go?"

I slid my hand beneath his jacket and hooked my fingers on his surprisingly tight waist. "Do you like to dance?"

"I'd love to dance," he said, tossing five one-hundred dollar bills to the table. "As long as it's with you." He tightened his arm around me as we walked toward the exit.

I wondered who still carried that much cash when I said, "You'd do anything with me, wouldn't you?"

"Is that an invitation?" He peered down at me with a wide grin.

"Drive fast. Warm me up," we stepped outside, leaving the restaurant, "and we'll see where the night takes us."

The valet brought his car around shortly after we hit the curb. Timothy towed me by the hand to the passenger side and I watched him open the door. "Wait one second," he said, twirling me around so that my back was pressed up against the window glass. Our eyes danced when he said, "You were such a joy tonight."

"I thought it wasn't over?"

He chuckled as he stroked my cheek with his thumb. "I've been wanting to do this since I first saw you." He dropped his head and pressed his lips against mine.

My heart stopped and I fought to keep my body from freezing up but it proved to be impossible. I'd known this was coming. Known that he'd make his move sooner or later. But when it finally came, I couldn't give it back.

He pulled me closer to him, demanding I open my mouth for him to explore.

I squeezed my eyes shut, not liking how the Madam dictated who I fucked and who I didn't. It took all the fun out of it. For me, it was about the experience. The act of living without fear. Yet, it seemed ever since Kelly unknowingly resurfaced my rape, that was all I felt when a man touched me.

Timothy poked his tongue against the seam of my lips, and just as I was about to open up for him I heard a man yelling from afar, "That's my girl. Don't touch her!"

My eyes flew open and I gasped, not believing my eyes. "Kelly?"

He rushed toward Timothy faster than my mind could comprehend. And I couldn't believe what happened next.

24

KELLY

My head spun with what she was saying.

It didn't make sense why she was telling me this.

I kept an ear on her words as my fist clenched.

"Okay, got it. Thanks," I said, ending my call.

Then I was in my car and racing across town as fast as I could drive.

I swore the Madam was purposely filling my head with doubts. I was a pawn in her game of chess, but after what she just told me, I couldn't leave it to chance.

Kendra was about to get fucked by another man and it was my job to stop it.

The tires squealed as I sped around a curve. My knuckles were white from how tightly my fingers gripped the wheel and no matter how fast I drove, I couldn't run away from the shit that my life had become.

My stomach clenched as I thought about Mario and what I might learn after meeting with him. The Madam already had taken a position in her head—I knew that much—so the reasons for her mind games had to be a power play.

I downshifted, letting the engine roar as I cautiously rolled through a stop sign. When I saw that it was clear, I hit the accelerator and sped off.

I dreaded what could be, especially after Adrianna Eastman surprised me at the cemetery. Once she involved Wesley Reid, there would be no turning back to how things once were. If the Madam *was* up to what we all speculated she was, then God help us all. Fear hardened my stomach as I imagined what Wes and Adrianna were going to do to counter-attack the Madam's pursuit.

The stress was enough for me to steal Kendra away and lose myself in her.

Not to mention, save her before something bad happened.

I needed her to know that I didn't mean to hurt her last night. I didn't like the way we'd left things, quiet and awkward, leaving us to only guess what the other was thinking. It was the pursuit of sex that introduced us, but it was something much deeper that had me speeding through the city in an attempt to get to her before it was too late.

A car honked when I cut someone off. Nearly getting t-boned, I continued weaving in and out of traffic. "Move it," I cursed under my breath.

Whatever that internal drive was, I wasn't sure. I wanted her to be mine and mine alone, but I wasn't in need of a girlfriend. We could fuck, be there for each other, and stall the engine there before it got complicated.

But I couldn't allow her to be with any other man.

It had to be me.

No exceptions.

I slammed on the brakes, skidding to a complete stop the moment I whipped my ride into the parking lot of the restaurant.

As soon as I stashed my gun in the glovebox, I caught Kendra and her date leaving. They walked through the front doors, hand-in-hand, with looks on their faces that sent me over the edge. Spots flashed across my vision as jealousy burned deep. From the moment I laid eyes on him, I knew I wanted to kill him.

He was seducing my girl.

Making my girl smile.

Holding my girl's hand.

My feet hit the pavement and didn't stop moving until I had my hands fisted in his expensive suit, tossing him over the hood of his car.

I heaved through heavy breaths, pointing at the man. "Stay down, asshole."

"Kelly!" Kendra screamed from over my shoulder.

I turned to find her wide-eyed and scared.

My blood boiled as it pulsed through my veins. How could she? After what I'd promised her? How could she go out with another man?

I took one step toward her.

She retreated, keeping one eye on the growing crowd surrounding us.

I followed her line of sight and saw that phones had been pulled from pockets and were now held on us, red-lights on. We were being filmed.

"C'mon." I stole her hand and marched with her in tow. "You're coming with me."

We hurried away, heading to the safety of my parked car, her heels quickly clacking behind.

"Kelly, are you crazy?" She worked to peel my fingers free, but my grip was too tight. "Let me go!"

She dug her heels in and I stopped, turned to face my doe-eyed beauty. "Don't be ridiculous."

"Me? Ridiculous?" She hit me square in the chest with the flat of her hand. "You attacked Timothy for no reason."

"No reason?" I growled.

"What did he do?"

Our eyes danced with nostrils flaring.

A camera flash hit my face and I lifted my gaze to find the same dozen pairs of eyes following me to my car.

"This isn't the place. We can talk in the car. Now, c'mon." My fingers readjusted their hold on her wrist as I began dragging her through the street.

"You can't just steal me away when you feel like it." She hit my arm. "I'm on a date. It's my job, whether you like it or not."

I leaned forward, pulling her along with me, ignoring her pleas for me to stop.

"The Madam is going to kill me." Kendra gripped me at the crook of my arm with her free hand and tugged on my arm. "I'm already on her shit-list. You can't be doing this, Kelly."

Once we reached my car, I spun her around, pinning her against the door. My thick arms caged her, forcing her to look me in the eye when she talked.

"You're such an asshole," she said, dropping her gaze to our feet.

I hooked her chin and pulled her eyes back to mine. "Who do you think told me you were here?"

Kendra's brows knitted as she swallowed.

"Hmm?" I angled her head to meet my eyes again. "Do you think that I just happened to be in the area? Or that I like having to chase you across town?"

"You don't own me."

My mouth crashed over hers. I considered her comment a challenge, and I was going to make it very clear that no matter what she thought—or what the Madam said—Kendra was going to be *all* mine.

I licked the seam of her lips, coaxing them open. She parted and pushed the tip of her tongue against mine. I knew she wanted it—knew she shared the same burning desire as I did. I stroked her tongue with stiff dominant strokes, digging my hands into her sexy body that I needed to mark as my own. I'd make it very clear that no man was ever to touch her. "You're mine," I said, biting her lip.

Kendra pulled away and gave me a questioning look.

I thrust my steeled cock into her soft mid-section. "You're not free to do what you want." I cradled my mouth against her neck, peppering kisses across her fluttering pulse. Her hands roamed the muscled valleys of my back. "If you want to be with me, there are rules," I breathed into her ear, causing her to shiver.

Kendra fisted my hair and pulled me away. I could see question marks flashing across her eyes. "Kelly—"

I silenced her with a heated kiss. There wasn't any reason for us to be having this conversation here, out in the open where everyone could hear. "I'll give you one chance." My fingers threaded through her hair as I tugged her head back so she could see how serious I was. "Think before you answer, because based on what you say, your tomorrow might not look like how you thought it might."

Her breath hitched and I could hear her heart beating wildly in her chest. The severity of my question was life-threatening.

I gave a swift tug to her hair. "Do you understand?"

She nodded.

"Then listen carefully." I leaned in and whispered the one question I had for her. And depending how she answered, it was certain to change both our lives forever.

25

KENDRA

"Yes." My arms flung around his neck. "Yes, of course I want to be with you." I hung off him, promising myself I'd never let go.

The question surprised me. It was like he needed to hear me say it. And I liked that he asked me, too. Because after I left his suite, I didn't know when or how I'd see Kelly Black again. My entire body twisted with regret since running out on him, but when I heard him just ask me if I wanted to be with him, my answer was flying out of my mouth before my mind knew what it was saying.

Kelly crashed his mouth over mine and I swirled my tongue over his, loving the taste that was every bit him.

"I'm sorry," I said, pecking his lips as I spoke. "This isn't how I wanted it to be. You should have never seen me in the company of another man."

I felt the tips of his fingers knead into my sides as he listened to me apologize profusely for treating him with such disrespect. I knew the tight hold he had on me was deep enough to leave bruises, but I didn't care. Because what I was feeling tonight was sheer happiness that could only be found when he was around.

Kelly held that kind of power over me. He came to save me from having to sleep with Timothy, and I wondered if he knew about Madam's instructions or if it was just coincidence of being in the right place at the right time. Either way, it didn't matter. Not now that he was the one kissing me.

He cupped the back of my skull and angled my head back, deepening our kiss. The way Kelly was kissing me now, with long, deep strokes, I felt like my heart was about to explode.

"The other night," I whimpered as he pressed his hardness against my softness. "I shouldn't have left."

He fisted my hair and tugged my head back, exposing my neck completely. "Don't you ever leave me again, you hear?"

"I won't," I cried against the pressure pulling at the roots of my scalp.

He dropped his head, flattened his tongue, and licked from my collarbone up. My nipples puckered into hot balls of fire and I was pulsing between the legs. Kelly nipped at my flesh with his teeth, causing my leg to hook over his solid thigh. The way he was working to slowly undo me, he had me writhing against his leg, moaning against his ear, eagerly pressuring him to finally use that muscle between his legs and send me to the stars.

"You better fucking not." He slammed his hips into me, like he too couldn't wait to get our fuck on. Except we still both had our clothes on and I was positive there were people still watching us, waiting for a fight to break out between him and Timothy.

My jaw snapped shut as I clamped his ear between my teeth. He growled and pressed more of his weight against me. He was so tall, his shoulders so broad. I was a small insect compared to this beast of a man, but even that had me set ablaze.

I snaked my hands up to his face and cupped his cheeks between them, kissing at his thick lips before sucking his tongue back into my mouth.

Kelly Black.

I adored him.

And I hated him all at once.

He was so infuriating but the way he was kissing me now, with such brute force, was unlike anything I'd ever experienced before. He was a man. A real man who was determined to unravel all that kept me tight. And in the process he made me believe that what we had was real. That I was not just a date who buttered him up when the time was right. No. I was his jelly, the jam he was about to spread.

My fingers gripped at his button-down, tugging it free from where it was tucked securely beneath his belt. The urge to touch him was completely overwhelming but I couldn't stop. Nor did I want to. Kelly Black had been on my mind since I first got a taste of his desire, and he'd been on my tongue like a lasting taste of the finest appetizer. I couldn't wait to see him again, and now he was here, grinding his length against me, promising to destroy me forever.

"The Madam is going to kill me," I murmured between labored breaths.

This was the second time I'd run out on the date I started the night out with. And each time, I traded in for something better. If the Madam didn't kill me first, then Kelly certainly would with the promise of orgasmic bliss he was surely going to shower me with tonight.

"You let me worry about her." His possessive hand squeezed my heavy breast. "Let's get out of here before I end up fucking you in public."

I grinded my sex on him, not caring about anything other than the need I felt for him inside me. "What about the contract?" I didn't mean to bring it up. Mentioning it was sure to pick a fight. But I needed to know.

"After I fuck you, you'll do anything for me." He pulled me against his hardness and I knew that if he fulfilled his promises, he was right—I would do anything he asked of me.

I kissed his strong lips and said, "Then let's ride, cowboy."

He squeezed my ass and chuckled before opening the door to his car, pushing me inside. I was so hot and bothered by our near fuckfest in public that I wasn't sure how I was going to survive the ride to wherever he was taking me.

I watched Kelly walk in front of the hood, taking one glance back to Timothy who was still standing on the sidewalk, dumbfounded by what the hell just happened.

Timothy had unbelieving eyes and I felt bad for him. And not just because Kelly tossed him to the ground. He didn't deserve that, and Kelly didn't need to take it that far. Beyond that, I could only imagine how it felt to see your woman leaving with another man. I made him believe he would be the one to fuck me tonight. Instead, it was looking like Kelly would do me the honor.

Kelly slid in behind the wheel. I smiled and he smiled back.

The truth was, Kelly needed to be the one to pop my escorting cherry. I was now thankful the Madam had made me hold out. Because without it, I would have missed this incredible opportunity with Kelly.

"Where are you taking me?" I asked.

"Does it matter?" He turned the key and started the engine.

Kelly was the one I wanted to be leaving with—the one I wanted nestled between my legs. I was his whenever, wherever, however he wanted his girl. He might not know it yet, but I did. "Not really. As long as it's private."

"Your wish is my command." He looked over his shoulder and sped off.

"Then I guess I'm all yours," I said as I lifted his hand off the gear shifter, draping it over my head as I reached for his steeled cock tenting his pants.

"My possession." He kissed the crown of my head.

It was sick, but somehow sweet, to think he owned me. "I'll be your possession," I said, stroking his stiff cock through his pants, "but only if you allow me to own this."

His eyes darkened as he bit his cheek. "Tonight, I'm all yours." He leaned his head back and pulled my face down to his lap.

My heart beat wildly in my chest as he left me breathless. Anticipation of what I'd find got the best of me. Slowly I unzipped him and what popped out was a long beautiful, thick throbbing cock with a purple crown fit for a king.

This time I'd be sure to love on it without pissing him off.

First, I kissed it. Then, I tasted it. And soon, my own desire had me bobbing up and down his hot satin stick, challenging myself to see how much of it I could fit into my mouth before gagging.

It was big.

It was thick.

And it was veiny.

Everything that I loved about Kelly's penis was there. I liked the way his hot flesh felt against my tongue. How I could make him twitch as my teeth lightly grazed up and over his head. The way his balls felt like huge marbles as I rolled them in my hand.

"Fuck me. That feels incredible," he said, sucking in a breath.

Kelly drove slow and with control. I didn't know if it was because I had him cross-eyed from how I was making him feel, or if he wanted to make the ride last longer than it would have otherwise just so I'd keep sucking his dick. It didn't matter why. I loved on him like I'd never loved on any dick before.

I felt the car slow to a stop. Kelly tapped my head and said, "We're here."

When I lifted my head, I felt disheartened that I couldn't make him cum by the time we arrived. I continued to pump his shaft, needing to spark a release.

"C'mon." He pulled my hand away. "Let's go up to my suite."

It was the same hotel penthouse he had brought me to before. I wanted to get up to that bed and continue our night, but why he didn't want me to finish him off first had me feeling like I was less qualified than I thought.

I pulled my hand away, sinking into the far corner of my seat.

"What's wrong?" Kelly lifted his hand to my face, stroking my cheek with his thumb.

I held his hand on my cheek, deathly afraid to ask, "Are you not attracted to me?"

"Why would you say that?" His voice was soft and compassionate. There was a glimmer of pain in his eye that made me believe that I was totally out of line with my questioning.

"Because I just sucked you off for the last fifteen minutes and couldn't get a release." I watched him struggle to tuck that huge thing back inside his pants. I hated to see it go and as soon as he zipped himself up, I missed it dearly.

"That doesn't mean I'm not attracted to you." He pulled me in for a gentle kiss. "I'm wild for you."

"Then what is it?"

"Kendra, baby." His eyes smiled. "I'm saving it all for when we get upstairs." He kissed me again. "That's where I plan to ruin you."

26

KENDRA

His dark eyes were glued to me as he sat on a chair in the far corner of the room.

My panties were the only fabric I had left on. Everything else lay bunched on the floor by my feet. I didn't know why he was taking so long in getting undressed. After giving him head in the car, I couldn't wait to milk his cock with my wet sex.

"You're not one to hurry, are you?" I said, watching him pull one shoe off. He promised to ruin me, and I hoped he would, but I'd test his stamina and see just how long he could last.

His tongue wet his bottom lip as he chuckled. "I'm a man who takes his time."

"That's a good quality to have." I could appreciate a man who took his time, I certainly didn't want him to hurry through me. But still. I wanted to know he was as eager as I was to get our fuck on.

"Lose them," he said, pointing to my panties.

"And what about you?" I arched a brow as I hooked my thumbs on the sides, beginning to shimmy my way out of the last barrier between him and me. "Are you planning to undress as well?"

His look alone drew my nipples tight. "Hang on." Kelly held up his hand as he kicked his other shoe free. "First, c'mere."

I eyed him for a second before submitting to his call. The room was cool from the air conditioner. It swirled between my legs as I hesitated. I was wet and pulsing with uncontrollable need to be fucked.

His pupils dilated as he raked me over.

I didn't know where to put my hands. An uncomfortable feeling made me hesitant in my actions. Second guessing myself, I first folded my arms and covered my chest. Then I let them hang. It was like he had me under his spell, my mind going blank, losing confidence with every passing second. This was Kelly's show and I didn't want to overstep my boundaries for fear of losing him again. I needed to remain strong.

I bit my lip, twirling my hair over my shoulder and seductively walking in long strides to the sexy man hiding dark secrets behind those hypnotizing eyes.

Once I was within reach, Kelly held his hand out and I placed mine in his palm. He had large, strong hands that were covered with deep lines that told a story of his ambitious life. His fingers closed over my thin bones and there was no escaping him. Not that I wanted to. It was time we stopped dancing this tango and got on with what I knew we both wanted.

God, did I *need* him inside me.

With him on the chair, I was barely taller than him. Even with me standing, he was such a large figure in the small room. Though I liked the feeling of hovering over him for once. It was a new angle for me to explore and I liked how his sharp angles cast shadows in new directions over his face. He had a thick head of hair and he was just as immaculate from up here as I knew he was from below.

He lifted my hand and turned me to the side.

Kelly needed to see his prize. Study the package that he kept fighting to take for himself.

I was proud of the assets I owned and wasn't shy to show them off. Though I was eager to get on with the action he promised me in the car, I was curious to see how this dark and mysterious man, Kelly Black, took his women. So I let him guide me and do what he needed to do to properly prepare himself for the impending onslaught I was sure to receive.

"Do you like what you see?" I asked as he dug his fingers into my fleshy hips, turning me so that I was facing away from him.

He trailed his finger down my spine, letting it fall through the crease of my ass still covered in my thin laced panties. "You're incredible." His deep husky voice sent vibrations across my skin.

"Thank you."

He slapped my ass hard enough to cause my heels to lurch up off the floor. "What was that for?"

"What?" His hands soothed the sting with a gentle massage. "You didn't like it?"

My eyes hooded over and heat leafed across my cheeks. "I did."

The flat of his hand spanked me a little bit harder. My hand flew over my mouth as I yelped.

"Good." He jiggled my ass. "It's perfect."

"You're a bad boy." I bit my pinky finger.

"You're a bad girl." He pushed my ass cheeks together and jiggled them again.

We both laughed.

"Now, turn to face me." His voice was firm and unforgiving.

Slowly, I twisted around to face him. There was a desire in his eyes, a look on his face that said tonight was only a test.

He pulled my hands away from my breasts. I didn't even remember when I had covered them up, but it must have been after one of his spankings. The tip of his finger circled the deep pigment of a peaked nipple. "You take care of yourself."

"I'm a girl who prefers perfection over going natural."

"And what about," his finger trailed down the center of my fluttering stomach, "down here."

My gaze cast down to his finger hooked on the hem of my waistband. I wanted him to pull it open, reach his hand inside and touch me. "Check for yourself."

He scooped my ass up with his big bear hands and pulled me to him. I tangled my hand in his hair as he peppered open-mouth kisses across my soft mid-section. "God, you taste amazing." His tongue lapped over my hip bones. He had my body on fire as electricity transferred from him to me. "Does your pussy taste as good as your sexy bronzed skin?"

"Get me naked and find out," I said, taking his hands off my ass and bringing them to the sides, forcing him to rid me of the thin fabric that kept his tongue from slicing open my throbbing cleft.

In one swift motion, Kelly yanked my undies to my ankles. I lifted one foot, then the other, stepping out of them before bending my knee and placing one foot next to his thigh, perfectly perched on the seat of his chair.

His rough hands roamed my silky-smooth legs before he reached between my thighs, touching me for the first time.

A light moan escaped past my lips as relief washed over me. I'd been waiting for this since I danced with him the night I was on a date with Oscar Buchanan. And now that it was here I panted, eagerly needing more. More of Kelly. All of Mr. Black.

"I like a woman who leaves a little patch of fuzz." He pulled at my curls and I thrust my hips toward his face.

"Is that right?" I held on to his head, touching my left breast with my hand.

He nodded, smiling as he slid his finger through my moist folds.

"Because I could shave it bare if you'd like?"

He pressed his wet lips against my belly. "If I like?" He peered up at me from beneath his brow.

"Anything for you." I tugged at the hair on his head, nodding.

He growled, continuing to stroke me. "Take off my shirt."

I did as he requested, starting with the top button. My hips writhed over his finger, grazing over my tender button, and I worked my way down his chest as far as I could reach without losing contact with his finger. "You'll have to do the rest yourself."

His brows raised.

"Because I'm not moving away from your hand."

His chuckle was a deep, satisfying baritone that only got me wetter. With his free hand he finished what I couldn't do myself, and with his shirt open and his chest exposed he pulled his hand away from my aching sex and replaced the void with his face.

My breath labored through the intensity of having his tongue over my swollen nub. He licked and sucked, slurping a quick taste down before pulling back. "You taste amazing."

"Do I have you hard yet?"

He lapped his tongue against my tightness one more time before standing. My fingers curled over his broad shoulders, helping him slide his shirt away from his shoulders. It was only fair that I could have something equally as appetizing to lust after.

Kelly's body was stone. Perfectly defined muscles that were hard and powerful but not outrageously big. I liked that. I didn't need a muscle-man. I needed a man with stamina, a man who could protect me when the time came, and the more I learned about Mr. Kelly Black, the more I was starting to believe he had those attributes I found completely irresistible.

I trailed my fingers over each of his steeled abs, and if I wasn't careful, he could send me over the edge by just looking at him.

"Raging hard," he growled, finally answering my question.

"You gonna do something about it?" I looked up at him, my tongue circling my mouth as I met his eyes. "Or should I just leave now?"

He picked me up and carried me across the room where he

tossed me onto the plush bed. "After I'm finished with you, I doubt you'll have the strength to leave."

My hand reached up and started playing with my tits. "Don't underestimate me. I may be small, but I have the strength of a Greek goddess."

"I'll be the judge of that." He smirked.

Kelly finished undressing himself and when his hardness sprang free, my sex clenched. He was a gorgeous man who was truly a gift from God. I was lucky to have him fight so hard to have me. Kelly deserved me. And I deserved him. He could take whatever he wanted from me after proving that I wasn't just some girl he could buy. I'd seen the intensity in his eyes when he found me with Timothy. There was no doubt that he thought I was something special. Something worth fighting for.

My knees fell out to the sides, as if tempting him to ravage me.

Kelly stroked his shaft, pumping the blood to the tip. His crown turned a deeper shade of purple. It looked painfully swollen and I was already aching for what I imagined it would feel like to have that thick girth drilling me to the depths of my core. When he lifted his gaze, his eyes were dark and entirely too sexy to comprehend. There was a danger in them that said he was about to turn up the heat and put the pressure on.

He stepped forward, grabbed me by the ankles and flipped me onto my stomach. I pushed myself up onto my elbows as he spread my legs. He settled between them, getting his face so close to my sex I could feel his breath cooling the arousal coating my pussy.

"You have a gorgeous cunt." He spread my pussy lips, dipping his finger inside my hot cavern.

My breath caught, loving the way he teased, poked, and prodded.

"You're so tight."

"Don't ask why," I muttered, thinking how the Madam had deprived me of sex for so long. This tight vagina was saved for

Timothy, yet here Kelly was, taking it for himself. The night couldn't have worked out any better, I thought as I got lost in his pleasure.

"Do you get this wet for all men?" He blew cool air over my softness. "Or only for me?"

I hadn't been this turned on ever. Kelly Black was right about one thing: He was going to be the one to unravel me. And if he kept this up, I'd do anything he asked.

"Only you," I mewed, glancing over my shoulder with hooded lids. "And that's no lie."

He pushed his finger deeper. I lifted my hips, angling my sex up for easy access. And when his tongue sliced me open, I closed my eyes and whimpered.

Kelly thrust his tongue into me for what seemed like forever. Time froze and my body temperature shot through the roof. He worked me to the point of boiling over in a matter of minutes and the moment I felt my core tighten, I cried, "I'm going to come."

He thrust his thick finger inside me with skilled precision, continuing to lap at my sex like a man who knew just what to do to make me lose all sense of self. "Do it. I want to know what it tastes like to bring my sweet *Bella* over the edge."

My hand fisted the sheets as I felt my pussy tighten around him. The room spun and my toes curled as my body shuddered through the first bit of my release.

"That's it." He continued working me. "But I want all of it." His tongue hit my bundle of nerves and that was it.

"Oh shit," I cried as I exploded through a blinding orgasm.

I felt his tongue slurp down all of my feminism and I smiled as the euphoric feeling draped over me. It had been so long since I last climaxed that this one felt like it was my first. "Mmm ... thank you," I murmured.

Kelly continued circling his finger over my pussy lips like he couldn't get enough. With my legs still quivering, I let him continue to play. It was the least I could do as I fought to catch my breath.

"It's perfect," he said. "You're perfect."

"You're not so bad either, Counselor."

He touched the tight muscle of my anus and I flinched. Fear rolled through my mind, thinking there was no way I could take a man his size in my tight little asshole. He was too big. I was too small. It wasn't physically possible and didn't want it to happen. Not today. Maybe never.

He chuckled and climbed over me. Kelly rooted his fists on either side of me, and I let out a sigh of relief when I felt him position his wide cockhead at my entrance. Then he slammed home and ravaged me until I saw stars being born.

27

KELLY

"Can I ask you something?" It was the first words out of her mouth since I shattered her world with several mind-blowing orgasms.

We laid in the king-sized bed sated, our heads surrounded by the many down pillows, our bodies wrapped in satin sheets.

"You can." The tips of my fingers grazed up and down the back of her arm as she cradled her ear over my slow beating heart. "But I can't promise you that I'll answer it."

She clucked her tongue then asked, "Why here?"

"It's my place." I stared up at the ceiling, watching as beams of light from the street below made bright streaks across the walls.

"But you told me before it's your home-away-from-home."

"It is."

"You want to know what I think?"

My brows raised. "What do you think?"

"I think it's your fuck pad."

"I suppose you're right. I mean I just fucked you, didn't I?"

"Kelly," she nuzzled her face into my hard chest, "you're not hearing what I'm saying. Let me rephrase. Do you take all your girlfriends here?" She lifted her head, resting her chin over my pectoral. "Or am I the exception?"

"The exception would be taking you to my main residence." I threaded my fingers through her soft hair.

"Would you make an exception then, for me?"

"Not a chance."

"Why not?" She frowned.

I locked my gaze with hers. Her eyes sparkled against the dark night. Kendra was gorgeous and it didn't hurt that she could keep up with my own unquenchable thirst for sex. But taking her back to my main residence? Forget about it. "You haven't earned it."

"What do I have to do to earn it?" Her face perked up. She was so beautiful. Her cheeks flushed an incredible pink from panting through the ecstasy I inflicted with my fingers, tongue, and cock.

"I can't tell you that." I took my eyes off of her and went back to staring at the ceiling.

"Why not?"

I closed my eyes and sighed. "Because then I won't know if you're sincere or not."

I felt her eyes traveling over my face for a minute before dropping her ear back over my heart. It beat in a slow rhythm, all thanks to her. Kendra was a sense of calm in my hectic world, and I liked the effect she had on me.

"The reason you ran out on me the other night—" I paused, thinking my words through before I spoke. "If I hurt you—"

"You didn't." Kendra didn't lift her head, wouldn't turn to look me in the eye, and if her voice wasn't as calm and unwavering—and as confident—as it sounded, I would have thought that she was lying. "Kelly, like I said, that was my fault. Not yours."

"I know I can get rough," I said, scrubbing a hand over my face.

"You did nothing wrong." Her voice was soft and comforting.

We held each other, choosing to be silent instead of filling the room with more doubt than what I knew we both were already feeling.

"Did the Madam really call you to tell you I was with Mr. Parker?" Kendra's fingers stopped kneading the hair on my chest.

"That's that asshole's name?"

She lifted her head and rested the point of her chin on my ribcage. "You didn't know that?"

"I don't need to know. But, yes, Madam told me where I could find you."

"What's your relationship with her, anyway?" Her brows furrowed.

"Business."

Kendra dropped her gaze and I could see her forehead twist with uncertainty. "Why would she do that?" She lifted her eyes back to my face. "Tell you to come find me?"

I had my suspicions. This wasn't the first time I thought about why the Madam would do such a thing. I was certain that it was her way of letting me know that as long as I lusted after Kendra, she'd have me by the balls. And there was no better way of showing me that than allowing me just one night to have Kendra all to myself.

The worst part of it all, though, was that I knew that Madam was right. I'd do anything to be with Kendra. But there was also another part of the equation that Kendra wouldn't know herself. And that was that if I didn't agree to take on Blake Stone's case, and do as the Madam wished, she'd take Kendra away from me and never give her back.

"I don't know," I whispered.

"It doesn't make any sense."

"*Bella*," I cupped the back of her skull, "it doesn't have to."

"I like that." She smiled. "*Bella.*"

"If fits you perfectly."

"Because you think I'm beautiful?"

"I know you are." I peeled my head off the pillow and pulled her in for a kiss.

She darted her tongue against mine. It was cool, with a hint of exhaustion from when I claimed her body as my own. But I craved it all the same.

"Tell me, *Bella,*" my hand smoothed down her spine, finding her sexy round ass, "have you never let a man fuck you in the ass?"

"You mean butt-fuck me?" Her brow arched.

I laughed. "I noticed you puckered up when I played with it."

"Let's not go there." She diverted her gaze and let her head fall back to rest on my chest. I knew she was hiding something but I wasn't sure what.

"Okay, then tell me this." My hand ironed up her back before squeezing her shoulder. I could feel her breathing. I liked the way it felt against me. "Do you like pain?"

"Are you crazy?" She blurted out. "Who *likes* pain?"

I pushed up on my elbows and turned to rest on one side. My hand smoothed her delicate upper thigh flesh, then I let my hand wind back and come flying down on her ass.

She lurched into me with protruding eyes. "If that's what you mean by pain, then yes. You can spank me like a child."

I tapped her ass gently, loving the ripples that moved across her body as I did it. "Good to know. And what about this?" I asked as I took her taut nipple between my fingers, closing the clamp slowly but never letting up on the building pressure.

"Ahh ... fuck, Kelly!" She slapped my hand.

My fingers released and she winced just as I slammed my lips over her mouth. She scooped my tongue up with hers and swirled it with heated passion. "Did you like me kissing you?"

"Very much," she purred.

I thrust my tongue against hers and said, "When mixed with pleasure it enhances the feeling. Wouldn't you agree?"

"It certainly does," she murmured against my lips. "Kelly," she paused, "that club I met you at, are you into those types of things? Is that why you're asking me these things?"

"Would it change your opinion of me if I were?"

She tucked her hair behind her ear and thought about it. "No. I don't think so. I'm just curious to what it is you're getting at with me."

"Just learning your boundaries is all." I pressed my lips against her forehead. She was a heady combination of sweat and sex, the taste riling me up once again.

We didn't need to be talking about the club. We would get there if it was meant to be. I'd continue to test her, put her through a series of demands, before making my final decision. It was important that I didn't scare her away. Sexing her up like what we'd had tonight would be enough to hold my interest until I needed to dive deeper into my dark underworld.

"I didn't think I had boundaries."

I tossed my leg over hers so I could straddle her. "You do," I said, pinning her arms to the bed.

"You barely know me."

"Trust me. You have boundaries. Everyone does. Some are just willing to travel further into the forest than others." My head fell to her neck where I peppered her skin with open-mouth kisses.

When I released her wrists, she wrapped her arms around me, working her fingers into my back. The need to possess every inch of her body consumed me. Kendra moaned beneath me and I couldn't help myself when I found her pebbled nipple between my teeth.

"Mmm ... Kelly," she moaned.

I kissed my way down to her stomach. It fluttered against my tongue, and when I sucked on her tender clit she whimpered a sweet tune that had me stiff. My hand moved down her silky leg and that was when I found it.

It was a diamond anklet, and one I didn't recognize. Needing to take a closer look, I sat on my heels and brought her foot to my chest as I inspected the jewelry closely. It wasn't the Madam's. Only in special circumstances would she allow for this kind of jewelry to be worn. And if she knew that I was to fight for Kendra tonight, the Madam would only risk so much knowing that an anklet could easily get lost in a scuffle.

"*Bella*," I tsked her. "You broke protocol."

She gave me a questioning look.

"You know you're not supposed to wear your own jewelry out on dates."

Kendra's gaze fell to the sparkles and a glimmer of adoration flashed across her eyes. "You know more about the Madam's business than I do."

"That may be."

"I forgot to take it off."

"It looks expensive. How is a woman your age able to afford such luxury?" I sucked on her toes. "Was it from the time you worked as an attorney? Or do you have another man in your life I should know about?"

She laughed as my whiskers tickled the inside of her ankle. "No. I don't have another man. It was from an inheritance."

I lifted her leg high and kissed the backside of her calf. "You come from money?"

"Hardly." She rolled her eyes. "No, I come from a past I prefer not to discuss."

I continued to kiss her leg before moving on to the other. It didn't matter where her money came from. I didn't ask because I didn't care. All I knew was that I didn't want her to be with anybody but me. She was mine. I'd claimed her tonight, and the taste of what I received sparked enough curiosity to want it to continue into the foreseeable future.

When I dropped her foot back to the bed, she stared at me with a suspicious look on her face. My cock was heavy again and I liked what she did to me. She was amazingly strong, but there were demons hiding behind those big, dark green eyes of hers.

"Then tell me how you came to work for the Madam." I lowered myself between her legs, trailing the tips of my fingers lightly over her stomach. She was so soft, and so small, I was surprised that I didn't break her with the things I did to her in order to get me off.

"That, too, is a long story that I'm afraid I just don't have the energy to tell right now."

My tongue circled over her belly button. "Just give me a hint."

"A friend recommended I do it."

"I see," I said, dipping my finger into her slick cleft. I worked her until I had her panting with her eyes closed. Then I pulled away, knowing she'd be begging me to continue.

"Kelly, please," she begged.

I pushed myself up and moved away.

"Really? You're going to walk away now?"

My feet hit the floor and I moved to the dresser, opening the top drawer.

"If that's how it is, then what's next?"

I turned and held up the piece of paper that held the script to the contract I needed her to agree to. "I'm going to get in the shower and by the time I come out, you're going to have signed the contract."

"Can't I join you?" She looked toward the bathroom.

"Sign the contract." I set it on top of the dresser, placing a pen near it. Then I turned back to her and said, "Then I'll let you fuck me again."

28

KENDRA

"Hey," I said in a hushed tone when Alex opened the door. "All right if I stay here tonight?"

"You know you don't have to ask." She barely looked at me before turning on a heel and rubbing her eyes. "I thought I gave you a key."

I knew by the sound in her voice that I had woken her up. "I must have left it at my place."

I followed Alex inside, tossing my purse onto the chair in the living room. It smelled like it had been freshly cleaned and there were even vacuum trails left on the area rug. "I didn't think you cleaned."

"I don't." She stepped into the kitchen. "Nash hired a cleaner."

I nodded as I continued to glance around, thinking that my own place needed a good scrub. It had been forever since I'd had the time to clean it and I wasn't about to hire anybody to do it for me. But with everything going on, and knowing that I didn't have any plans to invite anybody over, it seemed like a waste of energy. Energy that was better saved for Kelly.

Alex wasn't one to wake up easy, so I watched as she pulled two glasses from the cabinet and fill them with tap water. She was probably wondering why I was more interested in staying at her place than going back to my own, but she didn't ask, so when she handed me the water, I did it for her. "You can ask me, you know."

"Ask you what?" She blinked away the sleep.

It was late, and I knew it was kind of rude of me to wake her, but I didn't want to be alone. "Why I want to sleep here tonight."

"You know you're always welcome." She glanced toward a bouquet of flowers.

I was surprised that I hadn't noticed them sooner. The colors were bright and, naturally, it brought a smile to both our faces. I side-stepped and flicked the note I saw sticking out of the middle of them. After reading it, I said, "Nash misses you."

"You have no idea." Alex unconsciously parted her lips.

"And chocolates, too?"

She nodded, her cheeks glowing.

"Nice." I smiled. "What did you do to deserve all this?" I asked, picking up the box of chocolates, opening the top and stealing one for myself. "Wait. Don't answer that. Let me guess." I chewed the caramel chocolate, marveling at the way it brought my taste buds to life. "You wore that slut costume during a video chat, didn't you?"

A guilty grin spread to her ears.

"You dirty whore." I laughed, diving in for seconds.

"And he also sent me this." She pulled a white sapphire pendant heart necklace out from beneath her shirt.

"Wow." It was beautiful. I could only imagine how much it cost him. But I knew Nash thought she was worth it, so it didn't really matter what the price tag was.

Alex was glowing and I was happy for her, but also a little envious. The only gifts I was currently receiving were items the Madam provided—items she expected to get back after the date was through. If I wanted anything like flowers and chocolates I would have to purchase them myself.

"You look nice." Her eyes did a once-over of me. Then her

nose twitched, sniffing the air. She leaned forward as if she'd caught a scent.

"Whoever smelt it dealt it," I joked, leaning away from her.

"You smell like a man." Her eyes brightened like she'd caught me in a secret I was hiding from her. Except I wasn't hiding anything. If she wanted to know, all she had to do was ask. Chances of me being with a man tonight were pretty darn good. She just didn't know *which* man I'd been with.

"Don't you have something better to do with your life than be digging into mine?" I teased.

"Date tonight?" Her brow rose and formed a perfect arch.

I nodded, cleaning my teeth with my tongue, and rested my tailbone against the edge of the counter stool. Alex leaned against the counter with her arms folded as I told her about my date with Timothy, the meal we shared, and finished by saying, "The Madam specifically instructed me to fuck him."

Her eyes popped out of her head. "Did you?"

"Not exactly."

"How do you *not exactly* fuck someone?"

"That's just it." My lips tugged at the corners. "I *did* fuck someone. Just not him."

"Then who?" She was starting to wake up.

"The lawyer," I said, stealing a sip of my water.

"That Black guy?"

I tilted my head to the side, giving her a pinched expression. "You know how that sounds, right?"

"You know what I mean." She waved me off, rubbing her forehead.

"Yes. Mr. Black," I said, telling her how he showed up out of nowhere and stole me away from Timothy Parker.

"Kendra!"

"I know." My voice was muffled as I talked into my water glass. "The Madam is going to have my head. But it's not my fault."

"Except it kind of is."

I rolled my eyes. "If you saw what happened you wouldn't be saying that."

Alex glanced at the clock. "I've had a long day and need to get up early. Promise to catch me up tomorrow when it's not so late?"

I nodded, finishing my water. "Can I sleep in your bed tonight?"

"Yeah, of course." There was a flash of concern in her eyes but when I stood, Alex bent her elbow and I met her at the counter's end, hooking my arm in the crook of hers.

"After what you said about your bed, I haven't been able to stop thinking about what it would be like." I laughed.

"You'll never find a better night's sleep." She turned her head and smiled. "I can promise you that."

We practically skipped down the hall and it felt good to be with my friend again. And it didn't hurt that Kelly had blessed me with the release my body had been craving since the day Madam deprived me of sex altogether. I was so tight, it was any wonder I managed to keep my cool as well as I had.

We were both in high spirits and our futures were looking bright. Alex had her man and I was working on getting one of my own. I was feeling more like my usual self, and that was a good thing. Good for everybody.

Alex dove under the covers and, after stripping out of my clothes, I joined her. My arms draped over hers and our legs tangled down to our feet as I spooned her. "It must have been good sex," she said. "He's even on your breath."

With Nash out of town, it was back to how things were before she found him and I kind of liked it. Tonight was a simple reminder that if our worlds did turn upside-down, there was nothing to worry about because at least we still had each other. Just the two of us, laughing and talking about the boys we were dating. It was the perfect end to an incredible night and it couldn't have been more perfect.

"I didn't know it was possible to have so many orgasms in one night," I said, making us both laugh hysterically.

It was refreshing knowing I could tell her about my sexcapades without being judged or shamed. That was another thing I loved about her. The only difference now was that instead of being disappointed by the men I fucked, I was actually exhausted from my night with Kelly. That, too, was another reason to work myself into his life.

But then I started having regrets, thinking that maybe I shouldn't have left him the way I did. Maybe I should have stayed, joining him in the shower against his will.

Alex rolled her head toward me and asked, "Then why are you here with me and not him?"

It was like she read my exact thoughts. Maybe she could feel what it was I was thinking, or perhaps she knew me better than I knew myself. "The thought of spending a night alone with him is both thrilling and terrifying."

Alex turned her head, resting her ear back over her pillow. "You really like him, don't you?"

My mind ran wild with possibilities. "I do."

"Wait!" Alex flipped over so she was facing me, her body perched on a bent elbow. "Was he the one you were with the night I picked you up?"

My eyes closed. I couldn't look at her. I knew what she was thinking, what she would assume. "It's not like that," I whispered.

"Then what's it like? Because I'd like to know."

I hid my face in my hands.

"See, you can't even face the truth."

I flung my hands to my sides and looked at her straight on. "Please trust the decisions I make."

"I'm worried about you."

"Don't be."

"How can I not? When are you going to tell me more about what happened to you? You promised me you would tell me."

"And I will." I reached for her hand and she let me take it. My thumb stroked over her knuckles as I fought to find the strength to tell her about the time I was raped. "Just not now."

Her eyes searched for answers. "Kendra, have you sought help for this?"

"Help?" I barked out a laugh but it wasn't sincere.

"Professional help. If you can't talk to me—your *best* friend who you tell everything to—then maybe you can open up to someone who's not so close to you."

I let out a heavy sigh. Maybe she was right. Maybe I did need help. Never had I opened up about what happened. Instead, I tried to push it out of my life and act like it never happened. That strategy had worked for a while. But the truth was, I was broken, in denial, and perhaps even confused about the person I really was and the person I wanted to be.

"Will you at least think about it?"

Tears swelled behind my eyes and threatened to spill. With a quivering chin, I nodded. "I came here tonight because he still wants me to sign that stupid contract."

"You haven't signed it?"

I shook my head.

"What is it? Like, a pre-nuptial for dating?" The left side of Alex's face scrunched.

Inside my mind I was there, inside the room of the club where Kelly first presented me with the non-disclosure agreement. A part of me wanted to go down that road with him. But another part of me was frozen stiff scared, too afraid that once I did sign it, it would set off another emotional trigger leaving me paralyzed and distraught once again. "More like a non-disclosure."

Her brows furrowed. "Geeze, I thought we were past all this."

"As if." In a perfect world, there was no reason I shouldn't sign it. At least, I couldn't come up with a reason to keep avoiding having to do it, except to keep my voice. It was the only thing I had when it came to him, and I wasn't sure I could trust him enough to not lead me astray.

"Maybe I don't understand," Alex said, still confused as to what the big deal was. "If he wasn't the cause of your breakdown, then why are you avoiding it?"

"I'm afraid."

"Kendra," she angled her head, "if he was the reason you were so shattered, then leave him now and don't look back."

"He wasn't. I promise." But it was a half-truth. He'd set it off, but he didn't mean to. I perched my body weight on my elbow, a mirror image of Alex. "And get this."

Alex leaned forward, blinking.

"He asked if I like pain."

Alex's eyes rounded into big white balls.

Then I spanked her and twisted her nipple.

"Fuck, Kendra. What was that for?!"

"That's what he did to me." A big smile filled my face.

Her head slowly bobbed on her shoulders. "He's totally a member of Mint."

"My thoughts exactly," I said, collapsing onto my back.

"So if that's why he wants you to sign the contract, to take you to a club like that, will you do it?"

"I don't know," I murmured. "I guess I need to know more about who he is and what he wants to do to me."

"And then?"

"Then I'll know if I should dive in. Or forget about him forever."

29

KELLY

M y hand balled into a tight fist as I thought about the mistake Kendra was making in refusing to sign the agreement.

Despite my gritted teeth, I had to forget about her. At least for now. My mind needed to be cleared and focused for my meeting with Mario Jimenez. There was too much on the line to fuck this meeting up, and I had some questions for him that needed answers.

Maxwell pulled my SUV into the county jail parking lot, stopping in the front to let Giselle and me out. "Don't go too far," I said to him as my feet hit the ground.

"Understood, Mr. Black."

I closed the door and met Giselle on the other side. "Ready to learn the truth?"

"If we walk away with fewer questions than we came here with, I'll consider it a win." She smiled as we made our way to the front entrance.

We had prepared for this meeting, and now that it was here I was excited to hear his voice, listen to his story, and learn what he had to say. I promised myself that I wouldn't blame him for

Maria's death until I heard it all—seeking to find the truth myself. It wouldn't be easy, because those images of her mangled and bruised body were the type that sparked nightmares.

"If I lose my cool ..." I pulled the door open and Giselle passed in front of me.

"I won't let that happen, Kelly."

I nodded, loving how Giselle had the guts to ground me when my temper flared. It was one of the reasons that made us such a great team. She was smart, but she also had the strength to not let things get to her either. It was that calm collection that allowed us to find our own meaning of the truth in each case we worked.

The clerk at the front desk greeted us and we both signed our names in before unloading our pockets and sending our briefcases through the x-ray machine.

"Morning." I nodded to the officer as I stepped through the metal detector.

"Who are you here to see?" I heard a familiar voice say from behind.

I turned to find Oscar Buchanan passing and I said, "A potential client."

"Always secrets with you." He snickered.

"It's not that hard to figure out if you know where to look." I winked, retrieving my possessions off the x-ray's conveyer belt.

He chuckled and reached out to shake my hand. I took him with a strong grip as he leaned his face close to my ear. "Any new details on the dead girl?"

"Nothing worth sharing with the DA's office." My grip tightened on his hand.

He pulled away when I released. "I heard Blake Stone's lawyer has been dismissed by the judge. Can't say I was surprised to hear that."

Giselle glanced at her watch and gave me an anxious look.

"I'm going to be late."

"Are you going to take his case?" He tipped his head back and raised his brows. "It would be an opportunity for you. Don't you think?"

"Is that what you want?"

"You know I can't resist a good courtroom brawl." He laughed. "And besides, I need a reason to get back at you for stealing Kendra away. It would also give me reason to humiliate you in court."

"I didn't steal her."

He arched his brow.

"She left you for a better man. Let that one sink in." I hit his shoulder and paused to watch him swallow down the truth-bomb I just detonated on him. "Now, if you'll excuse me, I'm already late for my meeting."

"I'll see you around, Kelly Black," Oscar said as I hurried down the hall.

Giselle's heels clacked down the hall at a gallop. "What was that about?"

"Male posturing." I grinned as I opened the door to the private room where Mario was already waiting.

Mario lifted his head when we stepped in and I couldn't help but notice how he eyed me with suspicion.

"I'm Kelly Black, the criminal defense attorney you called." I rounded to the opposite side of the table before reaching across and offering my hand.

He looked at my splayed fingers before lifting his hand to shake with mine. "Thanks for coming."

"Let's dive right in then," I said, opening my briefcase and pulling out the files of notes Giselle and I had collected pertaining to his case. "There was a woman who put you in contact with me," I lifted my gaze and looked at him from beneath my brow, "can you tell me her name?

His brows drew together. He glanced at Giselle, then back to me, shaking his head. "No. It wasn't a woman."

I turned to look at Giselle. "Can you tell us who did, then?" Giselle asked.

"A big man came. I didn't catch his name." Mario's voice was soft but tainted with the subtle underlying fear of a man whose future was uncertain. "He told me that the only chance I had at being set free was to call you. And I believed him."

"Has the court appointed you a lawyer?" I asked.

He nodded, staring down at the metal table out in front of him.

"And you refused to accept their counsel?"

"I haven't refused anybody's counsel." His eyes shot up, darting between mine and Giselle's. "Look, I need to get out of here. I don't care who will do that, but I was told that if you worked with me, my chances were good."

I took a deep breath. "Mario—do you mind if I call you Mario?"

"It's fine."

"Do you understand the charges being brought against you?"

He rubbed his face and turned his head. "Whatever you've heard, I'm innocent. I didn't hurt that girl."

"What girl are you referring to, Mario?" Giselle placed both her elbows on top of the table and leaned forward.

"The one they said I murdered."

"Do you know her name?"

"Maria something ..." His hand waved through the air.

"You mean this one?" I pulled one photo of Maria out from under the pile and slid it over to him.

He couldn't keep his eyes off of the image. Though he gave no hint of either remorse or guilt, there were still more answers we needed before deciding to take him on as a client or not.

"Let's go over the timeline of that day." Giselle pulled her eye-glasses down, straightened her spine, and began reading over the dozens of papers she had laid out in front of her. One-by-one she plucked, pulled, and slid them over to Mario.

I stared, listened, and watched as Giselle filled in the gaps to where Mario actually was that day and what it was he was doing. And as they conversed, my thoughts naturally drifted to Kendra.

She made my blood boil, but I wasn't about to let her go either. If anything, her constant rejection to my non-disclosure only made me want her even more. I was going to have to find a way to rein her in, because if I didn't—

"Like I've told the detectives, for the hundredth time, I was in Mexico when this all happened."

I snapped out of my thoughts when I heard Mario mention Mexico. Mario's story didn't stray from his initial interview with the detectives. And that had me thinking there was a possibility that he *was* telling the truth. But there was still a reason Madam put us in touch and I needed to get to the bottom of that before anything else. "Mexico, you said?"

"I have to repeat myself again?" Mario sneered.

"We just need to understand the facts." Giselle put a damper on the frustration beginning to build between us.

"Were you there on business?" I asked with pen to paper.

Mario cocked his head to the side. "Why would you assume that?"

"Is there a reason I should?"

"Look at me, dude. I'm Mexican. It's where I'm from."

"Mr. Jimenez, are you employed?" Giselle asked.

"I'm in business for myself." He fell back into his seat and folded his arms over his chest.

"What kind of business are you involved in?"

"What does this have to do with you helping me get off? If you're worried about not getting paid, I'll put up the money right now. Is that what you want?"

"Do you recognize this man?" I pulled another photo from my stack and pushed it to his side of the table.

Mario leaned closer and studied the face for a minute before saying, "Looks like every other asshole in this town."

"Except you both have connections to the Santa Marta drug cartel," I said, needing to see how he would react to my accusatory statement.

"Look." He dropped his elbows on the table, letting a hollow thud ricochet off the bare walls. "What is this?" His shoulders rose and fell. "Your words are making me believe you don't want to represent me."

"I'm still deciding."

"Without you, I'll sit in here forever." He leaned back and huffed. "How can I help you make a decision?"

"Give me something to make me believe you're innocent." My gaze cast to the photo of Blake Stone I'd passed his way.

Mario began to talk. He told Giselle and me about how film producer Nash Brooks was after some missing money that was thought to be hidden inside some Hollywood studio, and how instead a young woman named Alex Grace found all $250K of it, neatly stashed inside a duffel bag.

My pen scribbled as fast as I could keep up, taking detailed notes on it all.

Everything he was saying was news to us and we kept asking questions. "How do you know all this? Were you directly involved?"

He shook his head but there was something about it that made me think he was hiding a detail to his story. "Word travels fast on the street. And then, the next thing I know, I'm being arrested for a crime I didn't commit."

Giselle and I shared a glance, realizing that this went deeper than either of us originally imagined. But that still didn't explain why the Madam had sent me here. *What was it she wanted me to hear?*

"Somewhere along the line I was framed," Mario mumbled under his breath.

It wasn't worth entertaining that idea. Maybe he was framed, but likely not. And, for his sake, I hoped that he was wrong. But the more I heard, the less any of it made any kind of sense.

"The evidence points to you," I said, tapping the image of Maria's lifeless body.

He had a pained expression when he looked at her image. "I don't know who she is." He lifted his head to look me in the eye. "I don't do *that* to women. You must believe me."

There was a glimmer of sincerity in his eyes that made me believe he was telling me the truth about her. "It doesn't matter what I believe. If what you're saying is true, you'll have to convince a jury that you're innocent."

"With your help." His eyes rounded. "Right? With your help." His voice grew panicked.

When I looked at Giselle she cast her gaze to her notes.

Then Mario pulled the photo of Blake Stone between his fingers and held it in front of his face. "If I tell you more about him, will you represent me?"

30

KENDRA

Alex was already gone to work by the time I woke up.

Without her there to fill the other half of the bed, I flipped and flopped, nuzzling my head deeper into the down pillow. It was big, fluffy, and softer than anything I'd ever owned myself and I couldn't get enough of it. I was completely in love and we'd only had one night together.

Checking the tag for a make and model, I swore to myself that I needed to purchase a pillow like this, and soon. Especially if Madam was going to keep putting a wall up between me and the men who were supposed to be fucking me. At least then I'd have an easier time falling asleep as my angst for orgasm stirred, attempting to rob me of a peaceful night's sleep.

My arms stretched above my head as I yawned.

With a day without a schedule, I wondered how I should pass my time and if it was worth staying here or going home. But as I spread my limbs out—reaching as far as I could in an attempt to touch the sides—I couldn't do it. Couldn't find the edge where the bed ended and didn't want to leave the warmth and safety it provided.

And these sheets, too. The way the satin felt against my bare legs sparked feelings of vacation. A trip away. Something to take my mind off of Kelly and what he was doing to me. I could see why Alex bragged about sleeping in this gigantic bed. It was heaven. And it was any wonder how she managed to get up every morning and leave it just so she could go to work and bust her ass. Her bed was too good to leave, but without her there to help me fill it, I started to feel lonely and depressed.

My eyes popped open and I let out a sigh.

Now I understood how she could get up each morning. Without Nash there to fill the void, what was the point? Comfort could only go so far before loneliness crept in to steal it away.

Tossing the covers off of me, I hit the floor running. I splashed some water on my face and threw on my clothes. Heading into the kitchen, I stopped at the colorful bouquet of flowers, taking the time to put my nose up to them.

Slowly, my eyes closed as my lips curled upward.

There was no better way to start a day alone than like this. When my eyes opened, I stole a chocolate for the road and headed to the door. Just before closing it, I turned to glance inside, thinking this luxurious apartment wasn't as nice without someone to share it with. No wonder Alex didn't mind me basically living here while Nash was out of town.

Heading to the elevator, I scheduled for a ride to pick me up. And by the time I made it to the location of my requested pick-up, he was already waiting. "You again," I said, sliding into the back seat.

"My friend." He gave me a warm smile in the rearview mirror.

I nodded, buckling myself in, thinking that he was becoming like a friend. It was the same Uber driver as I'd been getting these last couple of requests, and the familiarity was a good feeling.

"Hey. Can I ask you a question?" I asked as he set the car in motion.

He glanced in his mirror again, taking his eyes off the road for only a moment. "For my favorite customer, anything."

"You remember that place you took me the other day?"

His browse squished as he took a moment to think back to that day. "I remember."

I held his gaze and said, "Do you make drops to that club often?"

He flipped his blinker on and turned the wheel as we made a sharp turn onto a slightly busier street. Alex's place wasn't that far from mine, so I knew that I didn't have much time to get as much information as possible from my driver before our time was up.

"People request to be dropped everywhere in this city," he said, looking straight ahead.

"I understand, but I'm asking about that specific location." He didn't seem to want to discuss anything related to the club so I dug in my purse and slipped him a couple of twenties. "It's okay. This conversation will remain between us. No one else will know."

I was the first to break eye contact even though he was the one behind the wheel. But from the way he was looking at me, I knew he was wondering if I could be trusted with what he knew.

"What are the people you take there like?"

His eyes fell from the mirror and moved back to the road. He readjusted his grip on the steering wheel and said, "It's only women."

"So you weren't surprised to see me when you knew where I wanted to go?"

"No."

He made a look like he wanted to tell me something else. "What is it?"

"And I never take the same route when heading there."

My brows furrowed, wondering why that was. "Do you ever pick customers up from there?"

He shook his head. "I don't know how they get home, but I assume they find men to do it."

"I see," I said as he slowed to a stop a couple blocks from my apartment.

When I opened the door he twisted around and said, "I'm not sure what goes on there but I'm paid good money to take customers there."

"Who pays you?"

He shrugged. "I don't know how they do it. It's computers that make the scheduling ... way over my head."

"Thanks." He nodded and I shut the door, watching him turn the wheel and roll back into motion.

I knew there was something weird going on with the route he took the other day. But I still didn't understand it. Why him? And who was paying him to take women there? And why was it such a big secret?

Hurrying back to my building, I was lost inside my own thoughts. Once inside the lobby, I was greeted by my doorman, Mr. Anderson. "Ms. Williams," he smiled, "a gift was left for you."

I bit the inside of my cheek as I wondered who knew enough about me to be leaving a gift here.

Mr. Anderson dug behind his counter and pulled out a solid white box, perfectly tied up in a glowing red bow. *The Madam*, I thought.

"Any idea who it's from?" I asked.

"I'm sorry." He raised his bushy eyebrows. "The packaging is lovely, though."

"It certainly is," I said taking it into my hands. "Thank you."

"You have a wonderful day, Ms. Williams."

"You too, Mr. Anderson."

The Madam was always up to something new, I thought as I rode the elevator to my floor. This had her name written all over it. The packaging. The surprise. And she was the only one, besides Alex, who knew exactly where I lived.

Digging through my purse I pulled my keys and unlocked the door to my apartment. It felt good to be home, and with a day with nothing planned, there was nothing more I wanted than to draw myself a bath and let my body soak. But first I needed to calm my burning desire to open the gift and see just exactly what lay inside.

Pinching the bow between my fingers I tugged it open, pulling the top off next.

A flash of adrenaline tingled across my body the moment I saw the note laying on top. My hand flew over my mouth as I gasped in surprise. This wasn't from Madam, no, the gift had been given to me by Kelly.

I fell into my wooden chair, feeling my thrashing heart beat fast and wild in my neck. The temperature in the room exploded as the thought of Kelly knowing where I lived was both terrifying and exciting. I could only guess as to how he found out, but I was sure it had something to do with his connection to the Madam.

There was a reason I preferred to keep my life a secret. A million different reasons, actually. And I was fully aware of my paranoia. It was what kept me cautious and alive. My natural distrust for others was real, but I also wasn't going to deny that it felt at least a little bit good to know Kelly was thinking of me, especially considering I kept running out on him.

I leaned back in my chair, reading Kelly's note.

Bella, you can run but you can't hide. Consider this a peace offering. Wear it tonight. I'm taking you out. Yours truly ~ K. Black

A warm feeling spread up my chest as a smile filled my face.

I knew I'd promised Alex I'd tell her everything about my night with Kelly, but she was out the door much earlier than I expected and now I wasn't sure that it would even be relevant after tonight.

After setting the note down on top of the table, I reached into the box with both hands and pulled out a gorgeous deep purple chiffon sleeveless mermaid dress with heels to match.

I couldn't stop running my fingers over the material, thinking that his actions weren't like the ones I would expect from a man who had issues with commitment. Angel didn't know what she was talking about. Kelly fought for me, kept fighting for me, and it spoke volumes to the character of the man he was.

A heavy sigh left my chest as my eyebrows gathered in.

It was selfish of me to always be leaving him without saying goodbye, and I didn't know why I kept doing it, other than I was afraid of getting attached too quickly. I guess I always figured that if I left him first each time we fucked, then I couldn't get hurt. But that didn't mean that I wasn't hurting him. And for that, I felt like a bitch.

"If this is what you want—" I mumbled to myself, digging out the contract Kelly wanted me to sign, "—then I'll do it. If only to calm your worried mind."

I clicked the pen and dropped the ball to paper. Just as I was about to scribble my signature, there was a knock on my door.

My head turned over my shoulder and I debated whether or not to just ignore it, but the knocking never stopped. I dropped the pen and headed to peek through the door to find Jerome standing tall with his hands at his sides. "What did I do this time?" I said, opening the door.

"The Madam would like to see you." His voice was gruff and straight to the point.

"Now?"

"Now."

"I just got home and was going to take a shower—"

Jerome reached out and clamped his big sausage fingers around my skinny arms, tugging me into the hallway. "That can wait."

"But my purse. I need my purse!" I tripped and stumbled down the hallway as I heard my front door slam shut.

Jerome didn't let up and by the time we were inside the elevator, I gave up trying to fight him into letting me stay and get ready before I showed my face to the Madam.

Madam was waiting in the back of the limo, hiding behind a

wide brimmed sun hat, tear drop diamond earrings framing her angled face. "Kendra, doll. You were home." She clapped her hands.

Jerome slammed the door, sending my insides jumping, and immediately after that the wheels began to roll.

The Madam and I stared at each other for a minute without saying a word. I didn't want to be the first to talk. She needed to tell me what was on her mind and why the sudden, early morning meeting that just couldn't wait. "Kendra baby, tell me. Did you fuck him like I instructed?"

I shifted uncomfortably in my seat, wondering how much of my night she already knew about. "I did," I said, not bothering to specify who exactly I'd fucked.

Her eyes narrowed as she set her jaw. "Huh." She wet her lips. "Mr. Parker didn't mention that part of his night to me." She tapped her chin with her long, painted nail.

I could feel my lower back beginning to sweat and I hated feeling like I was being interrogated. But if she already knew about Kelly and me, which I suspected she did if Kelly was telling me the truth, then why not just come out and say it?

"Don't know what to tell you."

"You can start by telling me the name of the person you fucked."

My tongue clucked when I turned my gaze out the window. The fucking Madam. It was always games with her and because of that, it always made for tough conversations—conversations that didn't need to be dragged on if she would just get to the fucking point. I rolled my gaze back to her. "Do you know?"

"Of course I know."

"Then why does it matter if I say his name or not?"

"Because it changes the conversation when you hear it coming out of your own mouth."

"Look, I know how it looks, but believe me when I say that it's not my fault. I can't help being wanted by multiple men at the same time." My hands swiped through the air as I unleashed all my pent-up frustration. "You must know what it's like. Men are dumb. They do stupid shit when it comes to fighting for what they want. If you want to be angry, be angry with Kelly Black. He's the one who keeps doing this."

Madam's eyes were wide as she listened without speaking. "So you did fuck him?"

"Who are we talking about now?" I gave her a questioning look as confusion clouded my brain. That was the appearance I was hoping to give her, anyway, because the truth was, I was too afraid to admit what I already knew—that she called Kelly to tell him where I was.

"Kelly?"

"Yes." I slumped back into my seat, a feeling of defeat weighing me down. "Well, it was more like he fucked me. But, yes. We *fucked.* But that was the plan all along, wasn't it?"

There was a knowing glimmer in her eye that told me she finally understood that I'd connected the dots. Then again, maybe this was exactly what she wanted to happen. It was too early for me to care. Madam dug in her giant purse, then pulled out an envelope, handing it to me.

"What's this?" I asked, taking it between my fingers.

"A delivery."

"And what do you want me to do with this?"

"Deliver it."

"What if I don't want to?"

"Then Kelly Black goes away."

My gaze dropped to the envelope. It was thicker than the one before and by the weight of it, I knew it wasn't a date card like my last delivery where she initially set me up with Kelly. "What's this, money?" I joked, thinking back to when Alex found all that loot. It had the same weight to it, just not nearly as much as what Alex had found.

"I don't understand your attraction to him." She opened up her compact mirror to reapply her cherry red lipstick.

This time, I just stared, knowing that no matter what I said, she wouldn't understand.

"You need to be careful with Kelly." She snapped her mirror shut and tossed it back into her purse. "Like I keep saying—to deaf ears," she glanced at me out of the corner of her eye, "he's not the man you think he is."

"And what kind of man do *you* think he is?"

"You really want to know?"

"I do."

Madam dug inside her purse and pulled out a photograph of a man's face perfectly framed in a mug shot image. "A defense attorney who represents rapists."

Suddenly I felt ill. My hands fell over my belly as it twisted over itself. "What are you saying?"

"I'm saying Kelly sets rapists free." She gave me a curt nod. "In fact, he's meeting with this rapist-slash-murderer right now." Madam handed over the photograph of the accused but I refused to look. As far as I was concerned, representing a rapist was the same as the one doing the raping and I wasn't going to stand for it.

31

KELLY

"Why didn't you want him to tell you what he knows about Stone?" Giselle asked as we approached my waiting SUV.

Maxwell was waiting with the back door held open just outside the county jail, and I liked that we didn't waste any time when moving on to our next visit. The day was quickly slipping by and there was still so much that needed to be done before tonight.

"We need to fact check his story." I allowed Giselle to slide inside to the back seat first. "Then, if everything comes back just as he said, we know that whatever he shares about Blake Stone is true."

Maxwell shut the door behind us and walked around the front, taking the captain's seat behind the wheel. "Mr. Black, where to next?"

I barked off instructions to a production studio in Hollywood, and Maxwell knew it well enough to not have to resort to using GPS. He dropped the gear and set the car in motion.

"What do you think Mario knows about Stone?" Giselle pondered as she caught up on her emails.

"I don't know, but I'm suspecting it has something to do with the cartel."

"Do you think he's guilty?" Giselle lifted her gaze from her phone and moved her eyes over to me.

My fingers drummed with anxiety on top of my thigh. "I don't."

"You saw it too, then?" She tucked a loose bang behind her ear.

"I did." I nodded as the sincerity we both saw in Mario's eyes flashed behind my lids. A guilty man would have to be a magician to give off the kinds of looks he was showing us today. "And I believe what he said, too."

"We need to bring him on. If he didn't do that to Maria, it's up to us to get him off." Giselle's voice was confident as she prepared for the long battle ahead. "You know the DA will pursue the stiffest sentence possible."

I swallowed what little doubt I had and said, "Let's first see what Nash Brooks knows. Mario thinks he'll give us some answers, and if that's the case, then we'll see what he knows about Stone before agreeing to represent him."

"Sounds solid." Giselle agreed to the plan.

I pulled my phone out from my inside breast pocket and scrolled to a number I had stashed away from the day before. "Here. Put a quick call into Nash's assistant and let her know that we're on our way."

Giselle quickly dialed the number I gave her and I turned my head to the outside, thinking of Kendra.

She should have received my gift by now, and I hoped that she was free for dinner tonight. With her constant refusal to sign my contract, maybe it was time to change tactics. And I hoped that I could convince her that I needed this done in order for our relationship to move to the next step.

My cock twitched to life as I thought about how her tight

pussy felt wrapped around me, how she clung to me when her body shuddered through a climax.

Whether or not she was aware, God knew it was only a matter of time before I made her my submissive and did things to her that no man had done before. I'd light her body on fire and she'd beg me to put out the flames.

But none of that could happen until that damned contract was signed.

"Fantastic. Thanks for your help." Giselle ended her call and turned to me saying, "Nash is out of town. On location. However, his assistant director is at the studio, and get this—"

My brows raised with perked ears.

"His assistant director is none other than," she paused to purposely add to the suspense, "Alex Grace."

"The plot thickens." I pulled my sunglasses over my eyes. "Then let's see what she has to say about all this."

The moment we arrived to the studio, both Giselle and I invited ourselves into the building, following the signs that led us to a very dark room made for video editing. It was there we found Alex sitting behind a couple of bright computer monitors with headphones covering her ears. I nodded to Giselle and she gently tapped Alex's shoulder. "Alex Grace?"

Alex pulled her headphones off her ears. "Yeah, that's me."

"My name is Giselle and we'd like to ask you a couple questions about Nash Brooks. Can you give us a few minutes of your time?"

Her eyes darted between us. "What's this about?"

"It's about the quarter million dollars you found," I said, causing Alex's face to go pale.

Her brows pulled together. "I'm sorry, but do I know you?"

"I don't believe you do."

"Are you detectives?" She stood with a wrinkled brow and moved to the wall behind us, flipping on the overhead lights.

"Ms. Grace, you're not in any kind of trouble. A potential

client of ours mentioned that maybe Nash Brooks knew about the missing money and we were hoping he could shed some light on that."

Alex crossed her arms over her chest, leaned her back against the wall, and bent her knee. "Nash isn't here."

"We're aware. But we'd like to hear your version of events, if you don't mind."

"Sure." She told us the same story Mario had shared, filling in the holes where he couldn't, and as soon as she was done, she said, "All I know is that it seemed like someone was trying to frame Nash."

Giselle licked her lips. "Why would you say that?"

"Nash is a lot of things, but he's no killer." Alex's eyes widened. "Is that who you're representing? The man who killed that intern? Because if he did what the papers say, then he needs to rot."

"Ms. Grace, you said that you believe Nash was being framed." It was important I changed the subject before emotion took her rational thoughts away.

She nodded. "That's what it seemed."

"Who would want to frame him?"

She lifted herself up on her toes and glanced over my shoulder to see if anyone else was in the room. "Professor Ted Fields," she whispered. "But I thought this was over." Her head dropped into her hand as she rubbed her forehead.

"It's never over until the guilty is convicted," Giselle said. "I'm confused about one thing though."

Alex lifted her head.

"Whatever happened to the money you found?"

"I paid off my debts. It's stupid, I know."

"And the owners were okay with that?"

"Nash took care of it. I didn't ask too many questions at the time. Like everyone else involved, I just wanted to get it over with and move on with my life."

My eyes narrowed. "Where, again, did you say you found it?"

"Outside Mojito. The new joint on Rodeo drive. I'm sure you know the place."

I turned to Giselle. "Wesley Reid's new establishment."

"Is that it?" Alex dropped her arms to her side and bounced on her toes. "I really have lots of work that needs to get done by the end of today."

"One more question." I stepped one foot forward.

She arched a brow and cocked a hip.

"Do you think Nash murdered that girl?"

The door opened behind us and two of her colleagues walked in carrying soft drinks.

"Look," she said, leaning close and lowering her voice, "let's just say that I wouldn't be dating him if I did. If you need someone to talk to, ask that nosy reporter Sylvia Neil. She seems to have an interest in this particular case—more so than anybody else. Now, if you'll excuse me, I really have to be getting back to work."

32

KENDRA

T he Madam left me on the curb with more questions than when the day had started. And as soon as her stupid glossy limo was far enough away, I threw up my middle finger and told her to fuck off.

I didn't know if she was telling me the truth or if it was just her way to make me doubt Kelly. Regardless of her intention, it had worked. I was completely rattled. As I stood there, a sense of loss crept up my body causing my mind to frazzle.

Tonight was supposed to be free from drama. It was supposed to be the day I signed Kelly's contract. The day we officially took our relationship to the next level. And he was supposed to reward me with the onslaught of toe-curling orgasms that made me scream his name until the lights went out. But now, instead, I didn't know what I was going to say to him.

When a car horn honked in front of me, I blinked, turned on a heel, and stormed into my building.

Passing the front lobby, I hoofed my way to the elevator, ignoring Mr. Anderson's greetings completely. It wasn't that I wanted to be rude, it was just that I knew that whoever talked to me next was going to get more attitude than they probably deserved.

I swatted at the air, totally annoyed that there wasn't an empty car waiting.

My mind raced as I paced back and forth, waiting.

How could he represent a rapist?

We didn't know each other that well, and it wasn't like he hid the fact that he was a criminal defense lawyer. But defend a *rapist*? And to learn this only days after I had to leave him because he set off a trigger of my own past trauma?

A pinched expression puckered my face.

The thought of Kelly fighting to set this man free was sickening. I violently rolled my shoulders, suddenly feeling disgusted in the very clothes I was wearing. I knew what it was like to be a victim of rape. Every day I feared that I'd cross paths with my assailant. It wasn't just some made up thing to draw attention to myself. No, the feeling of paralysis was real—*crippling*.

A fucking rapist. *How could he?*

When the doors finally opened, I leaped inside, hurrying to hit the button to make the doors close. There was nothing I wanted more than to be alone with my thoughts and inside the safety of my own home.

My gaze sprang up off the floor just as my stomach dropped.

Shit.

He knew where I lived.

Kelly was here.

This morning. Or late last night.

He was here inside my building. *Fuck.*

Suddenly the walls began to close in around me and a feeling of claustrophobia nearly did me in before the ride slowed to a stop. I gasped for air as soon as the door opened, striding down the hall, fumbling for my keys.

Except I didn't have them.

Nothing was in my hands but this stupid package Madam insisted I deliver as part of my new job description.

Shit. Shit. Shit.

Jerome was so determined to get me in front of the Madam that we'd left without my personal items. No phone. No keys. No nothing. And, worst of all, I found my door had been left unlocked this entire time.

"You fucking bitch," I cursed the Madam. "You did this on purpose."

Stuffing the delivery package under my arm, I hesitated a second when opening the door. As it fell open, I peeked my head inside. Holding my breath, I listened. It was mostly quiet except for the pounding of my own heart.

Thump. Thump. Thump. Thump.

It felt like it was about to explode inside my chest.

My head hurt and my palms were gross with sweat.

Finally, I took the courage to step fully inside, feeling stupid for not feeling comfortable inside my own home. No one was here. Everything was exactly where I'd left it and when my gaze landed on the gift from Kelly, the tension between my shoulders released and I blew out a heavy sigh.

"You fucking asshole." I laughed as I touched the dress Kelly gave me to wear.

The Kelly I knew was a good man with a heart determined to win me over. He made me feel good and he wasn't anything like the picture the Madam painted of him. She had it all wrong.

I plopped down in the seat at the table, running my hand through my hair.

I was sure Kelly had his flaws, and whatever those were, who was I to judge? I was a shattered woman with a dark past and a history that, if discovered, wouldn't be so easily ignored.

When I took my cell between my fingers I noticed the time. I had to get going before the afternoon slid into evening. With no time to waste, I gathered my things, tossed my cell into a deep tote along with the package, and headed back out the door.

I had a driver requested by the time I reached the elevator. This time I smiled at Mr. Anderson who simply nodded as I hurried out the lobby doors, making my way to my pick-up spot, hopeful that it would be my new friend to drive me once again. But when I rounded the corner I frowned, realizing I wouldn't be so lucky to have two lifts by him today.

The driver greeted me and I told him where I wanted to go but, beyond that, we didn't say much else. Instead, my toes tapped and I couldn't stop fidgeting during the entire ride across town.

It seemed as if everyone was subtly—or not so subtly— warning me to stay away from Kelly. And though I refused to believe any of them, it was enough to plant my own seeds of doubt. I wasn't looking for an excuse or a reason to avoid having to ask him about why he was choosing to represent someone who did something so awful, it was just that with all that happened with Alex and that money she had found, I wondered if I should at least try to be a little more careful with the decisions I was being forced to make.

"Here we are, miss," the driver said, bringing me back to the present.

"I shouldn't be long," I said, glancing at the big warehouse building we were parked next to. "Would you mind waiting here until I'm back?"

"I can do that." His eyes met mine in the rearview mirror. "No problem."

I smiled and touched his shoulder before stepping out under the hot late afternoon sun. I had no plans to socialize with whoever it was I was supposed to be meeting. All I wanted was to make the drop and get my ass back home so I could get my thoughts straight before I saw Kelly tonight.

A shiver caused my body to shake as soon as I stepped inside the cold warehouse. "Hello?" The sound of my own voice echoed off the walls.

When no one answered, I perused the floor, seeing what it was they had in storage. Pulling the tops of several cardboard boxes open, I found everything from hair-dye and make-up to women's perfume. There were all sorts of different kinds of beauty products and I couldn't resist the urge to try a perfume for myself. I pulled the cap off and sprayed a little on the inside of my wrist, rubbing it in with my other wrist. I smiled at the floral scent and thought this wasn't so bad.

"Sure, make yourself at home," a man's voice called from behind me.

I jumped around with my hand on my chest, saying, "Holy shit. You scared me, dude."

He showed me his palms and took my wrist. I watched as he inhaled the scent of the perfume, closing his eyes as he did. "Beautiful."

Not wanting him to get the wrong idea, I yanked my arm free, frowning. He said *beautiful* but what I heard was *Bella*. And just like that, Kelly was there with me.

"Can I help you?" He gave me a full-tooth smile that made my skin crawl.

"Are you expecting a delivery?" I asked, looking him up and down.

He was decently dressed in a two-piece suit but his hair looked greasy and he could use a shave.

"Depends who is asking." He winked.

"I'm asking." He reached for my hand again but I took a step back, retreating.

"Watch it!" I said through gritted teeth, swatting his nasty fingers away.

He frowned. "Easy. If you wear my product, then I'd like to know what you think of it."

"I guess you're not expecting a delivery." I hurried past him, thinking that maybe I had the wrong place.

"I'll take it," he said from behind.

My heels dug in and came to a screeching halt. Slowly, I turned and said, "Take what?"

"The package." He stepped toward me and held out his hand, describing the envelope and its size perfectly.

That was enough to convince me he was my man. Reaching inside my tote, I pulled the thick envelope out and handed it over. He smiled when he took it and then said, "Stay awhile. We can get to know each other."

"You know I can't do that."

He gave me an arched look.

"Tootle-oo." I waved my fingers at him as I turned and left, thinking that I needed to demand more money from the Madam if she wanted to have me keep making deliveries for her. I could do dates because the men were classy, but this, *this* was pushing my limits.

My Uber driver was still waiting, as I'd asked of him. He had his arm out the open window and was listening to soft rock when I opened the door. "Everything good?" he asked as I got into the back.

"Everything is good," I said. "You can take me back to where you picked me up."

He nodded, took the vehicle out of park, and put the wheels in motion as I put in a quick message to Kelly.

Hey. Tonight is too far away. Want to meet me now?

When he didn't respond, I knew that if I wanted to get him to talk, I would just have to surprise him with a visit myself.

33

KELLY

With tabloid reporter Sylvia Neil wanting our connection to remain a secret, it was better that I took this one alone. Besides, Giselle could make some follow-up calls while I got to the bottom of this.

Maxwell dropped me in front of the hotel and I headed straight for reception, passing patrons conversing in the front lobby without so much as making eye contact.

"Good afternoon, Mr. Black," the woman behind the desk greeted me.

"There is a woman who will be visiting," I said, then went on to describe Sylvia Neil. "When she arrives, would you mind sending her up?"

"Of course. Not a problem." She nodded and smiled.

I tapped my knuckles on the wooden counter, turned, and headed to the elevators, thinking that this was the only truly safe place I had available. I knew what Sylvia was risking when meeting with me, disclosing the information she worked tirelessly around the clock to uncover. It was important I reassured her that our meeting would be done in, and kept, private.

Reaching inside my pocket, I pulled out my keycard and

swiped it in front of the elevator doors, causing them to immediately open. Stepping inside with furrowed brows, I couldn't stop thinking of all the power moves being played out around me. Something big was about to go down. I could feel it.

When the lift stopped on the top floor, I stepped into the hallway, making my way to my penthouse with memories of the first time I'd brought Kendra here. I still remembered the flower petals that trailed over the floor. Remembered the excitement in her eyes, the kind of bubbly spirit that still brought a smile to my face.

Tonight, Kendra. Tonight, you will see that I'm the man you've been waiting for, I said to myself, unlocking the door to my place.

As soon as I stepped inside, I could smell her. It was like she had been here this morning. All fruit and flowers. As my eyes traveled the length of each wall—into the living room and past the kitchen—I could easily see her there, floating on her feet as she made herself at home.

I flicked my wrist and glanced at the time.

Sylvia was running late and I wondered what was keeping her from me. Pacing impatiently, I moved to my bedroom, trailing my fingers over the bed where, again, all I could think about was Kendra.

God. I was getting hard just thinking of the last time we were here, rolling between the sheets. It was an incredible night. The way her moans grew louder as she drew closer to orgasm. How her needy body hungrily writhed beneath mine as I thrust in and out of her, growling into her ear as I came.

A chuckle escaped my lips as I cracked my knuckles.

We were made for each other. The hard-headedness found in both of us was a recipe that made for great, feisty sex. Now, if only she would sign the contract, then I could take our already great sex and turn it into even hotter sex.

A knock on the door took me out of my thoughts and away

from my *Bella,* Kendra. I hustled to let Sylvia inside. "Any problems getting access to the elevators?"

"Easy as pie." She smiled.

I invited her inside and watched her take in the grandeur that defined my place, soaking up the rich, luxurious details with her eyes. She had her hair pulled up in a messy bun, and with jeans and a loose-fitting blouse she looked like a reporter who had spent all morning typing away behind her desk. "Can I get you anything to drink?"

"Water would be great," she said, stopping at the bookcase.

I prepared two lemon ice waters and went to her, handing her a glass.

"Thank you." Her voice was soft and she didn't hesitate to steal a quick sip while she slid her finger down several book spines, reading the titles.

"It's a small collection I've been working on," I said, rocking on my heels, my hands buried in my pockets.

"I didn't know you read fiction." She glanced at me out of the corner of her eye.

"Hardly have the time it seems these days." I smiled. "But even defense attorneys need a little excitement in their lives."

She plucked a novel from the shelf and said, "Ever think you'll pen one yourself? I'm sure you have some fascinating stories from cases you've worked."

I tipped my head back and laughed. "Not my thing. What about you?"

She glanced at me. Her eyes were a hazelnut brown that lit up under her dark lashes. "Write a novel?"

"A writer like you, it must have crossed your mind a couple of times?"

Her eyes moved back to the novel as she shrugged. "I've thought about it," she said, sliding the book back in its place.

"And?"

"Huh." Her brows squished together as she inched closer,

peering over the top. It was an orchid flower on top of the book-case that stole her attention and I watched as she picked it up, bringing it to her nose for a smell. Her eyes closed when she inhaled in an attempt to catch any remaining scent that may be left over from before it was plucked. "Where's the rest of it?"

"Left over from the other night." I turned and moved to the couch. "Come. Let's sit."

She followed me to the living room, choosing to sit in the chair across from the sectional I sat in. We were separated by a glass-topped coffee table, and it was there we both chose to set down our sweaty glasses of water.

"Mind if I keep this?" she asked, holding up the flower.

"All yours." I nodded, not thinking anything of it. "So, Sylvia, anything new on the Maria Greer murder?"

She leaned back, crossing her legs at the knee. "That's funny, I was going to ask you the same. That's why you asked me to come today, isn't it?"

"I want to get to the bottom of it, just like everyone else."

"What have you been doing to get there?" She quirked a brow.

"Beginning here." I lifted my hand and pointed my finger down to the floor. "With you."

"Sorry, Kelly." She frowned.

My brows drew together, wondering what it was she was sorry about.

"I thought you heard."

"Heard what?"

"I want to uncover the truth about Maria's murder as much as you do, but I'm no longer working the story."

My spine peeled off the back of the couch as I leaned forward, resting my elbows on my knees. "And why is that?"

She let out a heavy sigh before bending over and digging through her bag. "This just came to my attention this morning." She handed me a one-page manuscript.

I took it between my fingers as a grave expression moved over my face. Then I read it line by line. "Who sent this?"

She shrugged as she leaned back, wrapping herself inside her arms. "It's the first death threat I've ever received and it has me scared shitless."

My head lifted to terrified eyes staring back at me. "Any idea who is making the threats?"

She shook her head, dropping her gaze to her feet. "It's coming through in email, but the message was encrypted so there's no way to track who's sending it."

"Fuck. I'm sorry. Is there anything I can do?"

"Look, Kelly. I love my job, but it's not worth dying over. Someone is clearly pissed with me digging into their lives and I know it has something to do with the Maria Greer case."

"What makes you say that?" I dropped my eyes back to the typed-up threat Sylvia had printed off, trying to piece together the connection between Maria and what Sylvia already knew.

Sylvia told me the same story Alex shared with Giselle and me this morning. How Blake Stone had stashed away a large sum of money in a studio and that the cartel who gave him the loan wanted it back after he got arrested on distribution with intent to sell charges.

"Does anybody else know about this?" The paper flapped between my fingers when I held it up.

She bit the inside of her cheek as her shoulders shrugged. "And, Kelly, that's not all. I received a call this morning—"

"From the same people who are threatening you?"

She nodded. "I assume. Whoever it was made a similar kind of threat."

"Do you think it could be the cartel behind the threats?"

"I'm not going to make any guesses." She played reporter, always protecting her stories and sources, but with Mario and Stone both behind bars, I wondered who was behind the threats. "If I step away, I'm willing to bet that the death threats. Will stop"

"Shit," I said, shoving my hand through my hair. "You need to report this."

Her head snapped up and she lurched forward. "No, Kelly. I don't want anybody to know about this. Promise me you won't tell."

I stared at the email, running through my options. Sylvia was an asset I couldn't afford to lose. Sure, I could turn to Hollywood Stars reporter Julia Mabel instead of Sylvia, but Sylvia was the one to first bring Maria to my attention.

"I went to see Nash Brooks today," I said.

Her leg stopped swinging and I swore she held her breath as she stared at me with big round eyes. "He knows about Maria," she blurted out. "I showed him the photos of her death before I handed them over to you."

I gave her a slight nod. "He wasn't there."

Her chest rose, then fell, with easy breaths.

"What do you know about him?"

"Besides that he's a billionaire film director?"

I nodded once.

"Maria Greer was also an intern of his."

My brows knitted. "Really?"

She nodded, a slight curl pulling at the corners of her mouth.

"News to me." I clasped my hands and hung my head. "Anyways, doesn't really matter. The police are convinced Mario is the killer."

Sylvia flopped back in her chair.

"What do you think?" I asked, lifting my head to meet her gaze.

"I think what I know. The evidence points to him."

"I'm not so convinced."

She blinked rapidly as her fingers gripped the sides of the chair with enough force to make her knuckles go white. "Do you think it could be Nash? I mean she was *his* intern."

"I don't know." I frowned.

I watched as Sylvia reached into her bag to pull out a pen and paper. "Visit this man." Her hand scribbled a name and address.

I read the name. "Wesley Reid?"

"Good. You know who he is." She tapped the pen against the paper.

"What's Wes have to do with any of this?"

Her mouth spread and curved into a smile. "Wes knows more about Nash and Maria than anybody else. Go talk to him. And after he talks, come find me. We'll compare notes."

34

KENDRA

"Can I help you?" The woman behind the desk lifted her head when I walked in.

Readjusting my grip on my tote, I slid my thumb through the shoulder strap and froze at the sight of her dazzling eyes. She was lovely in her professional suit that brought out her slim, perfect hour-glassed figure. There was no way she could be a defense attorney, I thought to myself. Her beauty caught me by surprise, as I wasn't expecting to be walking into someone like her when trying to track down Kelly.

Her makeup was applied to perfection and her long lashes highlighted her soft gaze. But there was also a hidden intensity in her eyes that I only noticed after staring deep inside them for longer than a second. A pang of jealousy hit my gut, causing me to clench at my side, realizing now just who Kelly worked with.

The woman straightened her spine and raised her brows when I didn't respond.

"Uh, yeah. I'm looking for Kelly. Is he in?"

I dragged my feet as I moved cautiously into the office. My head swiveled on my shoulders as I looked around, curious to learn more about Kelly and his firm. There was a palm in the corner, stretching to the ceiling, and a few spider plants whose limbs reached to the windows. It created a fresh ambience to what would otherwise feel like a stuffy office environment—an environment I was all too familiar with. Awards and diplomas lined the walls, and when my eyes landed on her desk, I read her nameplate – *Giselle Archer.*

"Mr. Black isn't in right now." She stepped around her desk, extending her hand in my direction. "Kendra, right?"

She took me in a surprisingly firm grip and I shook her hand, nodding, feeling slightly awkward being in Kelly's office uninvited and without warning. Now I didn't know what to say or what I'd do next. But something inside me told me that he wouldn't be happy to learn that I was stalking him. "Do you know when he'll be back?"

There was a hint of concern in her eye when she looked at me, but she remained strong and unassuming as she folded her arms over her chest. "What brings you in today?"

"It's nothing." I dropped my gaze to the floor, tucking a loose bang behind my ear. "I'll just come back when Kelly is here."

"If you leave your number I'll tell him you stopped by."

"Forget it. I'll talk to him some other time," I said, turning on a heel and pushing my way through the glass doors. Giselle never did pursue me, and I was thankful for that. I didn't need to bring her into my relationship with Kelly or my own personal drama. And though we had met before, I was happy to assume she had forgotten who I was.

My waiting Uber was exactly where he said he would be. Hurrying to get back inside, I opened the door and sank deep into the backseat, letting out a heavy sigh.

"Where to now, miss?"

I stared out the window as I thought about it. There was only one other place I could think of where Kelly might be. It was also the one place I didn't really want to go without first being invited.

But I'd come this far already and knew that I might as well

keep on going until I found him. I had nothing to lose, and I couldn't stop thinking about the allegations against him. I had a burning desire to get to the truth and see what he had to say for himself.

"You got it," my driver said after I barked off the name of the building, giving the names of the general cross-streets to go along with it.

He started the engine just as I swiped my phone alive. My thumbs typed up a quick text to the Madam.

Your delivery is done.

She responded almost immediately.

Well done, dear.

Keeping the Madam happy was essential to keeping my schedule open for the day. The last thing I needed was Madam to surprise me with a date tonight, especially since I'd already reserved tonight for Kelly—whether she knew about it or not.

My brows pinched.

Maybe they were the ones to conspire for his invitation and gift to appear in my apartment. It was proving tough to keep up with all the secrets that surrounded him. He'd seemed like a fairly easy nut to crack in the beginning, but I'd also known there was more to him after that first initial impression.

The driver made a right-hand turn into the park. Instantly, we were shaded by tall trees that flickered sunlight between the cracks like a disco ball spinning on the dancefloor.

It was then I wondered why Kelly failed to mention he worked with such a bombshell like Giselle. I couldn't get over how gorgeous she was. She stopped me in my tracks. I knew what a woman like her could do to a man with strong desires—desires like I knew Kelly had. It wasn't a good combination and could easily escalate into something more. I wanted to know how they came to be working together and if there was a history—a past beyond professionalism—that I should know about.

My mind swirled as I adopted a sullen look. We passed a couple in the park lounging on a blanket, enjoying what appeared to be a lighthearted, romantic picnic lunch. Cuts of cheese were spread across a plate and they each held a glass of wine. It looked relaxing and was the kind of day I wished I was having.

But, instead, I was dealing with mixed emotions for the man I wasn't supposed to let my heart be falling for.

The more time that passed, the more questions I had for him. There was so much I needed to talk to him about. It sickened me to think that I'd become one of those clingy girlfriends in only a short time. I despised those women.

But that was how I felt, and I wanted to lay my claim over him before another woman did.

How serious was he about me? And did he think of me as more than just an escort he could rent through Madam's services? I wanted to know. No. I *needed* to know. If I knew where he stood, then I could know where to stand.

As soon as we pulled up in front of the hotel, I knew that my chances of finding Kelly here were better than anywhere else at this point. He did say that his penthouse suite was his home-away-from-home, and since I didn't know where his main place of residence was, this was my only shot to knock on his door. And, besides, it was also safe for me to assume that this would be the place he would want to end our night. *If* he played his cards right.

When I pulled on the car door handle, it swung open and the driver turned his head over his shoulder. "Would you like me to wait for you again?"

My tongue wet my lip, as I felt bad for stealing his day away from other customers. But I hated driving in the city and I needed to get around, so I nodded and said, "Thank you." He seemed like such a nice guy. I knew that I needed to do something nice for him.

"Not a problem. I'll park over there." He pointed to the corner parking lot off to the side of the building. "Take your time."

I dug in my purse and pulled out the last of my cash, slipping him all three twenties as a special appreciation for being so patient with me today. "You're a doll," I said, sliding out of the vehicle like a snake slithering to the ground.

I fixed my hair and smoothed my hands down the front, feeling somewhat embarrassed for wearing only a petty chiffon tassel dress that fell just above my knees. It was nothing compared to how Giselle looked. And after all the running around I had been doing, I was sticky with sweat. If it weren't for the perfume sampling from Madam's guy at the warehouse, I would have needed to stop to get myself some deodorant. I could only hope that Kelly wouldn't think that I looked as disgusting as I felt.

With the front entrance in my sights, I realized that I was beginning to drag my feet. A hesitation sent waves of doubt over my body as I was suddenly very aware of the fact that I was about to barge in on his residence with accusations flying.

If he didn't already think I was a bit crazy, he would after today. And maybe, if I didn't damper some of the anger I was feeling boiling over inside, he would think twice about wanting a relationship with me.

The fear of our relationship ending so soon was real, especially since I was already busy stalking him because I questioned his trust. But I pulled the front door open with gusto, telling myself, "Fuck it. He's the one who has some explaining to do. Not me."

I marched with my shoulders rolled back and my head held high.

How real was this man who had managed to grab my attention for longer than one night? And was he worth the internal struggle I'd been dealing with since the Madam dropped the bomb of the client's crime he was representing?

If anyone could persuade him to think otherwise, I thought maybe I could be the one he'd listen to. Though I didn't want to have to tell him the story of my past. I wasn't ready to share that just yet—if ever. Hell, I couldn't even find the courage to break it all down for Alex, and she was my best friend, the one who I should be telling first. If anyone had to know, it would be her.

As for Kelly, maybe we weren't to that point in our relationship where I could offer advice unsolicited, but at least if I did, I'd know just what kind of man he was and whether or not he would be willing to take a woman's advice.

My chest tightened and I suddenly felt thirsty as a rush of emotions hit me like the strong impact created from a car crash. And the further I walked into the hotel lobby, the heavier it felt.

Past memories came back in a flood, remembering the night I rushed out after Kelly set off the trigger of my rape. Or the way I felt after the night he brought me back for a do-over, the way he unraveled me with orgasms that left me breathless and seeing stars. The highs and lows were the definition of our budding relationship and I was undecided on whether or not that was a good thing or not.

A couple burst into laughter at the bar and I turned my head to find them snuggling, wrapped up inside each other's arms. Then I couldn't escape wondering if I was right about his penthouse being a fuck pad, a place he seduced women. When I'd asked about it, Kelly had blown it off like the master lawyer he was, deflecting the question entirely with an answer of his own, but maybe I was right? Faces of joy surrounded me and I could only hope that soon I'd join them in laughter and happiness that they made look so easy to find.

"Hi." I stepped up to reception. "I'm here to see Kelly Black."

The woman behind the desk smiled. "Kelly Black, you said?"

I nodded and watched her fingers work the computer keyboard. "I'm sorry. He's not expecting any more visitors."

"More?" My voice raised an octave, surprised to hear that

maybe he was in fact here, now, inside the building. "Does that mean he's here?"

She just stood there frozen with a closed-lip smile.

"Look." I swallowed down the sandpaper scratching the back of my throat. "He's expecting me."

"And you are?" She raked me over with judgmental eyes.

I thought about whether or not it was worth saying I was family in hopes it might give me the response I wanted, but I wasn't sure I was willing to risk the fallout if she were to ask for some kind of identification. "A friend," I said. "A really close friend."

"I'm sorry. Without explicit instructions from Mr. Black, no one is to visit him."

"What can I do?" I leaned forward, silently pleading with her to allow me access to the private elevator.

"Call him and tell him you're here. But, without his approval, you'll just have to wait."

"I don't have a phone," I lied.

"I'm sorry. My hands are tied."

"Don't you remember me from the other night?"

She gave me a strong, searching gaze before shaking her head.

"I was here with him. Twice. I'm a regular visitor." I knew that was a stretch, but the way I saw it, I didn't have anything left to lose. "Always with Kelly. Can you at least call him yourself, or tell me if he's in or not?"

Her brow wrinkled. "I can't give out private information on our guests without violating hotel policy."

I pushed away from the desk, cursing under my breath. This was so messed up. People who followed the book must lead boring ass lives, I thought, knowing she wasn't going to give up Kelly's whereabouts. "Live a little," I mumbled just as my cell started ringing in my tote bag.

The lady behind the desk scowled—learning I lied to her

about my phone—as I dug it out, answering the call. "What's up, bitch?"

"Kendra, not now." Alex's voice spat through the tears I could hear falling.

"What's wrong?" My heels clacked across the marbled flooring as I moved to a quieter area of the lobby.

"I thought this was over." She sniffled.

"You thought what was over?" My posture stooped.

She completely broke down and there was nothing I could do to comfort her. When she needed someone to hold her, I was stuck with only words. "Breathe, baby. Tell me what's wrong."

I could hear her wipe her mouth before saying, "It's about Nash."

My heart stopped, thinking the worst. "Tell me everything. Is he okay?"

She let out a heavy sigh. "I don't want him to go to jail."

"Why would he go to jail? Did something happen?"

"Kendra, where are you? I need you."

"I'm trying to get up to Kelly's place."

"Why shouldn't I be surprised?" She laughed for the first time, making me feel better about whatever was going on.

I crossed my free hand across my belly and lowered my voice. "Now, tell me what's going on."

"Some people came looking for Nash. They had questions about what happened. You know, with the money and Nash's involvement."

"I'm sure whoever they were, they just want to get to the bottom of it." Then I thought about it some more. "Were they cops?"

"Lawyers." I heard some papers crinkling in the background. "Look, I'm just finishing up work. Can you stop by my place when you're finished? I really need to see you."

"Yeah, sure," I murmured.

"I'm worried sick for Nash's future and feel completely helpless knowing that he's so far away when all this shit is happening without him knowing."

"You should call him," I said, seeing my way to Kelly open up before my very eyes.

"Maybe I will. But I need you here."

"I'll be there as soon as I can." I told her that I loved her and hung up to find a couple making their way toward the private elevator that would take me up to Kelly's place.

The woman behind reception was busy with a customer so I hurried to the elevator, catching up to them just as he swiped his special entry card over the detector. I played cool, like I owned the place, and they didn't ask questions as I watched the doors close.

My mouth curved into a knowing smile, like I'd just gotten away with murder.

Finally, I was going to get my chance. I knew Kelly was here. I could smell him. And the receptionist should have known that she gave too much information away. It was she who led me to sneak up to his floor in the first place.

The couple that provided me the lift got out on the floor below Kelly's and I stayed on until the next floor, knowing exactly where I was going. When the doors slid open, I could still see inside my mind the flower petals Kelly had scattered on the floor, leading in a long trail to his front door.

I followed that trail, the trail that only I could see, with a beating heart full of excitement to see him. It felt like it had been so long, and despite knowing that the reason I was here wasn't great, I still couldn't wait to be standing next to him.

Then I heard his door open.

My gait slowed to a crawl as I watched another woman leaving. As soon as she turned, she held her head high and walked a straight line, heading directly for me.

My eyes were wide and I couldn't help but feel heartbroken, thinking the worst. Assuming that Kelly had been with her while making plans to be with me later, my insides twisted with agony. It hurt to think that maybe I wasn't his only fling. That he had others and that all his promises were superficial.

Her hair was balled on top of her head but I could imagine long brunette curls bouncing off her shoulders if she would let it down. Then I watched her head tilt and her eyes squint. "Do I know you?" she asked.

I blinked. "No. I don't think so."

"Huh. I guess you just have a familiar face."

"I guess I do," I said, glancing around her to see if Kelly would be coming out next. The door remained shut but the woman must have connected the dots, assuming I, too, was heading to Kelly's place.

"Ahh ... I see." She nodded.

My brows knitted.

"I know this might sound weird, seeing as we don't know each other and all. But keep your distance from him."

I arched a brow. "And if I don't?"

She leaned in, her breath sending jitters down my neck. "Then you'll be the next one to go."

35

KELLY

A s soon as the front door closed, my forehead hit it as I
let out a sigh.

My visit with Sylvia didn't go as well I thought it
would. Nothing could have prepared me to learn what she
divulged.

Worry sent heartburn spreading across my chest as I blamed
myself for getting her involved in Maria's murder case. Even
though it was she who had initially brought me the crime scene
photos, I was the one needing to know more about the information she had worked tirelessly to gather. Without Sylvia, my
defense for Mario wouldn't be as strong, and that, too, was
disheartening.

I splayed my fingers, bracing my weight against the frame,
letting my posture stoop further down the door.

This was quickly getting out of hand. I thought about how
quickly it all seemed to be spiraling down the drain with a
clenched stomach. I was concerned about the death threats she'd
received, needing to find a way to keep her working the case as an
investigative reporter. But, of course, I first wanted her to be safe.

And with the look in her eyes when she broke the news to me, I knew that it was no longer a possibility.

My eyes closed, letting my mind race.

It wasn't that she was weak. I knew she was the best they came. Right up there with Julia Mabel. Women like them had to be strong to do their work. They were harassed, intimidated, and offered bribes daily. Threats like the one she received, well ... this was new to me.

I pushed off the door and turned to face the open living area of my penthouse, my hands on my hips.

It was important I kept my head straight when filtering through this tangled mess. And when I looked on the bright side, I was convinced maybe this was for the best. Then at least the detectives and other proper authorities could take over the investigation where Sylvia left off.

But that would require letting them have what she'd already found, and with her recent threats against her life, I knew that convincing her to report this—or hand anything over to the authorities—wasn't going to be as easy as I'd like it to be.

My ears perked when I caught wind of a conversation coming from the hallway. Slowly, I turned and pressed my ear against the door to see if I could hear what was being said.

There was enough chatter to recognize both their voices. My heart skipped a beat and my manhood thickened—*Kendra.*

What was she doing here?

Reaching for the door handle, I flung it open to find Sylvia standing there with a smug look on her face. Over her shoulder, Kendra's eyes locked with mine, then the elevator doors opened and she disappeared inside.

"Kendra!" I held up my hand, rushing toward her. "What did you say to her?" I demanded, rushing past Sylvia. But by the time I reached the elevator it was too late.

I was surprised to see her. The date I'd requested wasn't until later tonight. I wondered how she'd found me, and what was so important that couldn't wait. It seemed as if she was always running away from me, and that was enough to keep my fist clenched. If Sylvia was the reason for her to run today, she should realize that I was working.

"You know her?" Sylvia asked, sauntering over to me.

I jabbed at the button to retrieve the other free car, hoping it would arrive shortly so I had a chance at catching Kendra before she got away. "What did you say to her?" I growled at Sylvia, thinking that she had something to do with Kendra wanting to flee.

"Nothing." Sylvia looked at me with innocent doe eyes. "Just that I thought she looked familiar."

The elevator dinged open and I stepped inside, dragging Sylvia with me. I couldn't afford to have her stay on the exclusive floor without supervision. She stumbled into the car behind me without protest, and soon we were on our way down to the lobby.

"Who is she?" Sylvia leaned into the corner with crossed arms.

The floors counted down and all I could think about was getting to Kendra. Why couldn't she have just called? I knew how it looked. She already thought my penthouse was my fuck pad. And now with Sylvia coming out just as she was arriving, this one wasn't going to be easy to explain or convince her otherwise.

"You're not going to tell me?" Sylvia huffed.

"It doesn't matter," I grumbled with my blood thrashing between my ears.

Finally, the car slowed to a stop and I wedged my body through the skinny slit as soon as the doors showed signs of opening. I immediately caught sight of Kendra's small frame and my legs picked up the pace, knowing she was only a few steps away from reaching the exit, leaving me to dwell in my own thoughts of self-doubt. My legs widened their stride as I was nearly at a running pace. "Kendra, wait!"

She glanced over her shoulder, saw me, and stopped.

My chest heaved as I fought to catch my breath, putting the brakes on once I was within arm's reach of her.

"I'm not happy with you, Kelly." She pursed her pouty lips and I wanted nothing more than to press mine against hers.

The crease between my brows deepened as my eyes darted across her face. She was so beautiful; sun-kissed skin whose softness I could still feel on the tips of my fingers. "What are you doing here?"

She flipped her long beautiful hair over her shoulder and said, "I needed to talk to you."

"Did you get my gift?" I reached out to touch her but she pulled away, leaving me feeling empty inside.

"I did."

"So we're on for tonight?"

She flashed me a questioning look.

"*Bella,* tell me what has you bothered."

A man in a business suit walked past and as soon as he was out of earshot Kendra said, "I can't explain it here."

With her unwillingness to explain, I could only guess what the hell happened to have her so concerned and needing to talk. It seemed urgent and I didn't like knowing that she was feeling so distressed and unwilling to let me help.

This time a woman passed close-by and Kendra dropped her voice. "Everyone is watching us."

"Then come up to my place." I reached for her arm again but she wouldn't do me the honor. I didn't care that everyone was focused on us. "We can talk there, in private, without staring eyes."

"And be the next whore you invite up?" She huffed and rolled her eyes.

"It's not what you think," I said, knowing she was referring to Sylvia.

"I gotta go." She made a move for the door but I caught her before she could leave.

"Stay. Don't go," I pleaded. "I'd like to hear what you have to say."

For a second I could see she was at least entertaining the idea of coming with me, but then she leaned close and whispered, "If you want to see me, make a request with the Madam."

"That's not how this works," I said, gritting my teeth. Then she pulled her arm free from my grip and hurried to the exit, pushing through the glass doors with a sense of urgency I'd never seen in her before.

I chased after her, unwilling to let her just leave without a fight.

"Just stop!" she barked at me, causing more bystanders to stop and watch.

"Never." My brows raised, not caring who was watching. "You tell me what's going on with you."

Something had her upset and I was determined to find out what that was. It pained me to see her look at me with uncertain eyes and pull away from my advances. That wasn't the woman I knew, or the *Bella* I'd been falling for. Whatever had her acting like this, we'd get through it together.

Kendra turned and laid the flat part of her hands into the center of my chest, pushing me back with a frustrated grunt. "Seriously. Please, Kelly. Not now."

I stumbled back and watched her slip into a waiting vehicle before I had time to stop her from leaving me completely. A man who had seen it all said something in my ear, but I ignored his comments, hanging my head and wondering what I did to let things go so astray.

"Oh, good. She found you," a voice said behind me.

When I lifted my head, I found Giselle striding toward me with a satisfied look on her face.

"Yeah. She did." I shoved a hand through my hair, watching Kendra drive away, thinking that this wasn't over. "Come inside. I'll explain."

36

KENDRA

I hid my face inside my hands the entire ride to Alex's. Right now, seeing her was more important than having to deal with Kelly. After what I'd just witnessed, I wasn't sure that I could see him tonight.

Tears streamed down my face and soon I was a bumbling mess.

I couldn't explain what just happened or why I was so upset. Maybe it was because he'd made me feel like I was the only one in his life. The pain of another possible lover twisted in my gut. She was not the first woman to give me such a stark warning to stay away from Kelly. That was the last straw, the one that finally pushed me over the edge. And I couldn't deal, didn't have the strength to ask the tough questions I needed to ask.

The driver made a sharp turn, sending me flying deeper into the back of my seat.

Normally I wouldn't have cared so much about being exclusive with a man. I'd been on the opposite side, sending warnings to women who threatened to take what I considered mine. It wasn't like any of this was new. But, for some reason, Kelly had me caring more about us than I knew I probably should.

Wiping my tears dry, I sniffled and bravely moved my hands away from my face. I could feel my eyes puffed up and swollen when I looked outside into the bright sunny sky. My hands clenched my hardened stomach, hating myself for letting my heart get involved with Kelly before knowing the facts of who he was. It wasn't like me to fall quickly over a man, and ever since meeting him, he'd managed to get me to do things I normally wouldn't.

The Uber driver caught me in his rearview mirror, getting me to smile.

At least I had something to be thankful for today. I didn't know where I would be without him. He was still waiting, just like he'd said, and his show of loyalty today was nothing short of incredible.

This time, I instructed my driver to just drop me in front of Alex's building as I wasn't in the mood to hoof it another few blocks. It was a risky move, but seeing what he'd already done for me today, I figured it was enough to make me trust him with this little piece of knowledge I reserved for only my closest friends.

Alex opened the door before I even had to knock. One look and we were both throwing our arms around each other, opening up the floodgates. Though we weren't crying about the same thing, it didn't matter. It felt good to be held, rocked, knowing that she would always understand no matter what.

Even though we were both an emotional wreck, between the two of us, I was always the stronger one and my strength didn't stop today. "I'm here," I said, petting her silky soft head of hair. "Everything will be okay."

She pulled away and caught my face between her hands. "Coming from the person whose face is drenched in her own tears."

We both laughed at the ridiculousness of it.

"Tell me what's wrong with you?" Alex asked.

"Not a chance." I smiled, threading my fingers through hers. "You first."

Alex squeezed my hand, pulling me fully inside her apartment, leading us to her couch where we both plopped down. She flopped her arm over my shoulder and I wrapped my arms around her stomach like a belt, never wanting to let go. In the center of the coffee table, a bag of potato chips sat open next to a container of vanilla ice cream. That was enough evidence to give me an idea of the exact emotional state my friend was in.

"I'm worried Nash might still be a suspect in the murder of that girl," Alex murmured, her voice cracking at the assumption she was making.

"What did they say?" I couldn't take my eyes off the ice cream. "What happened?"

Alex began telling me everything that transpired and the more she talked, the more I realized I knew who had visited her. "Alex, were you talking to Kelly?"

She thought about it. "I don't think he ever mentioned his name."

I sat up, scooting myself into the corner, needing to be sure Alex could see my face as we talked. "Did he look like the person we searched on the internet?"

Her head slowly nodded. "If he was, he was gorgeous."

I knew it to be true, but that wasn't what was important. "Did the woman give her name?"

"Giselle."

My eyes popped out of my head as I jumped to the floor, cursing, "Shit. It was him."

"I can't believe I didn't recognize him. I was so concerned with what they were asking me that I must not have even thought he could have been the guy you've been dating." Alex set her feet on the floor, leaning forward with her hands flat on her thighs. "I'm sorry, babe. But what does it matter?"

"It doesn't." I rubbed the back of my neck, tipping my chin to the ceiling.

"Is that why you were crying?" She reached her hand inside the bag of chips and tossed a couple into her mouth. "On the phone you said you went to see him."

"That's not why I was upset." I moved back to the couch and hugged my knees to my chest, suddenly not caring about the ice cream melting in front of me.

"Then what was it?"

I rolled my eyes to hers and sighed. "I was crying because I'm afraid to learn who he is."

"Does this have to do with that contract?"

"Yes ... No ... I don't know." Alex crawled from the opposite end of the couch to give me a hug. "Everyone keeps telling me to stay away, or that he's not the man I think he is, and the more warnings I get the more my mind is convinced I should listen."

"You need to listen to your heart."

"My heart is the reason I'm trembling," I admitted.

"It's okay to love." Alex rubbed my shoulders.

"It's too early to love." I rolled my eyes. "And you know who gave me the latest warning?"

"Who?"

"Remember that reporter who was after Nash?"

"Sylvia Neil?"

I nodded. "I found her leaving Kelly's penthouse just as I was arriving."

"Did she recognize you?"

"Said I had a familiar face but I don't think she remembered me being your friend."

"Shit. I'm sorry, Kendra. This is all my fault."

I turned my head, giving her a look. "What are you talking about?"

"I told Kelly to go talk to her. Well, actually I told Giselle. Said

Sylvia had an unusually high interest in what happened to the missing money. More so than anybody else I know."

I reached over to grab Alex by the hand, giving it a reassuring squeeze to let her know that I wasn't mad at her. She turned her eyes back to mine. "Did she say anything else?" Alex asked.

My head nodded. "She said that if I don't stay away from Kelly that I'll be the next to go."

"What the hell does that mean?"

My shoulders shrugged. "Your guess is as good as mine."

"You don't think they're sleeping together, do you?"

"I don't know what to believe anymore."

We sat there in silence for a long time, both of us collecting our thoughts. Realizing that I might have let jealousy cause me to overreact with Kelly, I regretted leaving without first letting him explain.

"I see why you're so fascinated with him." Alex rolled her head to me. "He's insanely attractive."

The back of my skull peeled off the couch. "Are you straying off the reservation, young lady?"

"No one can compare to Nash. You know that. And I'd *never* cheat on him."

My lips thinned as they curved. "We're supposed to be going out tonight."

Alex rolled her head back, letting her eyes stare up at the ceiling. "You should be getting ready then. Don't you think?"

"You think I should go?"

"Of course I do." She turned to look at me. "You have work to do."

I arched a brow, tilting my head to the side. "Even after all that happened today?"

"That's more reason to sit him down."

I nibbled on the inside of my cheek, wondering if I even had it in me to sit down with him after such an emotional afternoon.

"Besides, I need you to find out why he was asking about Nash, and if I should be worried for him or not."

"Oh, so this doesn't have anything to do with me?" My brow lifted higher on my head.

"Girl, it has everything to do with you."

"Is that right?"

She nodded with a confidence that inspired me to take action. "He needs to answer your questions honestly."

"And then?"

"Then you can finally introduce us." Alex smiled. "He needs to know that we're friends."

37

KELLY

Giselle eyed me as she passed the threshold into my top-floor suite.

I followed her, appreciating her look. It was stunning business attire, her collar left open and unbuttoned down to the center of her chest. Giselle radiated a sexuality all her own and, knowing Kendra, I bet that she also was wondering about me working with Giselle.

But it wasn't like that. Our relationship was strictly professional, a friendship that went back to the day I first hired her to come work with me at my firm.

Giselle dropped her bag and purse on the empty stool at the breakfast nook when I said, "Her name is Kendra Williams."

"I know. We met, remember? She came by the office looking for you."

My brows rose as I subtly nodded.

"She never did say why she was at the office, but with the look on her face, I knew something was eating her up."

"Seltzer?" I asked, pulling an unopened bottle from the fridge.

"And you've been seeing her?" Giselle nodded to the water as she lowered her tailbone to the stool on the opposite side of the bar from where I stood.

"Something like that," I mumbled, handing her the first glass I poured.

Kendra had tension in her face and whatever she had on her mind, she should have stayed to get it off her chest. Clearly, it was enough for her to track me down. I didn't like knowing that she was making assumptions without involving me in the discussion.

"That's great, Kelly." Giselle's sparkling eyes matched her smile. "I've been worried about the lack of intimate relationships in your life."

"It's complicated," I said, purposely avoiding eye contact.

Giselle was one of a few who knew my true life story and why I was the way I was. Though we never discussed it in great detail, she knew and didn't have to ask. She knew it all. The dark secrets that clouded over me, the very same ones I refused to tell anybody about. The ones that brought nightmares, and the ones that made me sometimes think the world would be a better place without a Kelly Black in it.

Of course Giselle would want me to find someone to share it with. Instead—before Kendra—I drowned myself in my work, letting it consume me to the point of forgetting about all the pain strangling what little love I had left inside my heart.

"From what I witnessed, I'd say so." She took a small sip, keeping one eye on me as she did. "But how did it start?"

"That's part of the equation that makes it so complicated." I rubbed my face inside my hand.

She gave me a questioning look from behind the rim of her glass. "Don't want to tell me, fine."

It wasn't that I couldn't trust Giselle with this kind of information. She wouldn't judge. But I also knew that in telling her, it might open up more questions than I cared to answer right now. "We crossed paths when doing some work with the Madam."

"Oh." Her lips rounded into a perfect *O*, lifting her brows a little higher on her forehead.

"Yeah." I pressed my palms flat on the counter, leaning my weight over my shoulders, hanging my head and letting out a heavy sigh.

She set her glass down. "I thought you were done with that lifestyle."

"I was." I glanced into Giselle's curious eyes from under my brow. She even knew about how the Madam had helped with the recovery to move on with my life after all the shit that happened not so long ago.

"But?" She reached out to blanket her hand over mine.

"Like I said, it's complicated." I pulled away, reaching for my glass. I gulped down more of my cool drink. "You caught the end of Kendra's brief visit today, but I think she got the wrong idea about Sylvia visiting me here."

"She saw?"

I nodded, explaining how they crossed paths in the hall leading to my suite.

"From a woman's perspective, it doesn't look good when seeing another woman leaving the place of the man you thought was yours." Giselle slid off the stool.

"I know," I said with a hollowness in my chest.

Giselle stepped around the side and rested her hand on my shoulder. "She likes you, Kelly. Now that I know why she stopped by the office, she likes you more than you may know. It's not that hard to see. If you're looking."

"Thanks," I whispered, reaching up to squeeze her hand.

"Mind if I use your bathroom?"

"All yours." I extended my arm toward the bathroom. Giselle passed through the living area, stepped into the dark room, flipped the switch, and closed the door behind her.

Tossing back the rest of my drink, I knew Giselle was right. Kendra liked me, and I had it bad for her, too. And no matter how many directions I was being pulled in, I knew that my relationship with Kendra had to come first.

There was pain in her eyes that caused my muscles to ache. She doubted me, thought the worst when she bumped into Sylvia. Giselle was right about that, too. It didn't look good.

But why didn't she stay and talk? There was clearly a lot on her mind. What it was, I could only guess. Maybe it was my demand for her to sign my contract, or maybe the Madam had put her up with another man tonight and it conflicted with our date. I didn't know and could speculate all I wanted without getting any real answers until I decided to call her.

Stepping into the living room, I dug inside my jacket which was draped over the back of the couch and pulled out my cell. Kendra's name was on the top of my list when I pressed the call button.

After the first ring, I swallowed. And when she still didn't pick up, the temperature in my core shot through the roof. I stood frozen, staring out the window overlooking the city skyline, holding my breath, silently begging her to answer. All I wanted was to know that she was okay, that she knew that I was here, wanting to listen. But when it went to voicemail, I hung my head and killed the call.

When my eyes opened, I found myself staring at the note Sylvia had jotted down for me to call Wesley Reid. Quickly, I moved to take the note in my hand.

"Hey, you never did say," Giselle joined me in front of the sofa, "how the meeting with Sylvia went."

Staring at Wes's phone number, I mumbled, "She's no longer working the story."

"What?" Giselle's mouth fell open. "Why?"

I lifted my head and locked eyes with her. "Death threats."

Her hand flew over her mouth as she gasped. "Shit. From who?"

"No idea," I said with heavy lids. "But she suspects that it's somehow related to her digging into Maria's case."

Giselle sat in the far corner of the sofa, crossing her leg over her knee. "Do you think its Mario's guys?"

Shaking my head, I said, "I doubt it."

Giselle was lost in thought for a minute before asking, "You still believe he's innocent?"

I turned to look at her. "Don't you?"

With wide dull eyes she said, "He's guilty of something, but not her death."

We had never discussed anything other than his connection to Maria's crime, but apparently she had been thinking what I had been thinking all along. Though I didn't care to know anything else about him. I just wanted to get Maria the justice she deserved without sending an innocent man to prison.

"What are you going to do?"

I held up Sylvia's note to call Wes. "Start with this."

Her brows pinched and I handed it to Giselle. She quickly read the scribble and asked, "What's he have to do with anything?"

"I don't know, but I'm about to find out," I said, hitting the call button on Wes's number.

The line rang as I tried to recollect the last time I talked with Wes. It wasn't like we were complete strangers. We crossed paths in various social circles, and with Adrianna finding me the other day at the cemetery, I knew it was only a matter of time before one of us would be calling the other.

"Mr. Black, if it isn't the lawyer who should be on my payroll," Wes answered.

"How are you, Wes?" I moved to the large windows as I talked.

"Adrianna mentioned what you two discussed the other day." I heard a door close on Wes's end. "I've been meaning to call about that, but it looks like you beat me to it." There was a smile in his voice when he talked and that made our conversation easier. If there was one thing I knew about Wes, it was that he liked to get straight to business.

"There's something else that I need to talk with you about."

"Yeah, what's that?"

"I prefer not to do it over the phone."

"It must be serious."

"It is." I glanced over my shoulder to find Giselle in the kitchen pouring herself another glass of seltzer. "What's your schedule like, are you free to stop by my office tomorrow morning?"

"I have a better idea."

I raised a brow.

"How about if you stop by Mint tomorrow night. Meet me there at 11."

Reaching out, I pressed the door handle down, opening it up to the balcony. Stepping outside I said, "You know I can't do that."

"Then I guess what you have to say can be said now."

"Wes—"

"Mint. Tomorrow. 11pm." Wes ended the call without me giving him a response. But he knew that I'd be there, and that was the exact kind of shit I expected when dealing with billionaire media mogul Wesley Reid.

I feared I was only digging myself deeper into Madam's personal drama. It wasn't like her and Wes were exactly friends, but what choice did I have? Sylvia said Wes had information pertaining to Maria's case, information I needed to know. But I also feared what Wes would say about my theory regarding Madam's sudden business expansion.

My gut twisted as I stared at my phone, deciding whether or not to try calling Kendra again. I had to. Her running out with a forehead twisted in distress was too much to bear.

Lifting my cell to my ear, Kendra answered after the second ring. "Kelly—"

"Don't you ever humiliate me like that again." My voice was

firm. "Not in my house. Not at my work. And certainly not in public. Do you understand?"

The line was silent but I could hear her breathing.

"Kelly, I know who that woman was."

My brows pulled together, knowing she was referring to Sylvia.

"I need to know, are you sleeping with her?"

I tipped my chin back, a smile curving my lips. It was almost laughable how ridiculous her fear was. "I'll explain at dinner."

"You can't even answer a simple question," she huffed.

"Where can I pick you up? I'll explain everything at dinner."

The shuffling on the line led me to believe she was considering her options. And when she finally agreed, I said, "Wear the dress I sent you."

"And if I don't?"

"Don't tempt me," I growled. "Maxwell will pick you up in an hour."

"Kelly?"

"Yes, *Bella?*"

"Make sure it's private. We have a lot to discuss."

38

KENDRA

The thrashing pulse in my neck subsided the moment Kelly threaded his fingers with mine, leading me inside the luxurious restaurant reserved for the elite members of southern California society.

We stepped inside to a warm greeting from the hostess. She was young and beautiful with a tight black dress accentuating her curves. "Reservation for Kelly Black." Kelly's voice was confident in its delivery.

"Of course. A private table for two." The young woman smiled, motioning for us to follow.

Kelly tightened his hold on my hand. It was both strong and possessive, and I liked knowing that he was determined to make this night perfect. Even after me storming out of his building earlier in the day, he showed no signs of wanting to trade me in.

We skirted the main dining area, taking in the chic and modern surroundings, listening to the romantic murmur of couples laughing and cuddling as they enjoyed their meals and drinks. The smells were Americana with a French infusion, and the combination was enough to stir my stomach. I was starved.

Alex and I had opened up a bottle of wine as she insisted she help me get ready. Though I refused to drink more than a glass—I didn't want to be too tipsy when I brought up my concerns with Kelly—Alex was happy to slam down the portion I refused to get lost in.

First, she'd done my hair, curling it into long waves that fell to my shoulders. Then, it was onto my makeup, a dark blue eyeliner with a purple mascara to match the dress Kelly demanded I wear. And through it all I couldn't stop thinking how it seemed like Alex was the only person in the entire world who believed in me and Kelly. She wanted to see this work, just as I had rooted for her and Nash.

"You look stunning tonight." Kelly glanced over his shoulder, stroking his thumb over the backside of my hand he held firmly inside of his. "Did I tell you that already?"

"Thank you," I said, blushing. He'd told me how stunning I was, like, fifty times already, but it never got old. The dress was gorgeous and I didn't want to be wearing anything but this.

The noise from the main dining area grew distant as the hostess stopped at a beautiful corner table for two. There was a freshly lit candle in the center and Kelly did the honor of guiding me into my chair before sitting opposite me.

Once we were alone, he insisted he hold my hands. And though we didn't say a single word, I questioned what was on his mind. For the first time tonight, I could see clearly into his dark eyes. His hold on me didn't match the quiet, dark demeanor that was a window into his soul. "I love the dress," I said, hoping to ignite some kind of conversation. "It was just what I needed."

"And you look lovely in it." His mouth curved enough to finally show off one of his notoriously sexy dimples I loved so much.

A glass of white wine was served and I gave Kelly a questioning look. "I don't have to have this."

A part of me thought I shouldn't mention how he didn't have to order me an alcoholic drink when I knew he wouldn't be drinking, but with the weight of tonight's discussion looming, I was happy to have more wine to help take the edge off.

"I insist." He lifted his usual sparkling water and made a toast. "To tonight."

We clinked glasses and I said, "So, let's get on with it then."

Kelly pulled his lips away from the rim and said, "Good. I'll go first."

"The pleasure is all mine." I set my glass to the side, settling in for what I hoped would be a conversation to steer us back on course. I needed to know if he was for real, if what we had started was worth committing to.

He leaned forward and narrowed his eyes. "I'd like to know why you keep running away from me."

The way he was looking at me, with a sense of amusement and intensity crinkling the corners of his eyes, was enough to send flutters across my chest and a wave of pleasure under my skin. I hated how handsome the man was. His dark skin looked incredible. The way it glowed against the soft ambience of the flickering candle had my nipples tightening up, ready to cut him apart. His sex appeal was dangerous and already making me forget the reason why I was here in the first place.

But I forced myself to remain calm, focusing on our future instead of jumping straight into bed.

"*Bella*," he grinned, "are you going to tell me?"

My lips parted as heat flushed up my neck.

Kelly looked dashing in his slim-fit three-piece suit. His tie was the same color as my dress and we certainly had what it would take to become LA's next greatest power couple.

I touched the diamond necklace around my neck and looked around, appreciating how far away we sat from other couples—the curious listeners who would otherwise be able to easily eavesdrop on our conversation. I didn't want to have my mind on strangers and whether or not they could hear what I had to say. It was nice to be given space, and privacy, knowing that we'd prob-ably need it.

"What was Sylvia Neil doing in your suite?"

"Is that why you keep running away from me?" Kelly leaned back against his chair, lowering his gaze but never once taking his eyes off of me. "You're scared that you might not be the only one in my life?"

My hand fell from my neck and came to clench my other in my lap. "Am I?"

The room began spinning as I waited for an answer. Kelly tilted his head and eyed me. My last breath of air caught in my chest and I refused to let it go free until I heard his answer. I needed him to confirm I was his only one. Because if I wasn't, I knew I couldn't go any further down this precarious path.

"No matter what I say," he tipped his chin up, "will you even believe me?"

My gaze dropped to the tabletop. I wasn't sure I would believe him. If I *could* believe him.

After all the warnings to stay away, there was enough doubt to make me believe that Kelly did have secrets, secrets that he didn't want me to know about. And for the first time in my life, I didn't have an answer. I was too afraid to admit that I liked him enough to already be afraid of losing him.

"Good evening, Mr. Black." We were interrupted by the wait-ress with a big smile. "Are you ready to order?"

Kelly glanced at me then turned back to the woman. "Yes."

I listened as he ordered, not understanding it, wondering if he even cared to know what I liked when it came to dining out. The waitress left without so much as an acknowledgement in my direc-tion and I just couldn't wait to ask, "What did you just order?"

"Our dinner."

"I know that, but do you even know what it is? Or that I'll like it?"

There was humor in his eyes when he locked his gaze with mine. "I wouldn't have ordered it if I didn't." He smiled. "It's a seven-course meal, beginning with egg caviar and ending with a chocolate Nutella crunch."

My insides stirred. To his credit, I couldn't wait. It sounded fantastic. "And what's in between?"

"A black truffle risotto for you—"

I was salivating already. "And for you?"

"Dry aged prime New York steak." He wiggled his brows.

It was like he'd done his research, actually having taken notes the few times we'd been together. Though I couldn't recall giving anything away for him to know that I was going to love eating here. Maybe he was just *that* good.

"Kelly, I'm—" I hung my head, tucking my hair behind my ear as I did. My throat constricted and I couldn't get the words out— the apology that I knew he needed to hear.

He slid his elbows across the table, opening his hand in an offer I debated whether or not to accept. After careful consideration, I did, and the moment I let my hands fall into the safety net of his large palms, he closed his fingers around them, letting his calm warmth spread up my arm, giving me the much needed confidence to get through tonight.

His dark eyes danced with mine as my mind wrestled to decide whether or not I should tell him about my reason for running out on him the first time. But even just thinking that I had it in me to discuss my rape had my pulse beating so fast I swore I was going to have a heart attack just sitting there. Pellets of sweat formed across my lower back and I knew that it wouldn't be fair to him, and certainly not to me.

"You can tell me anything." His eyes were unwavering, so strong and full of trust.

I swallowed down the lump that had formed in my throat, knowing that even with those amazing eyes—telling me that I could trust him—deep in my heart I knew that now wasn't the right time.

My gaze moved to my wine glass. Suddenly feeling dizzy, I didn't reach for it.

I feared that Kelly would leave me before our relationship ever even got started. Instead, I deflected. "Madam told me about the case you're working on."

He pulled back, releasing my hands. "Why would she bring that up?"

His dark brows knitted and there was a sense of betrayal flashing over them as I shrugged. "Maybe to make me question your own ethical boundaries?"

"Ethical boundaries? What are you saying? That I'm not a man of ethics?"

"That's not at all what I'm saying."

"Then what is it?"

"How could you represent a rapist?" My voice cracked with emotional pain that resurfaced from thinking about my own traumatic experience. Just saying the word brought so much suppressed agony to the surface, I even surprised myself.

My hands began to shake and, suddenly, the room felt much cooler than it actually was.

"That's what this is about?" Kelly's voice was rough and I could hear the anger building inside him. "Does the Madam want you to believe that since I represent a client charged with rape that I'm no different? That I'm a rapist, myself?" He turned his head and barked a disbelieving laugh.

My worst fears were coming to life. He was acting just as I thought he might, and though I knew his anger to be warranted, I wished that he would understand where I was coming from.

But without knowing my own story, how could he?

"I'm just trying to understand why you would do such a thing." My voice was much weaker than I wished, but Kelly was the sort of man who could do that to a woman.

"Would it change your mind if I thought the man was innocent?" He snapped his head back around to meet my gaze.

"Is he?"

Kelly leaned forward, resting his elbows on top of the table and hung his head between his arms, nodding. "I believe he is."

Relief washed over me, but that still didn't settle my anxiety in knowing that he and Giselle went knocking on Alex's door earlier today. "Did you learn anything from Sylvia? I mean, that's why she was there, right?"

Slowly, he lifted his head with a wrinkled brow. "You know Sylvia? How?"

"Alex Grace." I raised my brows. "The gorgeous Assistant Director to Nash Brooks." One brow arched as I gave him a stern look of my own. "She's my best friend."

Kelly openly stared at me with a slack jaw.

There was little doubt in my mind that it was anything other than this case that had him stressed out and feeling down. "Alex told you to talk to Sylvia. We connected the dots after I bumped into Sylvia coming out of your penthouse suite."

He leaned back, turned his head, and rubbed his face inside his hand.

"Kelly, I'm sorry for jumping to conclusions."

"You shouldn't know about this."

"But I do."

"I don't want to bother you with my work. It's an ugly world I represent."

"I understand that, but remember, I studied law." This time it was me who leaned forward, smiling. "And it's not ugly to represent a client you believe is innocent."

He nodded, and from the look he was giving me, I knew he was listening to what I was saying.

"I'm curious to know the details," the crown of my head pulled up to the ceiling, straightening my spine, "especially since it involves you, and my best friend."

His chest rose just before he let out a heavy sigh.

"Kelly," I reached out, wanting him to take my hand, "what do you need from me? How can I make your life easier? I don't want to add to your stress."

Slowly, he brought his hands up from under the table and clasped his fingers around mine.

"Baby," I smiled, "I'm your stress *relief*."

He bit his bottom lip and chuckled.

"But I want you to prove to me that I'm your only girl," I said, squeezing his hand.

His eyes twinkled with life. "Sign the contract."

"And we're in this together. Just you and me?"

His head nodded as one side of his mouth curled at the corner. "Just me and you."

I leaned back until my back fell against the chair. "Fine."

Kelly freed one hand and reached inside his jacket where he pulled a freshly printed contract out.

"You have it with you?" I gasped.

His eyes narrowed as he smiled. "I wasn't giving up on you, *Bella*."

Kelly brought his chair around from his side of the table, pulling out a pen as he did, and sat next to me. Without a word, he offered me the pen.

My tongue rounded my mouth as I straightened my spine, taking the contract between my fingers. Quickly, I glanced over the agreement, seeing that each line item was the same as before. Then, when I knew in my heart I was ready, I put pen to paper and signed my name. "There you go, Counselor, I'm officially all yours."

Kelly put his arm around me, pulling me closer to him. I was dizzy with his musky scent, getting wet as my fingers trailed over his tight body beneath that incredibly sexy suit he wore. And when his lips crashed with mine, I mewed, closing my eyes, thinking how much I had missed him.

He coiled his tongue against mine and I reciprocated his exploratory kiss, tugging at his suit as my stomach growled with hunger. He was hard, pitching a large tent that only seemed to stand taller the longer we kissed. His member was impossible to go unnoticed and I liked knowing that I was the reason for it.

Kelly kissed me with extreme intensity. I was both elated and scared for what floodgates I might have just opened up by signing that stupid paper.

By the time Kelly came up for air, the food was beginning to be served. It was our first course of egg caviar just as Kelly said it would be. He explained the dish and then told me to take the first bite—which he fed to me. I closed my eyes, not realizing what I was doing, and moaned as the explosion of delicate tastes worked their magic over my tongue.

Kelly laughed. "Is that not good?"

"Amazing," I said, wiping my mouth.

"Just save some for me." He smiled.

"Yours is right there," I said, pointing to his plate and laughing.

He shook his head. "The orgasms. Like the one you just had." He touched my pouty lip. "I'd like to see that same face on you after dinner."

My sex clenched at his request. "I'll try my best, Counselor." I smiled into his dangerous eyes, thinking I was in over my head with Mr. Black. But as long as he always put me first, it was a drowning I'd happily accept any day of the week.

39

KELLY

Kendra let my jacket fall away from her shoulders and headed straight for the floor-to-ceiling windows that overlooked the city skyline. "It's beautiful." Her voice carried through the room like a timeless classical tune.

"Nothing like it," I said, expressing my own appreciation for those twinkling lights I often found myself staring into late into the night when I was alone.

She glanced over her shoulder, smiling, and it was hard not to mirror her excitement. I liked that she was careless when dropping my expensive suit jacket to the floor. I had covered her with it for warmth after Maxwell dropped us off after dinner, and though I knew the material was worth thousands of dollars of hard-earned cash, in an instant it became priceless with the knowledge of what I was going to do to her once I had her out of more than just my jacket.

"Sometimes what you see on the surface is better than the truth hidden in the shadows." I stepped behind her, letting my hands squeeze her waist just before sliding around her tight midriff.

Her stomach fluttered against my touch but quickly settled.

"Can people see in?" She trailed her painted nails up and down my arm, driving the blood from my heart to between my legs.

My head shook before lowering it, nuzzling her neck. I peppered the soft flesh with hungry, open-mouthed kisses. The smell of wine filled my nose and she tasted like sweet-honey nectar. "You think I'd be so foolish to let just anybody have a glance into the privacy of my own home?"

She twisted herself inside my arms, hooking her hands around my neck. She hung there, staring into the depths of my eyes. "In this town? Not a chance."

We both laughed, as if she understood just how dangerous it would be to allow any sort of camera access into what went on here in my top-floor suite.

My hands ironed up her sides, cupping the edges of her firm breasts before falling to the globes of her toned bottom. "God, you taste amazing," I said, licking her neck.

Kendra stood on her tip-toes, taking my face between her hands. She pressed her lips against mine. My tongue demanded entrance and she happily accepted. It was a tongue-thrusting kiss that encouraged my shaft to only grow stiffer in its pursuit to lay my *Bella*.

"Now that I've given up my right to voice my opinion about you—" her fingers worked to loosen my tie, "—what is it you don't want me sharing with the world, Mr. Black?"

I unzipped the back of her dress, pulling at the shoulder straps, encouraging gravity to take it from there. "You," my husky voice said.

Kendra dropped her arms. Wiggling her body, the gown fell and pooled around her feet. With one hand on my shoulder, she carefully stepped away from it. She flicked her gaze up at me, her eyes hooded with seduction, and I found her amazing body tempting.

"We'll get there soon enough," I said, lifting her hand above her head, spinning her around so I could let my eyes rake over every inch of her beauty.

Her stealth black laced lingerie was made for her. I'd sized her up before, but until now, I'd only known two things. One: that her small frame would make her easy to toss around and contort to whatever position I desired. And two: that she was the most gorgeous woman I'd ever laid eyes on—since my wife left me. But now I noticed so much more that I had missed before.

"I'm not sure I can wait for long," she murmured.

Kendra had a defined under-layer of toned muscle. There was a birthmark on her lower left hip that resembled the state of Florida and a tattoo up her right side that read, "Lioness." A chuckle escaped my chest. The line fit her tenacious personality. I knew early on that Kendra wasn't one to take shit from anyone. It was the reason I pursued her, and the motivation to fight for her signature. And now that I had gotten it, we were one step closer to her becoming my new submissive.

"You'll wait as long as you have to." I licked my fingers and let my hand come flying down onto her ass.

She jumped into my arms, wrapping her legs tightly around my waist, diving her tongue into my mouth. I tilted my head, deepening our kiss as my fingers kneaded into her firm ass.

Kendra curled her tongue, panting against my lips as I worked to undo my belt. As soon as it was free, my pants fell down to my knees and I pushed the waistband of my briefs down, taking myself at the root and placing the tip of it to her hot center.

"Do it, Counselor." She reached behind her, pulling her underwear fabric to the side. "Show me your opening argument."

In swift motion, I plunged deep inside her. She tossed her head back, growling. I widened my stance, pumping my hips as she rode me like the wild cat she was. She was so wet, hot and needy, there was little need for foreplay.

Her cries filled the room and I growled as I nipped her neck.

She was light as a feather and her weight made it easy for me to slide her up and down my length, making sure to put her in the exact position I needed to get her to clamp her teeth hard over my ear.

"Fuck, me," she breathed, her hot breath moist against my ear.

I slammed into her with several quickened thrusts. Soon, she tightened her slick cunt around my cock, and then she went quiet while every muscle in her body tightened. A second later, the built-up tension exploded out of her mouth as she screamed in orgasm.

Slick with her arousal, I brought her to the window. My balls were tight as I remained buried deep within her, getting off on the feeling of her throbbing sex pulsing against my thick arousal. "I love your tight little cunt," I said, licking her ear.

She pushed her fingers through my sweaty hair and pulled my face around so she could kiss me. Her lips were cold from breathing through the shattering orgasm I just gifted her, but I knew I wasn't finished. Not even close.

Lifting her up, I pulled myself out of her hot cleft, placing her on her feet with her back facing me. Angling her hips up, I bent my knees and found her entrance once again.

My abs clenched as I hovered over her arched back. She was still eager, wet with orgasm and arousal, so I took my time playing between her slick lips. I ran the crown of my head between them, making her giggle with gentle teasing thrusts. Then, slowly, I worked myself back in, stretching her walls to fit my thick girth, one torturous inch at a time until her clit hit my scrotum.

Kendra was a hungry, sexual creature. And between her grunts and aggressive reach-arounds to pull me deeper into her, I was once again reminded of why I was so in need of her in my life. We were made for each other. We each had a huge appetite that few others could fulfill, and somehow we'd managed to find one another at the exact time I needed a connection.

Taking her long hair in my hand, I wrapped it around my wrist and quickened my hips. Flexing my ass muscles and rooting my legs firmly into the floor, she clawed at the glass like an animal trying to escape. Her skin was wet with sweat, and the feel of her hitting against me sent me into overdrive. I gritted my teeth and moved like a jack-hammer as I grunted through the heat spinning at the base of my spine.

Kendra growled, whimpering against the window, begging, "Yes. Yes. Yes."

Fire spread across my skin. I was close to exploding but refused until I couldn't hold it any longer. "Oh, shit. I'm going to come." My grip dug so deep I could feel it pinching her flesh.

"Harder," she cried.

I released her hair, letting those same fingers clamp around the other side of her waist. I drove into her fast and deep, pressing her tits flat against the glass. And when I closed my eyes, stars flashed behind my lids and then my body shuddered through its own intense release. "Ahh ... shit."

I dropped my head to my chest, feeling my cock twitch against her tight walls. Refusing to let her go, I held her there for a long time, the two of us silent in a fog-induced orgasmic bliss, both of us breathing hard.

With my cock softening, I pulled myself out and quickly reached for a tissue off a nearby shelf. Stepping to Kendra, I reached between her legs and cleaned my hot desire off her. "You're an amazing fuck," I said.

"Thank you." She worked on her hair as my eyes took in her flushed cheeks. "But I still don't understand the need for a non-disclosure for just fucking."

"Then maybe you'll understand after what I'm about to show you."

She lifted her gaze and looked at me with a sense of curiosity only women like her would have. "Let's see it."

Pulling my pants back up, I took her by the hand and led her to the back bedroom. Setting her naked ass on the edge of the bed, telling her to stay put, I retrieved a key and moved to the wall. "This is my secret."

Kendra's tongue moved between the seam of her lips before freezing at the corner.

I turned the key, unlocking the hidden wall. I turned to steal a glance at Kendra and she had big round eyes with a visibly pounding heart. And when I flicked on a light switch, all my secrets were revealed instantly. All my sex toys, the things I'd reserved for her, the stuff that had her panting like a dog in heat.

"That's your secret?" She didn't sound impressed.

"Not this." I picked up a whip, snapping it across the air above where she sat.

She cowered and ducked her head. "What the fuck, Kelly?"

I grinned.

Her hand covered her heart. "Then, what?"

"The secret is what I'm going to do to you," my eyes fell to the leather whip as I stretched it between my hands, "with this."

40

KENDRA

"Where's Jerome?" I asked as I entered Madam's office.

She sat quietly behind her desk with soft classical music playing in the background. I had to give it to her —she always had a way of making her office environment comfortable and classy. I supposed that was her goal from the start of this business. It was that same attention to detail she brought to escorting which made for comfortable dates I felt safe agreeing to.

I inched my way further inside and Madam held up a finger, telling me to be patient with her as she finished reading whatever paperwork she had laid out in front of her. Stealing a glance, it appeared to be a series of documents that wouldn't make any sense to me without knowing more about the specifics around them. I ignored it and turned my attention elsewhere.

"Ah, there." She breathed a sigh of relief, removing her gold-framed glasses from the bridge of her nose. "Kendra, doll. How are you?" Her mouth spread, then curved, before her smile reached her eyes.

"Can't complain," I said, holding up the last set of clothes I'd borrowed from her. She motioned for me to set the box on the loveseat in the back corner, which I did, fully aware that I couldn't let her know about what happened last night with Kelly. If she found out she'd kill me. "So, where's Jerome?" I asked again, turning back around to face her. "Out sick?"

"I have him running errands." She folded her hands in her lap. "He'll be back soon. Please, have a seat." She motioned to the empty seat with her hand. "Tell me how your delivery went."

I slid into the seat, setting my bag down at my feet. "Fine. Why?"

"Oh, no reason." Madam brought her elbows to her desk. "Emmanuel said you were quite flirty with him." A twinkle in her eye told me that she found that amusing, except it wasn't true.

"Emmanuel?" I quirked a brow, realizing that was what that creep's name was. Fitting, really. Only dudes with slicked back greasy hair could pull off a name like that.

Madam tilted her head to the side, her smile fading as she did. "The man you made a delivery to."

"Yeah, about that—" My fingers drummed the wooden armrest as I refused to break eye contact with Madam. "You should know that I didn't flirt with him."

"It's fine if you did, honey." She dropped her chin and looked at me from under her brow. "Business is easier when the men like you."

"I didn't," I said firmly. I liked his perfume. Not him.

"Not the story I was told." Madam frowned. "Then again, Emmanuel does tend to embellish his stories so maybe you're right."

My eyes rolled. *Embellish* didn't even come close to what actually happened. "I am right. I *always* am."

Madam backed off, dropping her gaze to the papers she was reading when I'd arrived. Together we sat in silence as I gathered my thoughts on how I was going to break the news to her.

"And you should know that I won't be going back there

again." I voiced my opinion like she didn't have a say in the matter. But we both knew otherwise. Madam held the control when it came to deciding what was, and wasn't, best for me.

"Sweetie, why?" Her eyebrows drew together when she looked up at me. "Sometimes I need you to help out with chores around the house."

"I can't do it. Unless," I paused to lick my lips, "you increase my pay."

Madam's eyes narrowed and the dark look she was giving me was enough to make my hands go clammy.

"I know what a brick of hundreds feels like in my hands," I blurted out. "And that was exactly what was inside that last envelope."

"You think that's what that was?" Madam tossed her head back and cackled like a peacock.

"Of course it was, was it not?" I pushed for a conviction.

"Darling, why is it always money that your generation wants?"

My shoulders shrugged as I found her question to be contradictory, considering it was coming from a businesswoman like herself. She liked money as much as anyone else in this town. Perhaps it could even be argued she was one of the greediest people around.

"I'm not asking you to tell me how it was made, where it came from, or what it's for. Honestly, I don't care. All I need is a little more off the top to make it worth the scum I feel crawling over me after dealing with men like Emmanuel getting all up in my grill."

Madam stared at me with an unwavering gaze for what seemed like forever. I could see her thinking over my request and a jolt surged through my body, thinking that maybe she would grant me my wish. "Are you not happy with our arrangement?"

I sighed heavily, giving Madam a pinched expression.

This was getting ridiculous. I didn't understand what it was with everyone and their stupid arrangements and contracts that needed signing. It was like they thought that with my signature they owned me.

But it wouldn't stop me from walking away if things didn't feel right. Because I would. This was a matter of survival. Plain and simple. Though it wasn't worth trying to understand it here, especially with the Madam breathing down my neck.

"I signed up to be an escort, go out on dates, be arm candy, entertain *your* men, and that's it. House chores," I shook my head, "are not my thing."

"But when it comes to doing Madam a little favor, what I've already given you isn't it enough?"

I had always been motivated by money. Hell, before I met Kelly I would have taken money over sex any day of the week. But now that I'd been sexed up by a man named Kelly Black who had made orgasms rain down on me, I didn't care so much about money. I would take Kelly's dick between my legs—no matter the amount paid to me—any day of the week before selling out to Madam's silly house chores.

"I wish you would allow me to have sex more often."

"Darling, Kendra. I guess now would be the time to tell you."

"Tell me what?" My body suddenly overheated.

"Baby doll," she smiled, "Kelly Black has booked you out for the next month." Madam dropped her gaze, smiling. "Exclusive to him."

My mouth opened. Then it snapped shut. My brows knitted as my gaze traveled over the walls, trying to connect the dots of what the hell she just said. I knew Kelly and I were a great fit, and the timing of his request couldn't be a coincidence. It was totally related to me signing that stupid NDA and me having him promise that I was his only one.

"He what?"

The Madam laughed. "You're free to do what he wants. One entire month. Just him."

I pinched my bottom lip. "He rented me for the next month?"

"Not how I would describe it, but yes." There was a glimmer in her eye that had me wondering what the catch was. "By the way, how was your date last night?"

My jaw clenched as my heartrate exploded through the roof. "What date? I didn't have a date." But even I knew my words lacked the sincerity I needed to convince the Madam I was anywhere but on a date with Kelly.

The Madam hooted through a fit of laughter. "You are really something else, darling."

Giving up on trying to keep my secret from her, I asked, "How did you know?"

"It was clear as day from the moment I saw you waddling into my office." She raised her brows, giving me a knowing look.

Suddenly I was aware of how I sat gingerly in my seat, and she was right about me waddling around. It looked like I had a stick up my ass, and no matter what I did to try to conceal it, I only made it worse. "And you're going to allow this?"

She tilted her head to the side, giving me a questioning look.

"A month alone with Kelly." I licked my lips, hating that I could still taste him on me. Of course Madam knew about last night. I hid sex like an alcoholic hid his drink from his breath. It was impossible and stupid of me to think that I could get away with it. Especially while sitting in front of an expert like her.

"He must have a way of convincing you he's not as bad as he truly is." She collected her papers, placing them in a neat pile before opening a bottom desk drawer.

"So this is my choice to make?" I asked, watching her dig around.

"This time the choice is yours to make, darling." Her head popped up and she had something in her hand. "But before you decide," she handed me a newspaper article, "I suggest you read this."

It was the story of Maria's death. I was aware of it. Hell, the whole town was. "I'm aware," I said, placing the article back on top of her desk, not bothering to read any more than the headline at the top.

"Then I also assume that you're aware of reporter Sylvia Neil—"

My head dropped in my hands. A headache was coming on. I could feel it. "Look, Kelly told me everything. I'm comfortable with what he does, who he represents, and the people he works with."

"But did he tell you that Sylvia's life is being threatened?" Her lips flattened into a straight line as she stared me down. "Did Kelly mention anything about that? Do you think that's coincidence, doll?"

I jumped up from my seat and clenched my fists at my sides. "Why are you trying to tear us apart? What is it about him that you hate so much? Or is it me you hate?"

"Being with a man for a month is a big commitment," Madam said coolly. "I want you to have the facts before you decide. Because I might not be there to save you if he drags you down with him."

"Really?" I crossed my arms, hovering over her. "Because it seems like you don't want us to be together."

"Kendra," her voice was soft with a hint of compassion, "I know about your rape."

My chest tightened and suddenly I couldn't breathe.

"And the family inheritance you received."

Warm feelings of embarrassment flushed my cheeks. Asking for more money only made me look greedy. I had money, and the means to afford a very comfortable life. It was the excitement in my life that I was lacking. And now that I'd found Kelly, my life was more complete than it had been in a very long time. "What are you getting at?" I crumbled into the chair.

Madam pushed back in her chair, stood, and came to rest her hand on my shoulder. "Honey, I know everything about you. It's my job to protect you from getting hurt. That's why I tell you these things about Kelly. The reason I want you to have facts—so you can make informed decisions."

"My life's story isn't a secret." I played like I didn't care, but I did. I kept more secrets than I knew was considered healthy. My past was fucked up. A life history that I tried every day to erase from the books. Stories that I didn't want anybody to know about.

"What I'm saying is that if you do decide to be with Kelly for a month," she squeezed my shoulder, "then you'll be acting more as his girlfriend than a date. You understand?"

My gaze was trained on the floor. I didn't respond because I knew everything she was saying was true. "How much did he pay to have me?"

"Sleep on it," she released my shoulder and pulled me to my feet, "and let me know what you decide."

I moped to the door with my head hanging.

"And Kendra, baby?"

My feet stopped dragging as I glanced back at her.

"Keep your phone on." She smiled. "You'll be making another delivery for me soon."

41

KELLY

The woman escorting me to the top floor hid her face behind a masquerade mask, the same silver color as her gown.

Mint was the popular nightclub that catered to the lifestyle of exposition sex, glamor, and social encounters with the elite who called LA home. It was here where Wes insisted we talk. Ultimately, I was fine with that because I knew that we would be uninterrupted.

The woman stopped at the security guard, who dropped the rope to the stairs leading to the top floor. "Mr. Reid is immediately to the right at the top of these stairs."

"Thank you." I nodded, passing security and beginning my journey up.

It was late and already crowded, but I knew that the party was just beginning. Peak occupancy would come around one in the morning and slowly dwindle until it was just a handful of hardcore members who refused to leave until the doors closed at dawn.

The bar at the top had florescent blue lights behind the many bottles of liquor. They were lit up like night lights and created a cool glow that spread to the dark corners of the room. The bartender nodded and smiled when he caught my gaze, and there were a handful of people sitting on stools, drinking and chatting.

I found Wes at the table overlooking the activity below. He had his arm around his woman, his back to me, quietly nipping at her ear, making her squirm. I approached slowly, unable to recall the last time we'd met face-to-face. It had been a while, and though we went our separate paths over the years, whenever we did come together, it was always a reunion of respect and friendship.

"Wes," I said as soon as I was within earshot.

He kissed her cheek one more time, then turned to me with a huge welcoming grin. "Kelly Black."

I reached out and shook his hand. He stood, deciding that a handshake wasn't enough. He needed a hug. We laughed, looked each other over, then he introduced me to his woman. "Kelly, this is Kami. My fiancé."

My brows raised, surprised to hear that he was engaged.

Kami was a natural beauty with brown hair that she had done in a French twist. "Mr. Black." She shook my hand, smiling.

"Kami." I bent and brought my lips to the back of her hand.

"Well then," she glanced at Wes, "I know you boys have some important business to discuss so I'll leave you to it."

Wes pulled her in for a quick, sizzling tongue-kiss before letting her meander to the bar behind us. "It's good to see you, Kelly." He tossed his arm around my neck, squeezing me again. "Can I offer you a drink?"

"A sparkling water would be great."

Wes glanced to the bartender and made a motion with his hands. "Here. Sit. It's great to have you finally visiting Mint."

I chose the seat closest to the railing, knowing that I would like to catch the shows below as we talked. "I like what you've done with the place."

"Me too. And it's only getting better as membership grows."

Wes pulled out the chair opposite me and sat. "Kami, what do you think of her?" His eyes sparkled like a man whole-heartily in love. "Isn't she the most beautiful woman you've ever seen?"

I stole a glance to the bar, seeing that Kami was a natural here at the club and a perfect match for Wes. "You're a lucky man."

His grin deepened as he nodded. "God, I know." He turned his head, drinking in all that his woman was. "What about you?" Wes turned his gaze back to me. "Do you have a special someone in your life?"

For what was intended to be a friendly question, it was loaded with a dark past Wes knew about. Kendra's green eyes sparkled in the front of my mind, and as I thought about how I was going to respond to Wes's question, I couldn't deny how crazy I was for her.

And with my request to the Madam to have Kendra as my own for an entire month, I couldn't stop checking my phone every five minutes hoping to receive a confirmation that the deal was done. With how well things were going between us, I knew that getting her away from Madam's controlling grip would allow me to personalize our relationship in ways that I couldn't do otherwise. And if it all worked out, then I could see what needed to be done to break her free from Madam's contract I knew she was bound to.

I lifted my eyes and said, "I've been seeing someone."

Wes's face hardened. "Through the Madam?"

A trumpet began to play below. The band picked up and a quick melody brought the house to its feet. Performers rushed to their poles, and women swung in their partners' arms.

I knew I could open up to Wes. There wasn't any reason for me not to trust him. His reputation was solid and in this town, integrity like what he had was a rarity.

"Yes," I said, causing Wes's eyes to darken, "but I'm not here to discuss the Madam."

Our drinks were served and Wes leaned back, nodding to the server in appreciation.

"Forgive me, Kelly," he sipped his bourbon, "but I just can't believe that you're still working for her."

I swallowed down a sip of my sparkling water, appreciating how it helped cool my body temperature. "It is what it is."

"Except that you and I both know that you could be doing so much better working with me," a glimmer of pride flashed over his eyes, "just like old times."

My gaze dropped to the liquid popping in my glass. After the accident, I'd been a mess and it quickly interfered with my practice, and my life. Everything fell apart, including Wes having to make the tough decision to let me go. He needed a lawyer he could count on, and at the time, I wasn't the person he needed me to be. That was when a mysterious woman wearing cherry red lipstick and hiding beneath a wide-brimmed sun hat came knocking. And whether I now regretted it or not, it was important to never forget that Madam was the one to help me get back up on my feet.

"Adrianna said you weren't looking too good the other day." Wes's finger circled the rim of his glass.

"She looks good," I said, knowing that Adrianna's road to recovery probably wasn't an easy one.

"I'm proud of her," Wes said somberly. "It could have been so much worse."

I leaned back and turned my attention to a pole dancer. I watched as she wrapped her legs around the metal pole and spun upside down. Addiction was a nasty disease and just thinking of it brought me back to thinking of the reason I was meeting with Wes in the first place.

"There's a case I'm thinking of taking on, and in my research I came across tabloid reporter, Sylvia Neil. You know who she is, right?"

Wes gave a firm, knowing nod.

I rested my elbows on top of the table and lifted my eyes to Wes. "Have you ever worked with her?"

"I prefer to do business with Julia Mabel."

My gaze dropped back to my hands, understanding his decision. Julia was a trustworthy source, too. "Anyway, Sylvia is the one who told me I should talk to you."

"Talk to *me*?" He arched a brow.

"Named you specifically."

"What about?"

"Nash Brooks."

Wes's head tipped back but he kept his gaze focused on me.

"Are you two close?"

"Close, as in, we're colleagues. Yes. Many of my clients have starred in Nash Brooks's films."

"Was he a member of your club?"

"What are you getting at, Kelly?" His brows pinched. "It sounds like you need to be directing your questions to him, not me."

"I tried." I sighed. "He's out of town. Shooting a new film." I reached inside my suit jacket pocket and pulled out the photos of Maria, laying them out in front of Wes.

He took a minute to study them before looking up at me with anger in his eyes.

"Do you recognize her?"

Wes studied the pictures again. "It broke my heart when the story broke. I'm ashamed of what happened to her." His voice was full of sincerity. Then he lifted his gaze to me and said, "Makes us all look bad, doesn't it?"

I swallowed down the guilt I felt inside my own aching heart. "Nash is into the lifestyle, too, isn't he?"

Wes frowned, nodding.

"Did you ever see him with Maria?"

"She was his intern. And if you know Nash, that's his thing.

He falls in love with his interns all the time. Maria was no different."

"Do you know what happened? How they broke up? Why he was no longer with her?"

Wes rubbed his face, shaking his head. "Traded up. Hell, I don't know."

"Ever see them here, together?"

"Nash visits Mint occasionally, but not like he once did."

"When did he stop coming?"

Wes stole a glance over my shoulder toward his fiancé.

"Was it before or after Maria's murder?"

He looked up and to the left, thinking before he spoke. "Before. Definitely before."

"And if it came down to it, would you testify in court that he stopped coming before Maria's death?"

"Shit, Kelly." He tilted his head, looking at me with pleading eyes. "I have enough bullshit on my plate already. I don't need to get myself involved in this mess. At least not until I know you've talked this over with Nash."

"Trust me, I will as soon as he's back in town."

Wes swallowed down a healthy portion of his strong drink. "When you talk with him, keep in mind he went through quite the ordeal recently."

I thought about my visit with Alex Grace.

"You know," Wes's eyes widened for added emphasis, "when his girlfriend found the missing Blake Stone money."

I twirled the thin plastic straw around in my drink. "I heard you were after the money, too?"

"Everyone was." He lifted his glass to his lips. "That asshole caused me more stress than I needed."

"I'm thinking of representing the man accused of killing Maria." My fingers stroked the sweat falling down the sides of my glass.

"What's his name?"

I debated whether or not I should say, but in the end I decided that if I wanted Wes's influence to help me work the case, it was in my best interest to tell him everything. "Mario Jimenez."

Wes dropped his gaze to his nearly empty glass and shook his head. "What's holding you back from representing him?"

"I need to know how he's involved, or if he's just a face to convince the city that justice has been served."

"And with what you know now, what does your gut say?"

"That he's innocent."

Wes picked up a photo of Maria again. "Nash would never take it this far. That's not what this place is about. Nash was a skilled Dom. All my members are." He glanced up at me with a knowing look, like he knew I understood exactly what it was he was saying.

"Would Blake Stone or someone he's connected to be capable of that?" I leaned further across the table. "Would they take it that far?"

"Now you're just ruffling my feathers."

I raised my brows.

"This connects to Stone?" He clasped his hands on top of the table and sighed. "And that's what Adrianna was talking about," he murmured.

"I don't know. I'm working through several theories right now. Help me decide which one's the right path to follow."

Wes sipped what little remained of his bourbon as we sat there in silence.

I turned my attention to the party below and quickly found myself staring at a woman who reminded me of Kendra. God, I missed her. Last night was incredible, and I hoped to God I'd have her to myself for the next month. Just the thought had my desire springing to life. If it hadn't been for her, I'd be having to find a way to deal with all this stress another way, and I feared that booze would soon find its way back into my life, not realizing the darkness that would then follow.

"Stone is enemy number one," Wes said in a grave voice. "If I had it in me, he'd be the first person I'd kill myself. Gladly. After what he did to Adrianna, and so many of my friends, and not to mention my own brother? That fucker deserves to rot in his own feces."

"So you think he could be connected to Maria's death?"

"You know what he's capable of. I just gave you a glimpse of what he did to me." He tossed back his glass, emptying into his mouth. "You tell me. Darkness follows him like the plague. So be straight with me, Kelly. What is the Madam up to?"

"Excuse me?"

"Adrianna followed you the other day. She said that you both had the same idea, and that she found you at Emmanuel's warehouse. So, what is Madam up to?"

I told Wes my theory. How I thought the Madam was interested in filling the gap in the market Stone left behind, and maybe that she was using Emmanuel's business as a front for her drug operation. The evidence was all there, and the fact that Adrianna was even onto Madam only firmed up my own belief. "It makes sense, right?"

"Unfortunately, yes." Wes nodded. He couldn't look me in the eye, instead he stared out over the club and I wondered if he ever thought how many people were here, dancing, snorting the same shit he wanted to rid this town of. "The Madam is capable of some pretty dark shit."

"I know."

"And I'm not even talking about the possibility of her taking over what Stone left behind, either." His eyes were intense as he held my gaze. "If your girlfriend is working for the Madam, you need to get her out."

My stomach dropped as fear for Kendra boiled in my intestines.

"Madam will ease her in, then turn her inside out. Whether it's for her own needs or some of her client's sick desires. Stuff like this," Wes jabbed his finger down on Maria's image, "will eventually get her killed."

"Are you saying that Madam might be behind Maria's death?"

"What I'm saying is that you might be oblivious to the reality of Madam's other clients and how they treat their dates. Without knowing the facts, I'm not sure that's what happened here with Maria, but it certainly seems like a possibility."

I swallowed the rock forming in my throat as I thought back to the day in the cemetery I visited my wife's grave. Kendra was new in my life and there was still a lot that we had to learn about each other, but I already knew that I couldn't bear the thought of having to bury another woman who meant the world to me. "So I guess you've heard Stone's attorney was dismissed by the judge?"

"Not surprised." Wes turned his gaze back to me. "He brought lots of good people down with him."

"And now the Madam is wanting me to represent him." I nodded. "With the intent to purposely toss his case. Put him away forever."

"Shit." Wes's nostril flared as if he didn't need to hear any more. His opinion had been made. The Madam was minimizing her risk with Stone by having me toss his case.

"The irony of it all is, I too want to see Stone go away for what he did."

"But we both know why she wants him gone."

I hung my head, nodding.

"And you can't do it because you have a reputation to maintain."

"Exactly."

"But why then represent Mario? How does this all tie to him?"

"Madam introduced us." My fingers squeezed my glass. "She knows he knows something about Stone that would seal the deal. Except now, the more I learn about Maria, I'm convinced Mario is simply a face to go down for a crime he didn't commit, to look like justice is being served. He's innocent. I know he is, and I can't just let him hang for a crime he didn't commit."

"This is so fucked up." Wes ran his fingers through his hair.

"I need to distance myself from the Madam, but I'm afraid I'm in too deep."

Wes smoothed his hands down the front of his chest, taking a minute to think things over. Then he turned his head and looked at me with raised brows. "What if I could give you a way out?"

"I'm afraid I don't see a way out of this. I'm too close to Madam's activities. If she were to go down, and with my rocky relationship with the DA, there would be no stopping his pursuit to bring me down with her."

"Kelly, I can help."

"What are you proposing?"

"I'll tell you, but first, help me understand something."

I rolled my wrist and flipped my palm to the ceiling.

"Why did Sylvia send you here?"

"Because you're the owner of Mint."

"Fine. But, Kelly, I think you might have missed something in Maria's case."

I leaned forward with the crease between my brows deepening.

"Did you know that Sylvia Neil *also* had one night with Nash?"

I shook my head. "News to me. She didn't say anything about that."

"Didn't think she would. Nash ended it, and she wasn't happy about it. Now, I'm no detective, but I am a man of logic, and if I had to guess, her anger gives her motive to have been the one to kill Maria."

"As a way to get back at Nash."

Wes snapped his fingers, pointing at me. "We can bring the Madam down, and bring justice to Maria."

"So what are you proposing?"

"All you have to do is trust me." His eyes sparkled with renewed determination. "And it starts with you telling Mario that you'll represent him. Can you do that?"

"I can do that."

"Then let's get to work."

42

KENDRA

R olling on my stomach, I squeezed my eyes shut and grumbled into my pillow.

My body ached. I had a slow pulse. And I felt no motivation whatsoever to get out of bed. The desire to take on the day wasn't there. Absent, completely gone from the normal excitement I felt when waking up to see what surprises were waiting to find me today.

I flipped.

I flopped.

Fatigue defined the way I currently felt, and with the house quiet, I wished that I would have slept at Alex's last night. Instead, I'd come home to be alone.

The Madam left me feeling like shit.

My life was awful, and with my secrets now exposed, the same one's that I didn't want anyone to know about, I feared what else the Madam knew about me.

I yanked the pillow out from under my head and let it come crashing down over my face. Pushing it tightly over my nose and mouth, I fought to breathe.

Then I screamed until my face went purple.

I could only speculate what the Madam planned to do with the information I knew she had. A pang of fear twisted my gut as I clenched at the cramp.

A million different scenarios raced through my mind, terrified to think that she might know enough to either bring me down or use it to blackmail me into agreeing to do something I didn't want to do—like make those deliveries.

I rubbed my face and threw my fists down into the soft mattress, hating myself for getting into this position.

I felt stuck and couldn't believe this was happening to me. I'd worked so hard to redefine my image and move on from the childhood that wasn't so great to me. And suddenly, it all came crashing to shore like a monstrous hurricane, swallowing me up in the eye of the storm.

Tossing my covers off, I marched into the bathroom and found myself staring into the mirror. It was an ugly sight. I shouldn't have done it. But I had to see the wreckage to understand the emotion that pushed the agony to the far extremities of my body. My eyes were puffy with dark bags beneath them. My hair was a frizzled beehive and I looked disgusting. Splashing water on my face did nothing for me.

After a quick sit on the toilet, I dragged my feet to the kitchen, sticking my head in the fridge. It wasn't that I was hungry, but I felt like eating, if only to temporarily push the stress out of my mind.

Reaching for the carton of milk, I brought it to my lips and immediately spit it back into the container. It was sour and left my tongue feeling tingly. Thinking I'd find better luck in the cupboard, I opened the door and tried my chances with the cereal. But it only proved to be worthless. The cereal was stale, and with me spending most my time away, I had nothing in the house to eat that wasn't expired.

My cell dinged, and when I went for it I noticed that it was my doorman app alerting me to a message.

Ms. Williams. You have a package waiting for pickup, it read when I opened it.

Initially I was excited, but dread came back to curl my spine. I was sure that whatever was delivered to my apartment was from Madam. Probably my next delivery. I wasn't sure how I was going to get out of this, or if she would let me. She seemed determine to have me be the only girl of hers to do house chores. Or maybe there were others. I didn't know. We never crossed paths with the other women working for Madam so I could only assume that their job descriptions were similar to mine—minus these special deliveries.

Knowing I couldn't let it sit there forever, I jumped into the shower, letting the hot water stream over my closed eyes in hopes that it would wash away the funk I woke up in.

I shampooed and scrubbed the soap into my skin. When my hand grazed my sex, I immediately thought of Kelly.

I was flattered by his request to have me for a month. There was nothing I wanted more than to spend more time with him. I had a deep desire to learn more about who he was, and I wanted him to learn more about who I was, too.

But I was hesitant to make the decision when feeling like there was more to it than just dating Kelly. There was something up Madam's sleeve. I knew it. I could see it in her eyes. The way she glared at me, like this was her plan from the beginning—a way to bring Kelly and me together for whatever motive she intended to fulfill. It all seemed too good to be true, and for that I remained cautious.

I blew out a heavy sigh as I turned the knob over to off.

After drying myself, I tossed on a bright yellow sundress and let my hair air-dry. The elevator was empty. I had it all to myself all the way to the bottom floor where I stepped out to find a smiling Mr. Anderson.

"Why are you smiling?" I teased as I approached.

"When do I not smile after seeing you?"

"Well, I'm glad you are. I'm in need of some joy to brighten up my morning."

"What has you down, Ms. Williams?" He frowned.

I liked how he was so formal. It must have been a generational thing, because in most circumstances I preferred to be on a first-name basis with the people I encountered. But the way Mr. Anderson said my name, he made it sound cool. "Just some shit I woke up with."

"Well, whoever the man is, he's lucky to have you."

"What are you talking about?"

He reached behind his desk and pulled out the small gift box I had been alerted to. "I assume this is from him."

I tucked my wet hair behind my ear, slowly taking the box inside my hands. I knew that it was from Kelly, and my heart resumed its normal lively rhythm. "Did he stop by?"

There was a mischievous sparkle in Mr. Anderson's eye that made me follow his gaze over my shoulder. And when I turned to look, I jumped off my toes, squealing. "Kelly!"

Kelly stood there in the entrance with his hands in his pockets, smiling.

My head spun back around to look at Mr. Anderson.

"I guess he never left." He shrugged.

Kelly was rocking on his heels when I turned back to him. "What are you doing here?" I asked.

He sauntered over to me with a sexual desire that drew my nipples tight. Kelly was unlike any other man I knew and I was thrilled that he was here. It was the exact surprise I needed to make me feel whole after the fitful night I'd had. His fingers clamped around my arm as he leaned in to kiss my cheek. "Mind if we talk upstairs?"

I nodded, suddenly feeling breathless in his presence.

"Thank you, Mr. Anderson, I owe you one." Kelly smiled to an obliged doorman.

We headed to the elevator, linked at the hand, and I tucked

his gift deep inside the palm of my hand, managing to press the button with a free finger. The doors opened immediately, and I was eager to get Kelly into my apartment so we could be alone.

He glanced down at me with glowing eyes. My toes curled as a desire to jump his bones rippled across my skin. And as soon as the elevator began whisking us up to my floor, I asked him, "How did you know where I live?"

"I'm Madam's lawyer." He grinned. "I know more about her employees than I should."

My shoulders tightened with fear of what else he knew about me. But with the way he was holding my hand, I didn't care. He possessed me, made me feel safe, and I liked that he was here. "And how many of them have you dated in the past?"

It was a question that was asked without thought, and I said it in a teasing manner but I was relieved when he said, "None."

"Can I believe you, Counselor?" I leaned my shoulder into him and he bent his neck, kissing my forehead.

I closed my eyes, letting the warmth of his lips rejuvenate my soul. And I kept them closed until the doors dinged open. "Sorry. If I would have known you were coming, I would have laid out a path of flowers."

He chuckled and followed one-step behind me.

My door was unlocked, not bothering to lock it knowing that I would be back up soon, and as soon as it swung open, Kelly began checking out my place. It was a mess, with clothes draped over the back of the sofa and gossip magazines lining both the coffee and dining room tables.

"You just wanted to see how I lived?"

He opened the fridge and gave me a look.

A flush of embarrassment spread across my cheeks. "It's been awhile since I went shopping."

He closed the fridge and began opening up cupboards.

"Sure. Go ahead. Make yourself at home." I folded my arms

and leaned against a nearby wall. "Or, if you're looking for something in particular, maybe I can direct you."

"Just browsing," he said coolly.

There was nothing to hide, so besides me thinking that what he was doing was a little weird, I let him freely dig into my life one stale-smelling cupboard at a time. "Then while you're doing that, maybe we can talk about your request to have me for a month."

Kelly gave me a wicked grin that clenched my sex. "I thought you'd never ask."

"Is it because I signed your contract?"

"Of course." He strode over to me with sex in his eyes. "Now that we made a commitment to each other, I can't allow anyone else to have you."

"Does the Madam know about our commitment?"

Kelly took me by the waist, sliding his hands to the small of my back, pulling me against his hard abs. "It's our little secret."

"But I haven't said yes."

He chuckled, bringing his lips a whisper away from mine. "But you will."

I raised my brow, wetting my lips. Then he kissed me.

My tongue swirled over his and I was thankful that I had brushed my teeth in the shower. There was still a hint of mint on my tongue, and when matched against the heat of his lips, it was heaven. "You're right, I will," I murmured against his thick lips.

He nipped at my lips again. "Aren't you curious to know what's in the box?"

I turned my head to the gift box sitting on my kitchen table. "Only a little."

"Open it."

His voice was firm enough to convince me that it couldn't wait. I reluctantly slid myself away from his protective, masculine grip and pulled the top off the small cream-colored box. I glanced to Kelly as my heart fluttered with excitement against my ribs.

When my eyes fell back to its contents, my hand flew over my mouth and I gasped. "Kelly, it's beautiful."

His white teeth sparkled like the black diamond on the ring he'd just given me. "Now that we're together, I want you to know that you'll never have to worry about anything. I'll take care of you. That's my promise to you."

My hands tingled and I felt like I was floating in the air. Kelly reached inside the box and plucked the round piece of metal between his fingers, slipping it on my ring finger.

Tears of joy clouded my vision. Holding it up to catch the light I asked, "And what does it mean to be Kelly Black's girl?"

He ran his rough hands up and down my arms, pressing his heavy girth against my belly. He had me wet and begging for him to take me here on the kitchen table. "I'll teach you what it means to be my submissive."

A flare of adrenaline zinged up my spine. I'd heard the term but knew little of what it actually meant. And after Alex and I had gone digging to find dirt on Nash, ever since coming across Mint and knowing the rumors that swirled around the nightclub, I couldn't deny my own interest in learning the lifestyle.

His hands moved to my ass. "And it all starts now."

Continue the series in Black Demands. Click here to start reading today!

AFTERWORD

Never miss a release. Sign up to my newsletter and stay in the know. Visit me at www.CJThomasBooks.com

ALSO BY CJ THOMAS

City by the Bay series

Ruin Me Box Set

Promise Me Box Set

Save Me

Take Me Box Set

Control Me Box Set

Hollywood Dreams series

Big Willy Box Set

Beyond Tonight Box Set

On My Knees Box Set

Capture Me

Heat

Hard

ACKNOWLEDGMENT

I want to thank all of my readers for being supportive with each new story I write. It's because of you and your willingness to WANT to read my stories that make this all possible. Mwah!

I also want to thank my editor, LNS, for bringing my stories to life and constantly providing constructive advice on how to improve my craft. The same goes to my street team and beta readers, for without you, I'm not sure I would have the confidence to continue living inside my characters' heads day after day.

And last but not least, my family for giving me the love and inspiration to keep writing.

Never miss a release date. Sign up for my Newsletter!
www.CJThomasBooks.com

Made in the USA
Middletown, DE
17 October 2017